HEX ON THE BEACH

KELLEY ARMSTRONG   **JEANIENE FROST**   **MELISSA MARR**

GODDESS OF SUMMER LOVE

By

KELLEY ARMSTRONG

CHAPTER ONE

I do not know how I became the goddess of love. Oh, I understand the "goddess" part. I am immortal, and I possess certain powers, and in ancient Greece, "deity" was the only language they had to describe us. We were lucky to be born in that world. A monotheistic culture has far different words for such a thing, as Denny—Dionysus—discovered when he over-imbibed in Inquisition-era Spain and started showing off his powers. Marius—Ares—had to ride to his big brother's rescue, roping me into it because Athene decided a little pyre-burning might teach Denny to hold his liquor. Yes, Athene still goes by Athene, and dear Lord do not spell it Athena. She once snuck a chisel into the British Museum to fix a statue.

No, I understand why the appellation of goddess. It's the "love" part I've never quite fathomed. Goddess of beauty, yes, and that is no show of ego. I know how I look, and if Fate had given me some say in the matter, I would have denied that particular gift. I suppose "love" arises from that. What else is a beautiful woman good for?

My powers have nothing to do with love. Or sex, though I am very fond of it, and rather good at it, as one might certainly hope to be after three thousand years of practice. No, I lack any powers of love or sex or fertility, and yet one can even find twenty-first- century sects that worship me in hopes of receiving those blessings.

I have no dominion there, and so after centuries of confusion, I did the only thing I could. I slammed down my banner and claimed the territory for myself. Aphrodite aka Venus aka Vanessa. Patron deity of lovers. Matchmaker extraordinaire.

And I am about to do what I do best.

MARIUS ARRIVES to the soft blip of the security panel as he lets himself in. He doesn't call for me. Doesn't ask where I am. He strides straight through to my dressing room as if by homing beacon. We have been friends since we were children and lovers since we were adults, and even if we are currently "on a break" —as we have been too many times to count—he is first in my life, and I am in his. As he says, "Venus and Mars, planets with the entire earth between them sometimes, but still always within each other's sight."

He doesn't say hello. We are far past pleasantries. He walks in, and I don't turn from the mirror, but I do watch him enter through it. I will never be past *that*.

Marius looks in his forties. We all do. Our immortality took hold as we passed our youth and settled into early middle age, which is a very comfortable place to inhabit. He is handsome, of course. Athletic, of course. Confident and self-possessed. He is Ares, after all. God of War. But every statue leaves out the best of him. The easy-going charm and the kindness. Most of all, the kindness.

He walks up behind me as our eyes meet through the mirror. Reddish blond hair curls over his forehead. Beard stubble signifies he is taking the long weekend off work, as do the chinos, a golf-shirt and loafers.

"You're looking very corporate," I say.

"Don't worry. I have my Hawaiian shirt in the car." He catches my look and grins, showing perfect teeth. "Hawaiian shirt. Deck shorts. Sandals. With socks of course. Memorial Day appropriate attire."

"I *love* the corporate look," I say.

"I thought you might. And I see we're still trying to pick an outfit."

His gaze moves to the clothing hanging from every surface of the room.

"You do realize it's a small-town festival, right, Vess? Not a black-tie dinner."

"I would prefer black-tie. Then I would know exactly what to wear. This requires subtlety. Kennedy invited us as her guests, to celebrate the opening of her new shop, and I need to blend. *Blend.*"

"Good luck with that."

I shoot him a glare.

He tilts his head. "Wait. Did you say Kennedy invited us? Pretty sure *you* invited us. In fact, I'm pretty sure the whole opening-gala weekend was your idea. You played fairy godmother, getting her new shop ready in time, everything moved from Boston to take advantage of the long-weekend crowds, and oh, why don't we make a grand opening of it, invite Aiden for the weekend, yes, what a lovely idea that has absolutely nothing to do with matchmaking." He looks at me. "Please, please tell me it has nothing to do with matchmaking."

"It is the perfect weekend to open her shop. The start of the summer season in a tourist town. The timing was tight, so I helped make it happen."

He motions sprinkling fairy dust.

"I am old," I say. "Excruciatingly old, and entitled to my whims and notions. I had a notion to help Kennedy, in partial payment for all the help she gave us."

"I noticed you dodged the matchmaking question."

"Kennedy and Aiden make a *perfect* couple. They just need a nudge."

He sighs and lowers himself into a chair. "They've only known each other for two weeks."

"And at this rate, it'll be two decades before either makes a move. I am accelerating the schedule. They're mortal, after all. They don't have the luxury of time. However, that is far from the only reason we're going to Unstable. I *do* want to help with the grand opening. I also have other plans. Other work to do."

His eyes narrow. "Other matchmaking?"

"Jonathan and Ani."

He groans.

"What?" I say. "You complain that I haven't given Kennedy and Aiden time. Jonathan and Ani have been friends since childhood. They've had time. Now they need help."

"Also Rian and Hope, I presume?" he says, naming Aiden's brother and Kennedy's younger sister.

I snatch up a dress from a chair. "Certainly not. They don't suit, and I have every intention of making sure that particular match *doesn't* happen. She's a child. He's the emotional equivalent of one."

"She's twenty. He's a twenty-four-year-old in need of some maturity, but I see promise there."

"Of course you do, because he's your hundred-times-great-grandson. If you want promise, you have Aiden. Rian needs a swift kick in the rear." I pull on the dress. "Thankfully, he is out of the country, so that is one fewer problem to worry about."

I slap on my accessories, turn and strike a pose. I'm wearing an unflattering brown sundress and equally unflattering glasses with my hair pinned up.

"Sexy librarian," Marius says. "I like it."

I scowl and switch to a pencil skirt and linen blazer, leaving the glasses and hair.

"Hot for teacher?" he says.

A hard glare, and I try outfit number three, a linen pantsuit.

"Mmm, speaking of corporate." He waggles his brows. "Can I be the misbehaving new hire, lady boss?"

I sigh and slump into the other chair. He rises, riffles through one of my closets and pulls out a simple but elegant sundress. Then he removes my glasses, sets them aside and unpins my hair before handing me the dress.

"Be yourself, Vess. No one expects anything else." He pauses. "If you do want to change up anything, may I make a suggestion?"

"Please."

"Don't play matchmaker this weekend."

"I am the goddess of love," I say. "This is what I do. I have a plan. They are all very keen on mysteries, so I have one for them."

He winces. "Please don't tell me you've invented a fake mystery for them to solve."

"Of course not. They aren't children. I'm bringing them an actual local mystery . . . with a few extra clues."

"Clues you planted?"

"Red herrings. Just a sprinkle."

"Here's a thought. Give them the mystery, minus the fake clues, and skip the matchmaking. They're all adults. If they're meant to be together, they'll figure it out for themselves."

He catches my expression and throws up his hands. "I tried. No one can say I didn't try."

I kiss his cheek. "You did. It was a lovely effort, and I appreciate it so much that I will let you be my plus-one at the weddings."

He sighs, deeper, and returns to his chair.

· · ·

WE'RE DRIVING TO UNSTABLE, Massachusetts, the paranormal capital of New England. Oh, yes, Salem gets most of the attention, but that's an entirely different thing. Salem is renowned for killing witches. Unstable is renowned for welcoming them. Witches, mediums, spiritualists, and dozens of supernatural species that do not actually exist. What *does* exist has made a home there.

I suspect there's at least one immortal in town. There's also the Bennett family, with three orphaned sisters Ani, Kennedy and Hope. They're curse weavers, distant descendants of Mercy —Mercury—the "trickster god" of our family tree. The Bennetts aren't immortal, but they did inherit that specific gift, just as dream shapers inherit my power, being mostly descended from me. The Connolly brothers are descendants of Marius. Luck workers, inheriting their talent from the god of battle luck.

The Bennetts settled in Unstable generations ago, and they openly ply their trade. That's the advantage to both the modern era and to living in a town devoted to paranormal tourism. The average person doesn't quite believe in things like hexes and curses, but they don't quite *not* believe either, especially if they find themselves drawn to a weekend in Unstable.

The Bennett family business is called "Unhex Me Here"— someone had a proper appreciation of Lady Macbeth. Their specialty is *un*cursing. Most of the objects people bring them suffer only from the stain of superstition. They love this watch they inherited from their grandfather, but they feel a little uncomfortable wearing it, especially since he'd been wearing it himself when he died. Could the Bennett sisters have a look, maybe lift any lingering unpleasantness? What Ani and Hope really sell is the soothing balm of reassurance.

Middle-sister Kennedy has found another way to use her talents. She tracks down cursed antiques and buys them cheap from owners who are in a hurry to get rid of them. Then she removes the curse, fixes them up and resells them. For two years, she had a shop in Boston, where she fled after her mother died of cancer. With both parents tragically taken so young, Kennedy had felt the need to escape the memories. Now she's sorted that out and returned to open a shop in Unstable.

Marius exaggerated when he said I invited us to Unstable for the long weekend. As Kennedy's shop fairy-godmother, I wanted to be there for the opening. So I booked Marius and I into a bed-and-breakfast. Kennedy insisted we stay at her family home.

I'd then asked whether she was sure there'd be enough room as Aiden would obviously be there too, given all the help he'd provided with the insurance claim. I knew she'd only invited him for the opening. With my prompt, she extended her invitation to the entire weekend, including lodgings at the Bennett home, and he'd cleared his schedule to accept.

So we are all staying at the Bennett residence for a delightful weekend, as the town throws open its doors and kicks off the summer season.

We arrive a little past four and park on a side street. The Bennett house is along the main street, which has been roped off for the upcoming festival. Stalls line the street, stretching almost to the Bennett house. In the distance, a Ferris wheel is being set up.

Marius whistles. "They really go all out," he says, scanning the street. "What do you say we sneak off tomorrow night, grab some elephant ears and give that Ferris wheel a whirl?"

"Yes, that is exactly what I want. Fried carnival food prepared under god-knows what kind of conditions followed by sailing into the air on a metal wheel that probably hasn't been inspected since Watergate."

"Good thing we're immortal, right?"

I sniff and roll my eyes. He knows I'll go on the Ferris wheel, and I'll eat the fried-dough monstrosity, and I'll enjoy it too, because he will enjoy it. Just as he will pick through the local bookshop with me and stroll the gardens on the edge of town.

When a peal of laughter rolls over, I pause and frown. It seems to be coming from the Bennett's yard.

"Sounds like a party," he says, picking up his pace.

"Sounds like a lot of people," I say, frowning.

"Uh, yes. Because it's a party, Vess."

"No, Kennedy said get-together. A backyard get-together with a few people."

He grins. "I have a feeling that Kennedy shares my definition of 'a few people.' Less than fifty for an intimate get-together."

He's right. It's definitely a party, with people streaming into the backyard and spilling out onto the driveway and front lawn. People their age—all in their twenties.

"We're going to be the old fogies," I say.

"Well, then you didn't need to worry about what you wore, right?" He glances over, brows creasing. "This is okay, isn't it? You like parties. You like young people."

"I do."

"But . . . ?"

I shake it off. "Nothing. This is fine." I walk over and take his arm, and we head into the backyard.

CHAPTER TWO

Marius is right. I love parties. I love mingling with young people. That is the advantage of my middle-aged appearance. Oh, I still get admiring looks and seductive overtures from the young men—and some young women—and I will admit I have indulged in both when Marius and I are on a break. But just because he isn't currently sharing my bed does not mean I want to line up a sexual partner each time I step into a room, and the thrill of constant attention soured a very long time ago.

I have spent my life aching to be seen as a *person*—forget "goddess," and certainly forget "goddess of sex and beauty." When I am with young people, particularly with Marius at my side, I get a glimpse of normalcy.

The problem with such a large party is . . . Well, perhaps I'm worrying too much on another's behalf. It is entirely possible that I am wrong. I hope I am.

We've settled in, post-introductions. Marius has a beer in hand, and I have a plastic cup of spiked lemonade. We're at the back of the large yard, shaded by two sycamores that must be over a hundred years old. We have lawn chairs—someone made sure of that right away, given our advanced age.

Hope sits on the grass before us, with a couple of her young friends, who are truly adorable in their youth and enthusiasm, as they chatter about college and summer plans. They include us in the discussion, because they are at that age. Young adults past their teen years, who chat with us partly to be polite and partly because they're coming to realize that not everyone their parents' age is an utter bore.

I catch sight of Ani every now and then, striding about in full organizing mode. She shares her sisters' dark hair and olive skin. Hope is considered the prettiest of the three, but it's a marginal difference only signifying that she has more regular features. She's the tallest, with a lithe, model-thin figure. Kennedy has the most athletic build, and Ani is the full-figured one.

As the oldest sister, Ani is the head of the family and takes that responsibility very seriously. *Too* seriously, if you ask me, so focused on her sisters and the business that she forgets to look after herself. Jonathan is here, too. He's the local librarian and physically smashes every preconception of that stereotype. Tall, handsome and broad-shouldered, with dark skin and dark hair cut to his scalp.

Jonathan is refilling ice, bringing out snacks and unobtrusively helping Ani because otherwise, she'd do it all herself. Ani and Jonathan will, of course, end up together. Just as soon as they both slow down enough to realize what they have. Or, I suspect, they already realize it—they just don't believe the other feels the same. Terribly frustrating for everyone looking on.

My gaze shifts to Kennedy, zipping about like a butterfly. If Ani is the party planner, Kennedy is the hostess, making sure everyone is greeted and introduced and no one is left awkwardly on their own. Barefoot, she's wearing the cutest floral sundress with a crinolined skirt that bounces along with her dark ponytail. The only makeup I can discern is a bit of pink lipstick. She doesn't need anything with her youth and flawless olive skin. As she flits about, her gaze keeps sneaking to the gate, and while she might just be making sure she doesn't miss any new arrivals, I suspect she's waiting for one in particular.

"Kennedy's looking for Aiden," Hope says, as if reading my mind.

"Who's Aiden?" one of her friends asks.

"A guy."

Her friend rolls dark eyes. "Obviously. But *who* is he?"

"He's from Boston." Hope puts on an exaggerated accent. "Went to Hah-vahd. Runs his own company. Comes from money. Old money. 'Debutantes and daiquiris at the country club' kind of money."

"Is he hot?"

Hope wrinkles her nose. "If you like gingers."

"Oh," both friends say in disappointed unison.

"Fortunately, Kennedy *loves* gingers," Hope says. "She thinks he's *totally* hot."

I give her a warning look, but she only grins. If Ani takes her role as big sister too seriously, Hope is just as devoted to her role as exasperating and embarrassing little sister.

I lean back in my chair, my leg brushing Marius's. He shifts his closer and reaches one hand to rest on my thigh as one of the girls asks him a question.

I find myself staring at his hand, at the strong familiarity of it, the warmth of it on my leg. It's a casual gesture of equally casual intimacy, but I still notice. I always notice, and in the last couple of weeks, I've done more than notice. He puts his hand on my thigh, and heat licks through me. The heat of lust and of longing.

We've separated many times in our lives. Sometimes, frankly, we just get on each other's nerves. There's no shame in that. Even when we're a couple, we've come to realize that separate residences help, a place to retreat to and be alone, making our days and nights together so much sweeter.

Other times, a fight drives us apart. An issue pushes us to the breaking point, and we retreat to our corners, unable to reconcile the issue without doing further damage. That's what happened this time.

Marius and I have children. Many children, some mortal and long gone, some immortal and still with us. Most are our children together. Some aren't. It doesn't matter. Whether or not we're both their biological parents, we are a family. With one exception. A daughter of his who cast me in the role of evil stepmother and will not let me out of it. To call her difficult undersells the matter. She lives up to her name: Havoc, goddess of discord. She is hateful and dangerous, and she only listens to Marius. To control her, he decided he had to keep her close, and that drove me away. Two years ago, he gently shooed her from the nest, but the damage had been done. I'd been beyond frustrated at him giving so much of himself to someone who didn't deserve it, and he'd been beyond frustrated by my inability to understand his sense of responsibility.

Now that Havoc is out of his life, we should be back together, yes? It never works that way. Once the crisis has passed, we grow closer in friendship as we circle the possibility of more with infinite care. Too much care, in my opinion, which correctly suggests that I'm not the one holding out. I want him back. Have for a long time now. And he circles, testing the water, making sure he will not get burned again. I understand, and I have to grant him that, as much as I burn myself watching his hand on my thigh.

Enough of that. This weekend isn't about repairing an old and fractured love. It's about cultivating young and new ones. And as soon as I think that, the backyard gate opens, and

Aiden walks in, and it only takes a split second for me to acknowledge that I was not wrong earlier.

When I'd seen this party, that prickle of anxiety hadn't been for myself. It'd been for Aiden. I've known him much longer than I've known Kennedy, and I took one look at this backyard bash and foresaw disaster. Now he has arrived, and I was not wrong. Not wrong at all.

I teased Marius about looking very corporate. The inside joke is that he *is* corporate. Over the millennia, he's been a soldier, a mercenary, a spy, and just about every other job possible for his particular skillset. In the modern world, hiring himself out as a mercenary would be a very different thing, no longer the honorable calling as it once was. He's now in the business of war, or at least the technology required by the modern theater of war. CEO of a small but very successful corporation. So yes, the twenty-first-century god of war *is* a corporate man. He does not, however, really look the part today. More like a middle-aged guy who might be up for a round of golf or a match of squash, and either way, will kick your ass.

Aiden is different. Aiden looks like . . . Well, Hope joked about country clubs, and that's where he seems as if he's headed. To an intimate soirée at a club so exclusive you can't get a membership unless your great-grandfather had one.

He is impeccably dressed, because he is Aiden, who has an enviable sense of style. Every color complements his fair skin and red-blond hair and green eyes. Every fabric drapes just right on his slender, athletic form. Every fashion choice is both timely and timeless.

All of that is lost on Kennedy, who wouldn't set foot in a Fifth Avenue shop even if she had a gift card. She'd sell the card —or donate it—and shop at the mall instead. That's the world she comes from, and it's the world inhabited by everyone else at this party, all the other young men in jeans and shorts, T-shirts and tank tops and in some cases, no shirt at all. This is a backyard party, where you drink your beer out of the can and the spiked lemonade out of plastic cups, and Aiden just showed up carrying a triple-figure bottle of white wine, while wearing a crisp white linen shirt with tailored gray pants rolled at the hems to show off blue espadrilles.

He opens the gate and freezes, eyes widening, and in that moment, he looks exactly like poor Kennedy when we'd taken her to a black-tie charity event. She'd frozen up, ready to flee, feeling out of her league.

I start to rise, in case Aiden beats a hasty retreat. He is a man of pride, and he is embarrassed by his mistake. He sees a yard full of strangers and realizes this is not his sort of party, not at all.

Before I can get to my feet, Kennedy is there. After all, she *has* been watching for him. She darts over to greet him, bestowing a smile so bright and genuine that he has no choice but to step through the gate. He nods at the party and says something with a quick wave at his clothing, and I swear I can hear their conversation.

"I think I'm overdressed."

"No, no, you look great. Come in. Please. Come in."

I smile as Kennedy ushers him through, deftly closing the gate to keep him from fleeing. Then Ani is there, taking the bottle, and Ani and Kennedy are laughing, probably joking about putting it away to enjoy themselves.

Crisis averted. I exhale and settle back into my seat to enjoy the party.

IT SEEMS I did not misunderstand the party invitation as much as I thought. Yes, there's a backyard bash, complete with beer and burgers, but the food isn't long gone before Kennedy is thanking everyone for coming and herding them on their way, with promises to see them at the town festivities. Then it is just us: Marius and myself, the three sisters, Aiden and Jonathan, and the party slows to more of what I had originally envisioned.

We sit in the yard as twilight falls. We break out Aiden's wine and Marius produces a bottle of lemony-sweet kitro from his overnight bag, and we talk. We just talk, the conversations made so much more enjoyable by the fact that the party is reduced to those who know exactly who Marius and I are. It is a relief not to play a role.

As twilight turns to full dark, Jonathan lights a bonfire, and we gather around, the wine and liqueur replaced by beer and sodas, the lawn chairs abandoned as we stretch on the grass, under the stars and around the fire.

"Are we telling ghost stories?" I begin.

"Do you have any?" Kennedy asks as she plays with her black cat, teasing her with a strand of grass.

"Not exactly," I say as I rearrange my legs. "But I did stumble across a fascinating mystery associated with your little town."

Marius throws up one hand, just enough for me to get the message. Yes, I am pursuing this, and he knows better than to try to stop me.

"Lots of mysteries around here," Jonathan says. "Which one did you find?"

"The tale of the disappearing teen," I say. "Lisa Lake. 1969."

"Ooh," Kennedy rocks forward. "Yes! It's the fiftieth anniversary."

"Is it?" I frown, as if calculating. "Imagine that. Seems like a perfect time to reopen the case."

If Marius rolls his eyes any harder, he'll rupture something.

"I believe someone is giving a tour on it this weekend," Jonathan says. "They asked us to put up flyers in the library."

Ani frowns. "Who?"

He waves. "No one from Unstable. The anniversary did come up at a town council meeting—should we recognize it for extra publicity?—but the general feeling was that it would be in . . ."

"In poor taste," Ani says. "A teenager disappeared."

"Well, yes, but also, do we really want to call attention to the fact that a teen disappeared at the same weekend celebrations, even if it was fifty years ago? They decided to allow the tour, which is being run by a historian from Columbia University. Unsolved mystery and all that."

"Odd that it's still unsolved," I say. "One would think that someone would have dived back in by now. It really is a fascinating story."

"This Lisa Lake is the one who disappeared, I'm guessing?" Aiden says.

"She did," Kennedy says. "Under the most mysterious circumstances. Does anyone want to hear the story?"

Ani groans.

"I take that as a yes," Kennedy says. "Refill your drinks and gather round for the tragic tale of Lisa Lake."

CHAPTER THREE

Everyone gets more food and drinks, and Jonathan stokes the fire. Then Kennedy begins.

"Memorial Day weekend. 1969. The summer of love."

Jonathan clears his throat. "The summer of love was sixty-seven. Also, Memorial Day didn't become an official holiday until seventy-one."

She glares at him. "Artistic license. Everyone knows what I mean. It was a late May weekend way back when."

"Ancient history," I murmur.

"Exactly. It was the sixties, when the summer of love came every year, and this one was no different. Unstable was having a massive celebration that brought people from across New England. Every campground and motel for fifty miles was booked. They say Old Man Cooper made more that summer letting out his fields for parking than he ever did planting crops. Bishop Street was so packed the fire marshal got involved and had to put up roadblocks, letting people in only as others came out."

"It was busy," Hope says. "Got it."

"I'm setting the scene."

Aiden nods. "Because the fact it was so busy allowed this girl to disappear unnoticed."

"No," she says. "The fact it was so busy makes it even stranger that she *could* disappear unnoticed. It suggests . . ." She waggles her brows. "Paranormal forces at work."

Ani groans. Kennedy cheerfully flips her the finger and continues.

"Seventeen-year-old Lisa Lake came to Unstable with her parents and younger sister. There was some trouble the night they arrived, which is why people here remembered them after the incident. It seems the Lakes were strict church-goers. Plenty of those around Unstable, where no one sees anything wrong with being spiritual *and* believing in spirits. The Lakes were different. It seemed Mrs. Lake had seen a flyer for the festivities that mentioned spiritualism, and she thought that meant it was a festival for God-fearing folks. One that wouldn't expose their girls to that free-love hippie nonsense. Imagine her horror when she discovered it exposed them to something far worse—the dealings of the devil."

"Dum-dum-dum," Hope intones ominously.

"Indeed," Kennedy says. "Now, Mrs. Lake, being very organized—if not good with a dictionary—had booked a bed-and-breakfast right in town. Prime pickings. When she complained to the owner, they quite happily offered to cancel the reservation. Not as if they couldn't fill it within the hour, probably at double the rate. But no, the Lakes had planned to spend the weekend in Unstable, and they were going to spend it there, whatever the cost to their eternal souls. That did not, however, mean they were going to do so quietly. Both Mr. and Mrs. Lake complained to every person they could. How could such a town exist in the modern, enlightened world?"

"Uh, because it *is* modern and enlightened?" Hope says. "Because it's not 1692 Salem?"

"People tried to tell them that. You know Unstable. Live and let live. Consideration and co-existence. Etcetera, etcetera. We might not have been flying the hippie flag, but only because those ideals weren't anything new here. So when the Lakes complained to locals, the locals calmly explained the roots of spiritualism and how it related to Christianity. They also assured the Lakes that they didn't need to believe in any of it to enjoy their weekend. It didn't help."

"Never does," Hope muttered. "Closed minds are closed."

"Closed minds, and open mouths. Afterward, despite how busy the town was, people remembered them. The very angry couple and their very embarrassed teenage daughters."

"Poor kids," Marius says. "Are we sure Lisa didn't disappear by sheer willpower? Praying the sidewalk would open and swallow her whole?"

"Oh, that's been a theory. It didn't happen on the sidewalk, though."

"Tell us, Kennedy, how did it happen?" Jonathan says.

She grins at him. "So glad you asked. Well, it was Saturday night, and the Lakes were enjoying a history tour. Although one might say 'enjoying' was an exaggeration. You see, while it was billed as a history tour, this is Unstable. Every tour includes ghosts, because that's what people want. This one started off very historical. When the first ghost appeared—figuratively— Mr. Lake complained, but his younger daughter begged to stay, which made others join in on the girl's side. Harmless fun, and all that. Just a ghost or two with their history lesson. Nothing wrong with that. Mr. Lake relented and on went the tour. Soon it reached the old theater."

Kennedy turns to Aiden, Marius and me. "You haven't seen it. We'll pop by tomorrow."

"Or maybe we could take that tour," I say. "The one for the anniversary."

"Ooh, yes. That'd be cool. I'd love to figure out what happened."

I try not to smile smugly at Marius.

Kennedy continues, "The theater is at the other end of Bishop Street. It's the oldest building in Unstable. Or the bones of it are, at least. It was one of the first houses here, and the owners sold it to the town shortly after Unstable became Unstable. It started life as the town hall, with the stables and the barn being renovated into a museum and a small theater. When Unstable established itself as spiritualism-friendly, the need for performance space grew. The town hall was relocated, along with the museum. Today it's a full-blown performing arts center. There's a restaurant and patio and gift shop in the house, a large theater in the former barn and a smaller one in the former stables. Tours usually end in the house."

"The ride exits at the gift shop," Hope says.

"The gift shop and the charming patio where you can enjoy a hot spiked coffee and a delicious slice of homemade pie. The town staggers tours so they don't all hit the theater at once. This particular tour reached it at about nine-thirty, just as dusk fell, when the real ghost tours are just starting up. They proceed around the house—after chatting up the charms of the patio—and into the smaller theater. At this point, the younger daughter complains of cramps. Her mortified mother shushed her, but the poor kid meant stomach cramps. She'd eaten a candy apple at the carnival and it didn't agree with her. Yet even when she clarified, her mother still shut her down."

"Nice," Hope says.

"Yep, parents of the year, they were not. But this is significant for what happens next. The tour proceeds to the lounge of the larger theater. All of a sudden, the younger sister can't take it anymore. She needs a bathroom right away. She races off. There's a bit of a commotion over that, and the parents stay behind, arguing over whether to go after her or continue with the tour. Lisa stays with the tour. It moves from the backstage to the auditorium. They're up at the front as the guide tells the story of a fair young milk-maid, Dolly, who walked into that very barn one day and never came out. Disappeared. And then, suddenly—"

"The lights go out," Hope says. "Plunging the theater into total darkness."

Kennedy turns to her. "Really? *Really?*"

"Did they?" Aiden asks.

Kennedy glares at her sister. "Yes, Hope stole the moment, but that is exactly what happened. It's part of the performance. Just enough time to give people a scare, but not enough for them to freak out. The lights go out, and milk cans clink, and the image of a girl with milking cans flits across the stage curtains. No one pretended it was an actual ghost. It was just atmosphere. Theatrics."

"But this time," Jonathan intones, "it was different."

"You, too?" Kennedy says.

"Adding my own theatrics."

She rolls her eyes at him. "Fine. Yes. This time it was different. The lights came on as the shadow play rolled. People gasp and cry out, and then realize it's a projection. Lots of laughs and elbowed ribs and 'you thought it was a ghost, didn't you.' Just like normal. But then the younger sister comes in and says 'Where's Lisa?' And Lisa is gone."

"All right," Aiden says slowly. "Not to state the obvious, but she must have snuck out the back exit when the lights turned off."

"The back exits were locked from the outside. Yes, total fire-code violation, but this was the sixties, and with the overcrowded long weekend, they'd caught people trying to overnight in the theater. So they chained them up."

"Out the main door?" Marius says.

"Closed. They would have noticed the lobby lights if it opened. They *did* notice when the younger sister came back inside that way."

"Backstage doors?"

"Her parents were in there, still arguing over whether to go after the younger sister. Also, to get backstage, she'd have needed to climb onto the stage itself, which is five feet off the ground, and she wouldn't have had time before the lights came on. She'd have been on the stage as the shadow played right over her. They'd have noticed."

"All exits were accounted for," Jonathan says.

Kennedy continues, "Lisa was standing right in the middle of the group. When the lights went out, she was there. Someone even heard her gasp. Lights come on, and she's gone. It took a moment to realize it, because her family wasn't there to notice, but there is no way she bolted out a door in those few seconds."

"Could she have been hiding in the auditorium?" Aiden says. "Ducked into the seating and waited for her chance to escape?"

"Nope. After sending his assistant for the police, the tour guide—fearing Lisa had been abducted—asked two people to guard the only unlocked entrance while several guests searched the building. When the police came, they kept everyone there while the building was again searched. Every inch was scoured. There are no windows—it's a former barn. No old tunnels. No basement. A small loft for storage, but that's behind a locked door and they still checked."

"You're forgetting the—" Hope begins before Kennedy's glare cuts her short.

"May I finish?" Kennedy says.

"It's taking a while."

Kennedy ignores her and turns back to us. "As Hope says, there is one more thing. Something that was discovered immediately. The younger sister ran in and asked where Lisa was, and everyone who'd been near her turned. Someone looked down. And that's when the younger sister started to scream. Where Lisa had been standing . . . there was now a small pile of ash."

CHAPTER FOUR

"Spontaneous combustion," Hope says. "It's the only answer."

Jonathan clears his throat.

"Fine," Hope says. "Tell us how spontaneous combustion is an urban legend. And then please explain the disappeared girl and the ashes."

"I don't have an explanation," Jonathan says. "But I am quite certain it's not spontaneous combustion."

"Spoil sport."

Aiden looks at Kennedy. "Continue, please."

"Thank you." She clears her throat and stretches her bare feet dangerously close to the fire. "Yes, spontaneous combustion was one of the theories. A heavily favored one. This is Unstable after all. There was an entire town symposium five years later on the possibility, with experts and skeptics called in to debate it."

"What are the other theories?" I ask.

"For the Lakes, the obvious answer was demonic activity. They were convinced that evil forces reduced their daughter to a pile of ash. Like a reverse Lot's wife and the pillar of salt.

Instead of a sinner turned to salt by God, she was an innocent turned to ash by Satan."

"Because she was *so* good and innocent that the devil himself rose up to smite her down," Hope says. "He could not bear to have such goodness in his den of iniquity."

"Uh-huh," Marius says. "So spontaneous combustion is starting to look good."

"Right?" Kennedy says. "No demonic smiting. Almost certainly no spontaneous combustion—sorry, Hope. The last possibility is magic. That's been the strongest theory. Something magical happened in that barn."

"*Bad* magic, though, yes?" Aiden says. "I'm presuming she never turned up?"

"She did not. Someone had to have magically killed her—evaporated her on the spot. Or they disappeared her—a magical kidnapping. The problem with those theories?" She shrugs. "We don't know any kind of magic that would do this. You can't curse someone into vanishing from the face of the earth." She nods to Marius and Aiden. "You can't give them such bad luck that they vanish." A glance at me. "Lisa was awake, so dream shaping is out, even if one could do something like trap her in a dream dimension forever."

"One cannot," I say firmly.

"Then, while we know a few other magical subtypes, we don't know all of them. The Olympians each have a power, right?"

I glance at Marius who makes a face. "Yes, and no. We have several powers, and sometimes they overlap. Our progeny get one specific power from us, such as luck working from me. There are also other immortals, from other cultures, but from what we can see, they share our core abilities, which suggests common ancestry at some point. The Olympians aren't the *source* of the power. That goes farther back. We come from an unusual family because we're all immortal and, between us, we possess all the known powers. Is that a fluke? Maybe. Or possibly, well, interbreeding. A genetic abnormality. If you want more on that, speak to Athene. But for what you're asking, no, none of those powers could make a human either disappear or turn into ash. Nothing remotely like that."

"Agreed," I say. "If this is magic, it isn't any type we've ever seen, and that makes it almost a guarantee that it isn't magic. The ultimate solution is more mundane." I sip my wine cooler and then say, casually, "What about this milk maid who disappeared? I hadn't heard that part of the story. Any potential connection?"

"There is no milkmaid," Jonathan says.

"Because she disappeared," Kennedy says, which makes Aiden chuckle. She looks over at us. "What Jonathan is saying is that there is no historical record of the milkmaid. It's town legend. However, given that it happened before there *was* a town and therefore no records or newspaper existed, I think we can concede the possibility that it did happen." She glances at Jonathan. "Yes?"

Jonathan pauses, and I can tell it takes him some effort to nod.

"I will concede the possibility," he says carefully. "In fact, I will say that I'm quite certain a young female farmhand did disappear. However, I suspect the truth is that she just up and left one day, with nothing remotely suspicious about it. She tired of the work or had another opportunity and snuck out."

Kennedy flaps a hand. "Yes, yes. Your objections are noted. Now, does anyone want the story?"

Hope waves her hand.

"You already know it," Kennedy says. "In fact, if I recall correctly, you dressed up as the milkmaid twice for Halloween. Once as a zombie. The second time as a headless milkmaid, despite the fact that is not part of the story."

"It was your idea!" Hope squawks.

"Oh, right." Kennedy looks around the group. "Does anyone else want to hear the story?"

"Just tell it, K," Ani says. "You know you're going to, whether anyone wants to hear it or not."

"I'd like to," Aiden murmurs.

"Thank you." Kennedy smiles at him and then looks out at us all again. "There was a farm, as I said, where the theater now stands. There weren't many people in the area, so most of the farm hands were new immigrants. This girl was said to be Irish. A teenager who came to America alone. There were several young women, who all shared a room in the attic of the house. That night, this young woman, whose name is lost but who is locally known as Dolly, suddenly remembered she'd left a candle burning in the barn after the night's milking or feeding or whatever you do with dairy cows at night. Anyway, she leapt up to run out to the barn. One of the other young women woke and asked what was the matter. Dolly told her and then raced off. This other young woman thought she should go with Dolly but, well, she was snug in her room and not eager to leave. So she watched from the window. She saw Dolly racing across the yard in her white nightgown."

Something scrapes across the wooden fence, and everyone jumps. Everyone, of course, except Marius, because it takes more than a spooky noise to scare the god of war.

"We all heard that, right?" Hope says.

Kennedy waves a hand. "Just a branch from the neighbor's yard brushing against the fence."

"Uh, there are no trees there, K," Hope says. "Also? No wind."

"Atmosphere," Kennedy says. "A little early in my story, but close enough. So Dolly is racing across the yard, with the barn looming in the darkness. She throws open the doors, and the other girl sees her stagger back, hand flying to her mouth as if—"

A rat-a-tat-tat, like a stick being dragged over the fence slats. Marius shakes his head and gets to his feet. Aiden starts to rise, but Marius waves him down and strides over.

"I know someone's there," Marius calls. "If you want to join the bonfire, just say so."

He reaches the fence. It's six feet high, and he's about five-eleven. To see over it, he has to boost himself up. But again, god of war, and there's no way he's going to hoist himself up a half-foot and dangle there awkwardly. Nope. He grabs the top and swings up to crouch on it like a cat.

Hope claps.

Ani turns to Jonathan. "Can you do that?"

"No, but I can see over the top."

"I'm guessing no one's there?" I call.

"Dum-dum-dum," Hope says.

Marius doesn't answer. He's listening and looking, and as his head swivels, I follow it to a spot around the back corner, behind a pergola.

"Nope," Marius says. "No one there. Must be the non-existent wind."

Marius hops down and creeps toward the pergola, where he slides into the shadows. A shape moves, but he moves faster, grabbing the intruder and flipping him onto his back.

"Ow," the intruder says from the ground. "Way to spoil my entrance."

Hope leaps up. "Rian!"

She runs over as I wince, and I catch Aiden doing the same. Marius helps Rian up, and the young man rises. On his feet, he turns, grinning, and puts his arms out for Hope.

"Surprise."

"Not the good kind," I mutter, low enough that only Ani hears it and shoots me a look of agreement.

I don't dislike Rian. He's not the kind of young man one can dislike. He's just, well, he's trouble, whether he intends it or not, and I'll be gracious and say that he does not. He's handsome and charming and wealthy, and he uses it all to full advantage.

Hope is fully ensnared in the tractor beam of his charms, and he loves it. I love it a lot less, as do Ani and Jonathan. Even Kennedy isn't keen on the pairing, and I can see her casting anxious glances at Hope and then over at Aiden, because having Rian here isn't only a problem when it comes to her little sister. As Aiden gets to his feet, he's already tense, the relaxed young man of a few minutes ago evaporating.

Aiden and Rian remind me of Paulo—Apollo—and Denny. The gifted and ultra-successful older brother overshadowing the screw-up younger one. That's how Denny sees it. For his part, Paulo always feels like the stiff and pompous sibling socially overshadowed by the fun, popular little brother. That is Aiden and Rian, and this is a social situation, meaning with Rian's arrival, Aiden is already foreseeing the end of what was shaping up to be an enjoyable weekend with new friends.

"I thought you were in Italy," Hope says, fairly dancing back to the fire as Rian slings his arm around her shoulders.

"I was. Now I am not."

"Weren't you there for weekend meetings?" Aiden says.

"I was." Rian shows his teeth a little. "Now I'm not."

When Aiden tenses, Rian walks over and slaps him on the back. "Relax. I rescheduled them. No one wants to work on the weekend."

Aiden seems ready to argue, and then rolls his shoulders and murmurs, "None of my concern either way."

"Nope, because you escaped the family business, and I have not."

"Rian," Kennedy says. "This is a surprise. Welcome to Unstable." She puts out a hand to shake his, but he pulls her into a hug instead. Kennedy allows it for one second before putting her hands on his shoulders and backing him up. "I wish we'd known you were coming."

"That would spoil the surprise."

"Yes," Aiden says. "But when one is joining a party—" He bites off the rest, as if realizing he sounds pompous, even when he only means to clarify Kennedy's gentle point, that an added guest may be an inconvenience. "Well, it's nice to have you for the evening. I'm sure you'll be going back to Boston tonight, perhaps returning to join in the local festivities tomorrow."

"Join in the local festivities?" Rian says with a laugh. He affects a British accent. "I say, old chap, you make it sound positively provincial."

I resist the urge to grind my teeth and lay a hand on Rian's arm. "Now, now, no need to snipe at Aiden when he was extending an invitation to join *his* weekend plans."

Rian has the grace to hesitate at that. The boy isn't stupid. Nor would he intentionally spoil Aiden's weekend. He just doesn't think things through.

"Right," Rian says. "I didn't mean to party crash."

"You haven't," Hope says. "There's plenty of room. It's a big house."

Ani clears her throat. "Not *that* big. The beds are full."

"Mine isn't," Hope says. She lifts her hands. "Joking." She turns to Rian. "There's a pullout couch, if you don't mind that."

"I do not mind at all. I've slept on a couch or two in my time. A floor or two. A jail cell or two . . ."

"Well, a jail cell is where you'll end up if I catch you creeping into Hope's room," Kennedy says.

"Kennedy!" Hope says. "I'm *twenty*."

Kennedy looks around. "Well, since my story seems to have been ruined." A mock glare at Rian. "I'm going to suggest that we head inside. It's almost midnight, and I need to be at the shop by eight for the final shipment."

"Breakfast will be at seven, then," Ani says. She pauses, and

I can see her mentally calculating whether she has enough chairs and food, now that Rian is here.

"I'll swing by early," Jonathan says. "I'll stop at the bakery first and bring a few extra pastries."

"And you don't need to worry about me," Rian says. "I'm never up before noon."

"Well, you will be tomorrow," I say. "If you're staying, Kennedy could use your help moving that last shipment." I pause. "Perhaps you'd rather head back to Boston after all? So you can sleep in?"

"Nah, I'm good." He puts his arm around Hope's shoulders, and they head into the house, chattering away.

CHAPTER FIVE

I'd hoped Ani might misunderstand the current status of my relationship with Marius and put us in the same bed. No such luck. As the consummate hostess, she shows us the spare room, which has a single bed and a futon, and then she says we can take this one or the master bedroom. I must, of course, murmur "This one is fine," and tell myself that it's better than sharing a bed and sleeping on our separate sides, reminded of the gulf between us.

Marius takes the futon, and I take the bed. We talk into the night, as we did when we were children, Marius sneaking into my room to lie on the floor, half to talk to me and half to protect me from the interest of his older brothers—and his father.

Marius's family. The Olympians. Zeus and Hera and their children. In some stories, I am Zeus's daughter. In others, I rose from the surf after Cronus threw his father's genitals in it. The truth is far more mundane. I was born to a family with immortals in their bloodline, one that had not birthed an actual immortal in generations.

I was an uncommonly attractive child, which my family

prayed was a sign they'd finally been blessed with an immortal. When I was ten, I drowned. The story is that I slipped off a rock. The truth is that my father held me under the water while my mother watched, so that they might test my immortality.

While immortals *can* die, we are not as frail as mortals, and so I recovered from the drowning, and my father promptly took me to the Olympians. He sold me to Zeus, who bought me as a brood mare. Marius wasn't joking about interbreeding. While there's less than the myths would have one believe, it did exist. In myths, Hera and Zeus are full siblings. In truth, they are first cousins. As an immortal with no known blood tie, I was prime breeding material.

The stories cast Zeus as the philandering scoundrel of a husband, and Hera as the vengeful harpy of a wife. The stories are lies. Oh, Zeus fooled around, every damned chance he got, and consent was not required. There's no "charming scoundrel" there. He's a bastard in the first degree.

With a husband like that, Hera devoted herself to hearth and home. I became one of her children, and I was treated as such, by her and most of their children.

The oldest of their brood was Hector—Hephaestus—an already legendary craftsman whom I avoided, because his stares made me uncomfortable even from the moment I arrived. Next was Athene, the intimidating eldest sister who made it her duty to teach me everything her younger siblings refused to learn. Then Paulo as a kind but distant older brother, already a man when I arrived. His twin, Artie—Artemis—was the athlete of the family, who despaired of ever making a hunter of me, but let me tag along anyway. Denny was the teen brother who'd swoop in with presents—usually stolen—and tease me mercilessly before vanishing again to his own pursuits. Marius came next, and then Mercy, the wild child, the only one younger than me, and as adorably annoying as Hope is to Kennedy.

With the exception of Hector, I loved all my foster

siblings. Yet Marius was different. The day I arrived, I put on a brave face. Mercy had hugged me and said we were going to be "such friends" before bouncing off to bed. At night I was left alone in my room, crying into my pillow, in this strange place amidst all these strangers whose names I couldn't even keep straight. Then someone scratched at my window. I'd dried my tears and looked out to see eleven-year-old Marius in the courtyard with a bowl of figs.

I knew I'd been sold as a future wife, and it made me wary of Zeus's sons, even this child, a mere year older than me. Marius didn't try to lead me anywhere, though. We sat in the central courtyard, lit by moonlight, and we ate figs in silence. At the time, I thought I'd fooled him with my dried eyes. Now I know better. He realized I'd been crying. He'd heard me, and that's why he brought the figs. It's also why he didn't talk, not until I broke the silence by thanking him.

"You must miss your parents," he said. "Your mother, at least."

I had to stop and consider that. Then I shook my head. I did not miss them. Nor was I glad to escape them. I just missed my home, the certainty of it.

"Do you have sisters and brothers?" he asked.

I shook my head.

A quirk of a smile. "Now you have lots. That must be quite frightening. Would you like to know more about them?"

I nodded, and he gave me a rundown of his siblings—their interests and their powers and what to expect from them.

"I like Hermes," I said—that being Mercy's name at the time.

Marius rolled his eyes. "Everybody likes her, for the first couple of hours, until she drives you up a wall with her incessant chatter and pranks. She loves pranks." His face softened. "She's all right, though. She'll enjoy having another sister."

"What about you?" I asked carefully. "Do you mind another sister?"

He tilted his head, a gesture I came to know well. Marius would never be considered the "thinker" of the family. The opposite, according to myth. But then the myths also paint him as a violent and blood-thirsty warrior who is a coward at heart, and he is none of those things either. That night, he considered my words with great care before answering.

"I don't really need another sister," he said. "A friend, though? I would welcome a friend."

And so it began. The defining relationship of my life, the strongest and the most treasured. We grew up together. When it came time to marry me to one of Zeus's sons, I prayed it would be Marius, but he wasn't considered among the possibilities. He was but a child, a boy of fifteen. Little matter that I was fourteen myself. That was different. I was a woman, and in need of a husband. I went to Hector, and the less said about that, the better. If Marius is the defining positive relationship in my life, Hector is the defining negative one.

The myths all say that Aphrodite cheated on Hephaestus with Ares. There, the myths are correct, and I may have regrets in my life, but that is not one of them. The opposite, in fact. I cannot imagine how I would have survived without Marius.

For years, I tried to be a "proper" wife to Hector. As loyal and devoted as any husband could want. But Hector never wanted a wife. He wanted a possession—the most beautiful woman in Greece, on his arm and in his bed, and gods forbid I should want or *be* anything more.

I *was* more. Marius saw it, and I saw him, when he became a man, and by then, marriage was nightmare cage for both my body and my soul. I loved and respected Hera, but I would not be her, content to subsume my own self playing wife to an abusive bastard, focusing all my love on my children. I adore my children, but I would never put that pressure on them.

All that is in the past, at least as much as it can be. There are hiccups, such as this one with Marius, but I will take what he can give for now. This rift will mend when it is ready to be mended, and I have learned not to rush it. We have, quite literally, all the time in the world.

Others do not have that time, and so I will focus my attention there this weekend. Set this little mystery in motion, and give Kennedy and Aiden a push toward each other, maybe Ani and Jonathan, too, if I can manage it. Also keep Hope away from Rian.

Two pairs of seedlings to nourish and coax closer to one another. One pair to separate, gently, encouraging them to flourish in their own rows. I am Aphrodite, goddess of love, and if I cannot tend to my own garden right now, I will tend to others.

WHILE I GO to sleep alone, I do not wake that way. Marius is beside me, which would be so much sexier if he wasn't fully dressed, lying atop the covers, staring at the ceiling.

"Good morning," he says, without glancing over.

I want to comment about the bed not being big enough for both of us, but there are only two ways that can go. I can seriously grumble, and he'll get up, which I don't want. Or I can tease and make some ribald comment, and things will get uncomfortable quickly.

It reminds me of when we were in our late teens, coming into adulthood and the realization that we were not children together anymore. Coming into the awareness of the attraction smouldering between us. In the days before we were ready to act on it. The days when we weren't sure what to make of it and whether the other felt it and if so, what to do about it. This feels the same. There is a wall here, as much as there had been when I was married to Hector. Only this wall is of our own making, and we are even less certain how to tear it down.

No, let me be honest. I am less certain Marius *wants* it torn down. I am utterly confident in his love for me. I haven't always been, but I no longer doubt, for one moment, that he loves me, that I am as important to him as he is to me.

Loving me is not the same as wanting to be my lover again, and this is what I truly fear. That someday he will have had enough. That he may already have had enough. That I am, quite simply put, more work than I am worth.

What do I have to offer him, beyond what we currently have? Sex. No matter how good that may be, it's hardly something he can't get elsewhere. We've always had the understanding between us that sexual fidelity is not the true measure of our devotion. Sex is a physical act we enjoy together very much, and when we are not together, we do not begrudge the other finding it elsewhere, no more than we'd expect them to starve if we were not there to dine with them.

Yet there's more to sex than the act. There is intimacy between those who love each other, and that is what I miss most of all. That is what I fear he has decided—that he can do without sex and intimacy when it drags along all the complications of being my lover.

I am difficult. I am demanding and fickle, at one moment wanting to be left alone and the next, desperately needy. He has never complained. He rolls his eyes if I joke that I am "high maintenance." Yet I am not truly joking, and so I am afraid that this is the thing wedged between us. He wants nothing that brings heartache and pain and strife. Marius is happier in a life that runs smoothly. The god of war is, ironically, not fond of confrontation, having faced too much of that in his professional life to want it in his personal one.

So when I wake to him beside me, I only say, "Good morning," and I don't comment on the narrowness of the bed. Don't grumble or tease. I just wriggle over to lay my head on his shoulder, as I would when we were teenagers, lying together and staring up at the stars.

"Is everything okay?" I ask softly.

"Everything's fine. I just wanted to ask what you need me to do today."

I lift my head and lean over his face, my hair tumbling down. He makes a show of spitting it out of his mouth. Before I can tuck my hair back, he does it for me.

"I am saying, Vess, that I agree to assist with your scheme. To help you pull off this mystery tableau."

"Really?"

He chuckles. "Yes, really."

My eyes narrow. "What's the catch?"

"No catch. I just decided that this is important to you, and while I disagree in principle, I don't see the harm. I know that whatever you have planned, it's intended to be fun, rather than deceptive. So I'm in."

"You're tossing me a bone."

He sighs. "Vess . . ."

I push up until I'm sitting. "You're worried that I'm still recovering from earlier this month, from what happened with Hector. You think I need a distraction and want to help me get it."

"No, Vess."

"Then you're humoring me. You don't think I should do this, but there's no harm, so you're going to give it to me."

"Yes, I believe I just said that. It is not, however, a cookie. If I'm humoring you, it is in the most well-meaning of ways. Like you going to that technology show with me in Vegas last year."

I open my mouth to ask whether he feels obligated to do this *because* I went to that show with him. Or because he feels bad about what happened earlier this month and his role in it.

Instead I zip my lips because I had, only moments ago, been

fretting about how difficult I can be. Fretting that he's had enough of it . . . and then jumping straight into defensive and difficult mode when he offers me something I want.

"I'm being a bitch about this," I say. "Sorry."

He tenses, and then takes my face between his hands. "No, Vess. You are not being a bitch. I wish you wouldn't—" He bites the rest off and kisses my forehead before levering up. "It's agreed then. I am your willing assistant in this endeavor. Now, you take the first shower, and I will start coffee."

"You shower. I'll make coffee." When he tries to protest, I wave it off. "I wasn't planning on showering anyway. Or wearing deodorant. If I can't duck attention with an ill-advised outfit, I shall do it with my natural body odor."

"Mmm, sexy."

I swat him and reach for my wrapper as he heads from the room.

CHAPTER SIX

B reakfast is more than an hour away, so I'm not surprised to find the kitchen empty. I'm sure Ani has everything ready to be popped into the oven for warming and baking, allowing her to spend the minimum amount of time banging around the kitchen this morning. She has, naturally, left out a plate of mixed coffee pods and sugar with a note that there is cream and milk in the fridge. There are also plates of both muffins and fruit. I make two coffees and take a muffin and two apples. Then I text Marius that I'm taking our pre-breakfast treats outside to enjoy the sunrise.

It's a little late for the sunrise, but it makes an excellent excuse. As I step onto the deck, I'm so busy thinking of where to sit that I don't realize anyone is out there until I hear Kennedy's laughter and Aiden's answering chuckle.

I stop so quickly I slosh the coffee. Before I can retreat, Aiden is there, taking the coffees from me as Kennedy hands me a napkin for the droplets spattered on my arm.

"I didn't know anyone was out here," I say. "Let me go back inside."

"No, no," Kennedy says. "I was just talking Aiden's ear off, as usual. Chattering away. He'll be grateful for the rescue."

She's teasing, but then there's a slight pause before Aiden murmurs, "Of course not." It sounds perfunctory, as if he's just realized he should say something. Of course, what he should do is tease her back. Joke that yes, thank goodness I showed up to save him.

That's what Kennedy would do. It is not what Aiden would do, and that two-second pause was him madly trying to figure out what to say and realizing that the longer he says nothing, the worse it seems. So he made the most perfunctory response possible, and Kennedy colors, thinking she really is boring him with her chatter.

I have my work cut out for me here. But I am up to the task.

"He certainly didn't seem to *need* rescue," I say.

"I don't," Aiden says firmly. "Which Kennedy knows. She just likes to tease me." A mock stern look her way that makes her relax. "We were discussing the mystery from last night."

"Oh? It is a delicious one, isn't it? I'm surprised it hasn't been solved by now." I take my coffee back from Aiden. "Perhaps it just needs amateur detectives with a bit of luck on their side."

He gives the faintest smile as he shakes his head. "I believe it will require more than that. However, we are intrigued." A quick glance at Kennedy. "Or I am, at least."

"I am, too," she says. "And being the fiftieth anniversary, I think we should solve it."

"I absolutely think you should solve it," I say, sipping my coffee as casually as I can. "You have a knack for that sort of thing. You should revisit the scene. Look for clues. Oh, and Jonathan seemed interested last night. Perhaps he and Ani could dig through archives. See what they find."

"Sadly, they're too busy for research duty," Kennedy says.

"There are events at the library, plus Jonathan is on the town council. And Ani has volunteered for everything, as always."

"Mmm, well, yes, but—"

"Plus, I have a new shop to open." Her shoulders sag. "Which is exciting, of course. Especially right at the beginning of the season, and I have you to thank for that, Vanessa." She waves a hand. "Forget Lisa Lake. If the case hasn't been solved by now, it won't be. This weekend is about preparing for my grand opening."

"I'm sure that won't take up all your time," I say. "Not with Aiden there to help you."

They both hesitate. Then Aiden says quickly, "I will help, of course. As much as I can. I did promise—"

"You promised nothing. You did more than enough with the insurance claim. Family comes first."

I turn slowly on Aiden. "Family?"

He grimaces. "I woke to a five a.m. string of texts from my father, who woke to a three a.m. flurry of phone calls from Venice. It seems Rian's idea of rescheduling is to send out e-mails as he's boarding a plane. He was supposed to be the face of Connolly Enterprises at a critical meeting with investors today. They are not happy. Our parents are not happy."

"Which has nothing to do with you," I say.

Behind him, Kennedy makes a face, telling me she's pointed out the same thing.

"It is how they operate," Aiden says, sipping his coffee. "I need to speak to Rian."

"So you get the early-morning texts while he gets to sleep in? Despite the fact you have nothing to do with this and are not part of the family business?"

"I am here," he says. "Enjoying the long weekend, and he shirked his duties to join me. Therefore, it is my responsibility." He rolls his shoulders. "That sounds bitter. I apologize. It's best for all if I handle the situation as swiftly as possible. Speak to

Rian. Smooth things over with my parents. Help him smooth things over with the investors. And then . . ." A faint smile for Kennedy. "I am yours for the remainder of the weekend."

I want to argue. Kennedy's practically ready to explode with everything she wants to say about this. But we both stay silent. We've made our opinions known. If we push, Aiden will feel obligated to defend his family, because they are his family after all.

"I should wake Rian and get this over with," Aiden says, with all the enthusiasm of a man facing a date with the firing squad.

"No, no," I say. "Let him sleep a little longer. You two enjoy your coffee."

Kennedy shakes her head. "I should see if Ani needs help in the kitchen. Get that done before I need to leave for the shop."

They head inside, brushing past Marius as he exits. A quick good morning to him, and then they're gone, leaving him frowning after them.

He comes out and shuts the door. "Maybe you should rethink that shower, Vess. You're driving everyone away already."

He sees my expression, and his smile fades. "Everything okay?"

I sigh. "Just seeing my plans disintegrate around me, hopes and dreams swirling into nothing on the winds of fickle fate."

"Huh. That sounds bad."

I pat his shoulder. "I will marshal my resources and overcome the obstacles."

"I do not doubt it. Now tell me what you need me to do today."

WHAT I NEED Marius to do is help Kennedy, who has lost both Aiden and Rian. Ani and Jonathan offer to pitch in, but

Kennedy reminds them they have a full schedule getting ready for the weekend, which launches today. Hope promises she'll be by as soon as she's done running errands. As for Aiden and Rian, they say nothing because they aren't there. They take breakfast on the porch, which moves to breakfast under the pergola as Rian's voice rises. Because clearly what Aiden needs —after his brother ruins his weekend—is for that same brother to snap and shout at him.

Families. Sometimes, they're like the Bennetts, so close and loving you wonder whether they're accepting applications. Sometimes they're like the Olympians, where family gatherings are either heaven or hell, and you can never tell which until everyone's there and it's too late to escape. Then there are the Connollys, where you don't even need to have met the parents to want to declare them unfit, adopt their adult sons and invest a fortune in sibling therapy.

By seven-thirty, I'm at the shop with Kennedy and Marius, just as a moving truck pulls up in front. Earlier this month, Kennedy's Boston shop was, as she puts it, "trashed." By Havoc? By Hector? We still aren't sure, but it'd be one of the two, partly because they were looking for something and partly because they are both, as Kennedy would put it again, assholes. Kennedy also jokes that they actually did her a favor. As traumatic as it was at the time, it helped her realize she wanted to move home to Unstable, and the insurance money made that possible.

Unstable's main street—Bishop—has some houses that have been converted to shops and some businesses that also serve as houses, like the Bennetts'. It also has a proper downtown core, and that's where Kennedy is renting her new shop. The location has seen a carousel of businesses open and close over the years. As fads change, businesses in Unstable shift, keeping up with trends. Most of those are owned by longtime residents who simply alter their focus when the old one goes out of style. This particular site has been leased by a string of outsiders, all trying and failing to make a go of it.

According to town legend, the store is cursed, which is why locals won't rent it. As one might expect, Unstable is a superstitious town. Two untimely deaths, decades apart, meant that locals were loath to set up shop here, and then when the outsiders' businesses failed, that only added to the curse.

The shop is not cursed. Kennedy would know if it were. It is as if the universe reserved this spot just for her, prime real estate in downtown Unstable, where the so-called curse is free advertising, given that she's running a shop specializing in formerly cursed antiques.

Kennedy and Marius help the movers, and I supervise. I am excellent at supervising, at least when the alternative is lifting and heaving and grunting under the weight of heavy boxes. The moving truck is gone by nine, and we're helping Kennedy organize the final shipment.

What the truck brought aren't cursed antiques or even previously cursed ones. Those take time to accumulate. Kennedy lost seventy-five percent of her stock in the destruction of her shop, and what remained was mostly small items, such as jewelry and bric-a-brac. To reopen, she needed stock, and I've helped with that. One advantage of being immortal is that I have developed an excellent eye for antiques—I remember what was rare at the time, and I can spot both a bargain and a fake at ten paces. Like many immortals, I supplement my own income buying quality items and storing them as nest eggs. Kennedy and I spent a weekend video-conferencing as we scoured auction listings online until she had enough to open her new shop.

As Kennedy cleans and polishes, Marius rearranges under my supervision. We have an audience, too, a steady stream of both locals and early tourists peering through the windows. Also a steady stream of people knocking on the locked door until Kennedy decides it's wiser to leave it unlocked and hand out opening-weekend flyers.

The problem with that is every time the bell jangles, she's hoping it's Aiden. I'm about to suggest re-locking it when a couple walks in, and Kennedy hurries over to greet them. They're a middle-aged couple, perhaps in their late forties. Kennedy introduces them as Mitch and Jackie. He's the local "tech guy," who's come to finish setting up the inventory program. She's a medium specializing in retrocognition.

"No excuse for me being here," Jackie says. "Other than curiosity."

"I was going to invite you to a private tour," Kennedy says. "Please, look around. If you get a glimmer from anything, let me know. We could make up notes for those ones. Mention what you see in their past. I'd include your name and a stack of your business cards beside each."

"That would be lovely," Jackie says, and she begins making her way around the room, touching and peering at objects.

Behind Jackie's back, I lift my brows, and Kennedy shrugs. Retrocognition is the ability to channel history from objects. Athene's descendants have a variation on it, known as past perception. My brow-lift asked whether Jackie actually has the power. Kennedy's response means she isn't sure. In other words, Jackie seems to have some hint of a talent, which could suggest a weak dose of past perception, making her a very distant relative of Athene or another immortal.

When the door flies open again, it's Hope, who sails in clutching a flyer. She holds it in front of her and bounces on her toes. "Who wants tickets?"

Kennedy takes the flyer as I walk over. It advertises the Lisa Lake tour, with advance tickets available for each night this weekend.

"We're going, right?" Hope says. "After we talked about it last night? We have to go."

Kennedy points to the window.

Hope squints out it. "Little early for corndogs, isn't it?"

"I'm not pointing at the booth outside my window. I'm pointing at the sign in it, which announces the grand opening at seven tonight. The tour starts at eight."

"So open at seven and kick everyone out at eight. Short and sweet." She catches Kennedy's look. "Kidding. Maybe Saturday then?"

"Which tour is this?" Jackie asks as she comes over. She takes the flyer as Kennedy passes it over. "Ooh, Lisa Lake."

She turns to her husband and waves the flyer. "I told you someone was doing an anniversary tour."

He wrinkles his nose as he glances over from the computer. "I thought the town wasn't going to allow that. It's in poor taste."

"It's a true-crime mystery, Mitch."

"About a real girl who really disappeared."

She puts a hand on her hip. "I thought you liked the story."

He lifts one shoulder. "As a fascinating town legend. Not as an opportunity for outsiders to capitalize on a local tragedy."

"But renewed interest could solve it," I say.

"Do we want it solved?" He swivels in his chair. "What if it turns out to be a crime? Being the site of a mysterious disappearance is good publicity for Unstable. Being the place where a teen girl was abducted and murdered?" He shakes his head. "I think we should keep the mystery."

"But if something did happen to her, wouldn't we want to know? In case whoever is responsible can still be brought to justice?"

Mitch shakes his head and returns to the computer.

"If you kids are interested, you should talk to my aunt," Jackie says. "She was the assistant tour guide that night."

"Mrs. Ricci?" Hope says. "I didn't know that."

"You could interview her," Jackie says. "She adores talking about it. These days, no one asks."

"We'll do that sometime," Kennedy says.

"Why don't I have her come by? I know she's dying to see the shop."

Hope looks at her sister, her gaze pleading.

Kennedy smiles. "That would be lovely, if she has the time."

"She will."

CHAPTER SEVEN

It's almost noon when Aiden does arrive, looking pale and drained. He comes bearing a giant picnic basket filled by one of the local shops.

"Food!" Kennedy says, throwing down her dusting cloth. "Please tell me that's food."

Aiden manages a tired smile. "Sandwiches, meat pies and salads. Also wine. Yes, it's only lunch, but for some reason I felt the irresistible urge to buy alcohol."

"I bet." Kennedy takes the basket from him and busies herself with it, saying "How'd it go?" with studied nonchalance, as if asking about the weather.

"I smoothed things over with the investors and convinced them it was a misunderstanding."

Kennedy's shoulders tighten, and I know we both long to point out that this was not Aiden's job, as he does not work for his parents. But that'd be the tenth verse of a very old song that he knows by heart and does not need to hear again.

"And Rian?" Kennedy asks carefully as she lifts out a box of steaming meat pies.

"He's somewhat less happy with me."

Kennedy wheels, her hand flying over her mouth as if clamping back a reply.

"Yes, I know," he says, exhaustion sighing through his words. "I pull him out of a scrape, and he acts as if I'm the one who pushed him into it. This time, at the risk of defending him, I think there's more to it. He's just not telling me what it is. He seems . . ."

Aiden glances over at Marius and me. "And no one needs that lunch-time conversation. How have the preparations been proceeding?" He glances around. "It looks ready."

Before Kennedy can answer, I walk over the basket. "This is lovely, Aiden. Do you mind if Marius and I take a plate and slip out the back? There's a lovely little garden there, and we can enjoy a picnic for two while Kennedy explains what still needs to be done."

While you tell Kennedy about this morning, what happened with your parents and Rian.

That's what I mean, and Kennedy acknowledges it with a nod of thanks before saying yes, we should take our picnic outside, where she's set up a patio table beside the neighbor's garden.

We're in the midst of dividing the food when the doorbell tinkles again.

Jackie walks in, escorting a white-haired woman in her seventies. Jackie pauses as she sees the food. "Oh, are we interrupting your lunch?"

Kennedy casts a quick glance at Aiden but rebounds with a smile as she bustles over to escort them in. "Not at all. Please, come in and join us. Jackie told me about your connection to Lisa Lake, Mrs. Ricci, and we're dying to hear the story."

As HER NIECE SAID, Mrs. Ricci is delighted to be asked for her story, which she can recite as it if happened last week. She's also visibly annoyed with the tour guide—Ms. Dowling—for not talking to her. Mrs. Ricci had reached out as soon as she heard about the tour, having her niece pass on a message for the guide. She'd never heard back, and she's understandably miffed about that. It helps us, though, as she's happy to dish on every last detail, which Kennedy writes down. And then it's time to get ready for the opening.

IN THE PAST TWENTY-FOUR HOURS, Fate has upended nearly all my carefully laid plans. Having a few succeed seems even crueler, giving me a teasing glimpse of victory before snatching it away. The backyard party got off to a rocky start, but then came the bonfire, where I snagged both Aiden and Kennedy with the story of Lisa Lake. Jonathan and Ani weren't quite as enraptured, but they were intrigued. Bait taken. Then Rian showed up, and that threw in a wrench that keeps gumming up the works. It distracted Aiden. Kept him away from Kennedy. Slowed Kennedy's opening preparations, which meant she had no time to pursue the Lisa Lake mystery . . . Oh, but here's a witness! A living witness to the disappearance! Wonderful, except everyone is too busy and distracted to chase mysteries.

I have miscalculated. I readily acknowledge that. Even without the Rian disaster, Kennedy's focus would be on opening her shop. That is the important thing. Launch this new venture. Save the mysteries and the romance for later.

Logically, I know that, but in my gut, I see opportunity slipping away. With this new shop, Kennedy loses her ties to Boston, where Aiden lives and works. They've only known each other a couple of weeks. That bond may have been forged in fire, but it's too new to hold without more to bind it.

Marius would say I can't make this happen. I can prepare the garden, but I can't force love to grow there. I want to, though. I don't know why it's so important to me—critically important—but I need to see some glimmer of success.

For tonight, though, I must put the mystery aside. Forget that there is a tour on Lisa Lake starting soon. There will be another tomorrow and again on Sunday. Tonight is all about the shop. Tonight is all about Kennedy.

"It's going well, right?" she whispers as she walks over to stand beside me. We're in the shop, thirty minutes after the doors swung open, and it is wall-to-wall people, with tourists lined up outside, impatiently waiting for the locals to leave.

"Maybe I should have had a private opening last night," she whispers. "Just for residents."

"Those people outside don't realize these are your neighbors," I whisper back. "All they see is that you are very, very busy."

Hope and Jonathan are escorting people around the showroom, while Ani darts about checking the levels of tea and coffee and baked goods. Marius is talking to an older couple admiring an Edwardian wardrobe. Across the way, Aiden shows jewelry to a trio of teenage girls who don't give a damn about the old necklaces—they just want to scope out the hot older guy.

"Are the snacks too downmarket?" Kennedy frets. "Aiden offered to supply wine and cheese, but that felt too fancy. It *is* an antique shop, though. Maybe coffee and cookies makes it seem like a cheap vintage store." She pauses. "Or maybe I should have angled *toward* cheap vintage. It is a tourist town, after all."

"Kennedy?"

"Yes?"

"Breathe." I lay my hand on her arm. "You're doing fine. You've done this before. Just another opening day."

"Uh, no. At my last opening, I threw a party and no one

came except my sisters and Jonathan. It was four days before I had a customer."

"Then see how far you've come?"

"Yes, I've come home, to where people know me and will actually show up." She takes a deep breath. "It's fine. All fine."

Something cuts through the chatter. Was that a distant scream?

I glance around, but no one else seems to have heard it. Must be from the Ferris wheel.

Kennedy's gaze goes to Aiden. "Aiden needs rescue before anyone thinks he's flirting with those girls." She shakes her head. "He really thinks they're interested in those necklaces, doesn't he."

"Oh, if they were a decade older, he might—*might*—realize there's another reason they're hanging on his every word. But given their youth, no, he's not going to see it, because that would be wrong. Yes, go rescue him. Maybe you can throw them to Rian." I scan the shop. "Where is the boy, anyway?"

"If he's not beside Hope, he's not here. He was supposed to come by." She looks around. "Maybe he realized Aiden would be more comfortable without him."

"All the more reason for him to show up," I murmur.

Kennedy shakes her head. "He's not like that. He'd do it to needle Aiden in fun, but he's not a total asshole. Not really an asshole at all. Just very good at playing one." She clutches her clipboard to her chest. "Let me go rescue—"

"Kennedy," Ani says, appearing from our other side. "I need your help. I've recruited Jonathan to start shooing people toward the exit, in favor of actual customers, but they aren't moving fast enough. You should do an announcement. Thank them for coming, joke about making way for paying customers. From you, it'll be cute and funny."

Kennedy steps forward. "Hey, everyone!"

Jonathan's whistle cuts through the chatter, and everyone turns.

Kennedy steps onto a small colonial stool. "Thank you all for coming! It means so much to me. I was just telling Vanessa how no one showed up at my last shop until four days after my opening party."

"Hey, I did!" Hope calls.

"You don't count. Also, you didn't buy anything. In fact, I'm pretty sure you still haven't paid for that hair comb you took."

"Family discount!"

The crowd laughs.

"Anyway," Kennedy says. "Speaking of buying things, it seems I have a line up of potential customers out front. Which is lovely, but you guys are my priority. Always. So I'm offering you all a gift. In ten minutes, everyone remaining in the shop will get a free . . ." She turns to Jonathan. "Drumroll, please?"

He obliges, beating out a rhythm on a tabletop.

"A free curse!" Kennedy shouts. "Yes, that's right! Curses! You get a curse, and you get a curse. Everyone gets a curse."

People laugh and start filing toward the exit.

"Wait! Don't leave before I pass out the curses. Who knows what you might get. It could be a—"

A clanging bell drowns her out.

"Hey, Kennedy!" Someone calls. "We're leaving. No need to call the fire brigade."

"Whoops!" she says, shouting to be heard over the bells. "Wrong curse!"

Outside, the waiting line ripples as people head out toward the street.

Ani swears under her breath. "I'll tell them we'll be clear in a moment."

She edges through the exiting crowd. As the door opens wide, fire engines whoop. Someone shouts.

"Ghost! They saw the ghost!"

"And called the fire department?" Aiden says as he reaches us.

Kennedy's already moving toward the door as he clears the way for her. I follow. We reach the sidewalk. It's chaos, people running up the street, pulling out their phones and cameras, the shop queue disintegrating as the street crowd surges behind the fire trucks.

"It's the theater," a woman says when Aiden asks. "There's a fire at the theater."

"And a ghost!" her friend says. "They saw the ghost of that missing girl. The one from the sixties."

"Lisa Lake?" Aiden says.

"That's the one. She appeared and then burst into flame. Her ghost spontaneously combusted!"

W e're outside the theater complex. On the road, because we can't get closer. The police and fire department have it blocked off.

Marius strides back to us, using his powers to cut through the crowd.

"It was the tour," he says when he arrives, after doubtless charming an officer or firefighter into talking to him. "The Lisa Lake tour reached the theater for the big reveal. The guide was walking them through it, and the lights went out. The locals figured that was part of the show—recreating what happened that night. But the lights were only supposed to dim. They went out, and someone spotted a girl in the auditorium. A girl dressed in sixties clothing. Then she disappeared, and the seat where she was standing caught on fire."

"A ghost that spontaneously combusted?" Hope says.

He shrugs. "There was an alleged ghost, and there was a definite fire. It's out now, and they're interviewing the tour folks to figure out what happened."

Kennedy exhales. "Okay, well, that was some unexpected

excitement, and I lost my line, but the night is young and the coffee is hot. We should get back to Ani and Jonathan—"

As if hearing his name, Jonathan appears, his head bobbing over the crowd as he makes his way over.

"Everything okay at the shop?" Kennedy says. "Please tell me you've come because we're flooded with customers and you need help."

"Sorry, K," he says. "I came to say they shut us down."

"What?"

Before he can answer, another siren sounds, this one an alarm. He waits until it shuts off.

"Chief Salazar is shutting down all the businesses along Bishop," he says. "They've had four security alerts so far. No sign of trouble, just alarms and sprinklers going off. She has no idea what's happening, but she isn't taking chances. Everyone's closed for the rest of the night."

"MAY we ask where you're taking us?"

It's past midnight, and Marius is leading Aiden, Kennedy and me through an empty park. We'd been heading off to bed— exhausted from the long day and disappointed by the end of it —when he'd culled us from the herd and snuck us outside. Now we're being shepherded toward parts unknown.

When I ask the question, Marius ignores me and motions for silence. There are still people out on Bishop Street. The shops may have closed, but the carnival booths have not, and people are enjoying the warm evening.

"You're kidnapping us, aren't you?" Kennedy whispers. "Hope mentioned you've had some experience at that."

"Oof," Marius says. "Low blow. Deserved, but still low. Yes, I am temporarily kidnapping you. I promise to have you home in an hour, none the worse for wear. I am the most gentlemanly of kidnappers. You may have heard that, too."

Kennedy rolls her eyes but follows him around the block. When I spot a flashing light, I slow.

"Is that the theater?" I say.

"Yes, we're breaking in."

"To the *theater*?"

"For a good and righteous cause." He motions us across the road. "Satisfying our curiosity."

"Uh, it'll be under guard," Kennedy says. "By the *police*."

"O ye of little faith. Would I bring you all this way if I couldn't get you in?"

"Uh-huh," I say. "Let me guess. Whoever told you what was going on earlier also slipped you a phone number, invited you to come back anytime you want to . . . chat." I waggle my brows.

"I'm not sure we have any eligible women on the force right now," Kennedy says.

"Oh, I didn't say they had to be eligible. Also didn't say they had to be female." I waggle my brows at Marius again.

As Kennedy laughs, Marius rolls his eyes, and Aiden tries valiantly but unsuccessfully to hide a blush.

"No," Marius says. "Having no intention of following through, I didn't make any such promises to anyone. That would be wrong. Useful, but wrong. I'm getting us in with my other talent. A sprinkle of luck."

"I can help," Aiden says. "Though I doubt you need it."

Marius claps him on the back. "Thank you. I should be able to handle this, and I will spare you the balancing, which is much worse for you than it is for me."

If Aiden uses his power of luck, the laws of balance inflict a counter-weight—a period of *bad* luck. The same as Kennedy needs to curse an object if she uncurses one. The immortals aren't bound by those restrictions. Marius only needs to regulate his use of luck because he can run out of it, and then he *will* need to balance, which he'd rather avoid.

We reach the theater complex. We've come in along the

back road, and Marius takes us through a yard. Earlier I thought he'd gone into the Bennett house while we were having commiserative cocktails in the garden. He'd obviously snuck out to plan this route.

We scale the fence behind the old stables. I don't complain about that. In truth, I tend to reserve my grumbling about such things for when they serve a purpose. I am very good at playing the princess. It is the role I was cast into even before Hector took me to wife. The beautiful but useless and not terribly bright goddess to be placed on a pedestal and worshipped because, really, that's all women like her are good for.

I'll play the part to get out of unpleasant tasks—dear lord, you cannot expect me to lift that dirty box—or to amuse Marius—but what if I break a nail?—when the truth is that I've done my share of scaling fences and crawling through trenches and wriggling through tunnels. I've been a spymaster's lover and partner. Sitting on the sidelines is dull. Clean and safe, but dull.

I climb the fence, and I creep through the garden, and I trust Marius when he says, "Okay, go!" and then I sprint across the open ground right behind him, with Aiden and Kennedy following. Marius's luck ensures that the two officers on guard choose that moment to patrol around the building and don't return to investigate any noises.

We make it through the rear exit door, which has conveniently been left with the latch not-quite-secured, proving Marius was indeed here earlier. Once we're inside, he gently closes the door and then turns on a flashlight that casts a diffuse light. Kennedy takes out her phone for a light and Aiden does the same.

We pause to get a look around. It reminds me of many rural American theaters, summer-stock playhouses in small communities. Rows of chairs like one might find in a school auditorium. A stage at the front with the requisite heavy velvet curtains. All very simple and tidy, the sort of place where you expect to pay fifty dollars for a good seat and enjoy a pleasant evening of decent community theater.

Marius motions us farther in before he speaks. While the building is soundproofed, he's not taking any chances. Once we're halfway up the center aisle, he waves at the rear door and two flanking the front.

"Three exits," he says. "According to an old plan of the theater, at the time of Lisa's disappearance, there were only two. The one to the front left was added in the nineties to bring it up to code."

"You've done your homework," I murmur.

"One cannot solve a fifty-year old mystery without delving into historical records. The mystery we're solving right now, though, is much more recent."

"What happened here tonight," Kennedy says.

"Yes. Now, according to those on the tour, the guide was taking them through the *original* tour of that night. Recreating that while superimposing the story of Lisa Lake."

"A tour within a tour," Kennedy says.

"Or that was the claim, though we already know the guide didn't bother speaking to Mrs. Ricci. Ms. Dowling was using *only* historical records. Comparing recollections from this evening's tour with Kennedy's notes from Mrs. Ricci, tonight's version missed a few of the early stops, added on two others and completely mangled the town legend."

"In other words, Ms. Dowling is winging it," Kennedy says.

"I think she realized no one actually cares about the original tour and devoted her research to the disappearance, which she apparently got dead on. I don't believe any of the deviations were significant, but in a mystery, everything must be accounted for. Up until they reach the theater, there's not much Ms. Dowling can say about the Lakes. The family wasn't noticed until the younger daughter's gastrointestinal complaint began.

Now, according to someone on the tour—who has already posted to TikTok—"

"To what?" I say.

"To a video-clip social-media sharing site. I'll show you sometime. Now, according to the TikTok poster, all the pre-theater content on the Lakes was a rehashing of the trouble they caused before the tour, which of course, may be significant."

"If, as you theorized, Lisa was so embarrassed by her parents that she prayed for the ground to swallow her and it did," Kennedy says.

"Or something like that. But on the sixty-nine tour, no one noticed them until the theater."

"Wait," Aiden says. "Didn't they complain about the tour right from the start? They raised a fuss there, yes?"

"They did," Marius says. "Huh. I wonder if the guide missed that part, too. Or the young woman who posted the video was late joining the tour. Either way, the main event happened . . ." He stops at the front of the auditorium. "Here. Both that night and tonight."

He crouches and shines his light at the dark red carpet. Someone has painted an X on it, the paint faded almost to illegibility.

"This is supposedly the spot," he says. "Lisa stood here to listen to the guide, who was over there." He motions closer to the wall. "The guests clustered around her. Tonight, Ms. Dowling recreated it. She asked the group to stand there and imagine it was 1969. She led them through it. When the lights went off, she gave a little shriek, which made people laugh. It turns out that while the lights *were* supposed to extinguish, they went out early. That's why she cried out."

"Was someone operating the lights?" Kennedy asks.

"Excellent question, and the answer is yes. A high school AV student had been hired to dim the lights and run the old milkmaid shadow play. She was up in the rafters waiting for her cue. Instead, the lights turned off without her. She was afraid she'd done it, and tried to turn them back on, but nothing happened."

"The lights were cut from another source," Aiden says. "Perhaps the breaker was flipped. That would overrule her switch."

"We will investigate that. For now, we can only say they went off early, and it was not—it seems—the AV girl. The early darkness caught the guide by surprise. She presumed the AV student got ahead of herself, and so after her initial surprise, she waited for the milk-maid shadow play. But there's something twenty-first-century tour attendees have that they didn't in the sixties."

Marius turns off his flashlight. Then he points at Kennedy's and Aiden's phones, shining into the darkness.

Kennedy nods. "So when the power goes off, even if people think it's part of the show, someone will turn on their phone light to be a jerk."

"Yep. So the lights go out. The tour guide yelps. And within seconds, there are multiple cell phone lights shining. That's when they see Lisa."

He turns on the flashlight and aims it toward the auditorium. The beam lands on a row of seats near the back. "She appears there. A light-haired girl in a plaid dress, like the one Lisa was reported to be wearing. She's walking along the row. Then there's a bright light and a loud bang, similar to a police flash-bang. When it clears, that seat"—He points at one with a black mark—"is on fire."

"And Lisa is gone," I say.

Kennedy's already walking down the aisle, Aiden on her heels. They head along the row. Kennedy pauses at the charred seat and then leans over and inhales. She waves for Aiden to do the same and he murmurs something we don't catch. Kennedy nods.

Kennedy turns to Marius. "Someone must have taken a picture of her."

"They tried. Several people got blurry shots of seats, not able to focus in time. Two had their flashes go off, which left an overexposed picture of what was described—girl with light brown hair, wearing plaid dress. Someone without an automatic flash got a dark photograph of the same."

"How long did she appear?" Aiden asks.

"Maybe five seconds."

Aiden bends to check the floor as Kennedy taps something in on her phone.

"Okay, I have a photo," she calls after a second. "I found one on Instagram. It's been Photoshopped to make it as clear as possible. The girl's face is turned away. Light brown hair, worn long and straight. Plaid dress. But I also have a photo I saved earlier today from the old news articles on Lisa. It's not the same dress. Yes, I doubt any of us thought 'ghost' was the answer, but in case there's any doubt, here's the proof. Similar cut and color for the dress, but not identical."

Aiden straightens. "I presume the police removed anything they found here, but I suspect there's evidence that the device was indeed some form of flash-bang. There's the smell of fuel on the chair. Some sort of accelerant. The person playing Lisa sets off the device and causes the fire, and then . . ."

He looks around.

Kennedy says, "She could have made a run for it, if the device was blinding enough. Out the exit. Or hid in another row and escaped during the confusion afterward."

"Two actors, then," I say. "One cuts off the lights at the source and the other plays the part of Lisa Lake."

"But to what purpose?" Aiden says as he and Kennedy rejoin us.

"That's the million-dollar question," Kennedy says. "The flash-bang and the accelerant suggest this wasn't a last-minute prank. Too elaborate. Yet, at the same time, not elaborate enough. The police will easily find the traces of accelerant, and armchair detectives will easily see the differences between the dresses."

"If the goal," I say, "was to start a new legend, then they did a haphazard job. Which suggests that is not the intention."

"So what is it?" Kennedy says. "I'd blame the tour guide, adding in theatrics, but she was obviously startled and, if anything, this could mean her next two tours are canceled."

"Unless *that* is the goal," Marius says. We all look at him. "Someone may have wanted the tours canceled. May also have wanted to stop anyone from trying to solve this mystery."

"Wouldn't this increase interest?" Kennedy says.

"Not when it's proven fake. Anniversary weekend tours could be canceled. The site of the original crime is already sealed off. Tales of a vengeful ghost *would* work in Unstable, but by next week, everyone will know it's a hoax. Interest will die out, and people will move on."

"Leaving the disappearance of Lisa Lake unsolved."

"Exactly."

CHAPTER NINE

I'm at the shop the next day, helping Kennedy. Hope is with us. There's been no sign of Rian. He'd apparently been MIA at the grand opening because his parents dragged him back to Boston. Quite literally. They sent an SUV to pick him up, with no advance warning.

As Kennedy muttered when she found out "Gotta love parents who kidnap their own kids." Rian was recalled to the home front, and that had Aiden fretting this morning, so Kennedy insisted he drive to Boston and check on him. Aiden promised to return by lunch and spend the afternoon helping in the shop. In other words, par for the course this weekend. A ruined Grand Opening, followed by an exciting late-night bit of sleuthing, and then couple-separating family drama.

The pendulum of Fate swings back that morning, as we discover, to my relief, that the ruined opening was not a portent of things to come. The shop is busy enough to keep Hope, Kennedy and myself hopping all morning, with Marius helping customers carry items to cars, as we sell half the large items to antique-shopping tourists.

Of course, that starts Kennedy fretting that her grand

opening looks more like a going-out-of-business sale. One worried text to Ani, and within an hour, three locals show up with antiques to sell on consignment. I'm not always a fan of small towns, but when the right people live there, they can be a wondrous thing.

We also have five people stop by to ask about a "cursed" object they own: either selling it or having it uncursed. The family business is closed this weekend to focus on Kennedy's shop, but a note on the door directs people here. Those who fear grandma's silver vase is cursed now have two options in Unstable: pay to get it uncursed or sell it to Kennedy as is. In Boston, she'd kept the phrase "formerly cursed objects" to herself. In Unstable, it's a selling point.

A young couple is inquiring about one of those right now—a Victorian pendant brought from the Boston store that actually had been cursed. Kennedy is regaling them with the tale when the local police chief comes in. Kennedy looks startled, but the chief only nods and motions that she'll speak to Hope instead.

I walk over as the chief asks Hope whether there were any problems with the shop last night.

"Any sign of intruders? Anything missing?"

Hope shakes her head. "We have a security system. It didn't go off. Most things of real value are too big to steal. The jewelry and whatnot goes into the safe at night. Kennedy opened that this morning. Everything present and accounted for."

"Good."

"I heard other alarms after the fire," I say.

The chief looks from Hope to me. Hope performs the introductions, and then Chief Salazar addresses me directly with her answer. "We're still investigating, but there seemed to be a few break-ins and a few thefts. Oddly, unrelated."

"Unrelated to the fire?"

She shakes her head. "No, I'm sure they're related to that.

People taking advantage. I mean that the shops with the triggered alarms had nothing stolen. It was other shops that did."

Kennedy walks over, catching the end of that as she brings the necklace to wrap for the customers. "Diversion, then? Set off the alarms, and then rob other shops that are still open?"

"That's a theory," she says. "Seems elaborate, though. We'll know more when we get a full accounting of what's missing."

Kennedy and I exchange a look.

"What about tonight's Lisa Lake tour?" I ask. "We bought a block of tickets, but I'm presuming it's been cancelled."

"There will be extra security, but we wouldn't do that to Ms. Dowling. She put a lot of work into this tour. She's sold out Saturday and Sunday, and has asked to do another one Monday. The council is considering it, though some people aren't happy about that."

"Because of the thefts?"

"No, they just don't like dredging up that history. Mitch Keeling came to see me this morning, with a few other concerned citizens. I told them to speak to the mayor, but I can't imagine anything coming of it. We gave her the permit, and no one's eager to withdraw it halfway through the weekend. Especially when there's a film crew coming out tomorrow night to tape her tour." She slaps the counter. "I should move on. Checking in with all the businesses."

"We appreciate that," Kennedy says, and the chief heads for the door as four more people come in.

THIS MORNING OVER BREAKFAST, when telling the others what we discovered last night, Jonathan had offered to compile what he could on the Lake case from the town archives. After the police chief leaves, I head to the library to see what he has. At breakfast, he'd been discussing it with Ani, so I'd presumed they do it together, but instead I find him alone in the library, which is closed except for special events.

"Where's Ani?" I ask as he lets me in.

"Volunteering, volunteering and more volunteering." He takes a stack of books to the counter.

"I thought I heard you two saying something about spending the morning together?"

"At the dunking booth," he says. "That's where she is. But it was slow enough that I decided to come back to the library and gather what you guys are looking for."

In other words, my attempt to bring them together actually meant that they *lost* precious weekend time together. Wonderful.

"Oh, but it's such a lovely warm day," I say. "You really should be out at the dunk tank."

"And I will be. I got your text as I was leaving, so I stuck around to give you the bad news in person."

"Bad news?"

He heads for the door, waving for me to follow. "The archives are Lisa-free."

"What?"

"Someone checked out all the records. Which is odd, because we don't normally allow those to leave the library. I also can't find a record of the check out, so my guess is that another librarian let someone take them, probably Ms. Dowling."

"Isn't that a bit odd?"

He laughs as he reaches for the door. "It's Unstable. I can say that we usually don't let someone borrow our archival material. I can also say that they're supposed to check out whatever is taken. But if I'm not the one on the desk, the rules are more like guidelines. We have one librarian with Alzheimer's and while she never works alone, whoever's with her could have been busy at the time. Or it was the other librarian, who decided to bend the rules for a professional interested in local history. I'll track down the archives, but it won't be this weekend."

"You wear a lot of hats in this town, don't you?" I say as we head out. "Head librarian. Town councilor. Volunteer worker."

He shrugs. "I like to get involved."

"You and Ani both work very hard, for your careers and your community. It must not leave much time for personal lives." I rap his arm as we pause behind the library back doors. "Young people need to be careful of that. Work-life balance. When's the last time you've been on a date?"

He glances away and rocks on his heels. "It's been a while." He comes back with, "But that's not me being busy. Just . . ." He wrinkles his nose. "Still bouncing back from a bad experience. It's an old story. Meet a girl, think she might be the one, and then she's not."

"It's a good thing you realized that in time."

"Oh, I wasn't the one who realized it. Totally out of left field for me." He locks the door. "But, yeah, in retrospect, it was probably for the best. We weren't a match."

"Uh-huh." I take out my sunglasses and put them on as we step into the gardens. "And what about Ani? Is she seeing anyone?"

He pauses, and his eyes narrow. "Oh, no. No, no, no."

"No, what?"

"Please tell me you are not trying to match make."

"Why not? You and Ani are obviously very—"

"Very good friends. Lifelong best friends. Naturally, we should end up together. As we have been hearing since we were, oh, roughly five years old."

"And it's not what you want?"

"Who knows what we want?" he says, with genuine frustration in his voice. "No one will back off enough for us to figure it out." He sighs. "They mean well. But it's as if the whole town has bought tickets to our wedding, and we're ruining everything by not actually getting married. My parents, Ani's sisters, the entire town—they're all part of a giant conspiracy to get us together."

"And you just want them all to back off. Give you breathing room."

"Yes." He exhales. "That was more than I meant to say. Just please don't add to the fray." He clasps his hands together, raising them, mock pleading. "Please, please, please. Let us be friends. If there's more there, let us find it on our own."

"EVERYTHING OKAY?" Marius asks. I'm in the Bennett's living room after dinner, everyone else out in the backyard.

"I made a mistake," I say. I glance over his shoulder and lower my voice. "With Ani and Jonathan. I should leave them alone. They don't need anyone else interfering."

He shrugs as he lowers himself onto the sofa with me. "Didn't seem like you were doing much interfering. Just little nudges that weren't really working out. They've both very busy this weekend."

"They're always very busy. I just hate to see . . ." I exhale. "I can joke about mortal lifetimes, but I hate to see opportunities slipping away. I want to grab people and shake them and tell them how quickly it will be over. How much they can miss by doing the wrong things and throwing away their lives but also by doing too much of the *right* thing."

I exhale. "I'm not making sense."

He entwines his fingers with mine. "You are to me. You're worried that Ani and Jonathan are so caught up in their careers and their community and helping others that they're missing out on each other. Except they're not." He waves toward the back. "They're out there right now, staking out a corner of the yard and talking like they've been separated for weeks."

"Which means—" I cut myself off. "Which only means they

truly enjoy each other's company, not that they need more. Not yet at least."

"They're moving at their pace," he says. "They aren't even thirty yet. They have plenty of time if that's what they want." He leans back, hand still in mine. "I'm more worried about Aiden. At least Ani and Jonathan *have* balance. Work, family, community, friends. Aiden?"

He shakes his head. "Work, work, and also work. Family, too, but not in a good way. With Kennedy, I think he sees the possibility of more. That's a start. I'd just like to figure out what the devil is up with Rian."

"Have you talked to him?"

He grimaces. "Tried to, but he's not sure what to make of me. He cracks a few 'god of war' jokes and escapes as fast as he can." He pauses. "He reminds me of Denny. He comes off as the wild child, the black sheep, proud of his place in the flock but . . ." He shrugs. "There's damage there, just like with Aiden. Just like with Denny."

"Kennedy said something like that earlier. I just wish Rian wouldn't make things so difficult for Aiden. He—"

The patio door whirs open.

"Vanessa!" Hope calls. "Marius! Tour time!"

She runs in waving her phone. "Thirty minutes to go. You're both still in, right?"

I smile as we stand. "We wouldn't miss it."

CHAPTER TEN

As Marius said earlier, the tour allegedly follows the one Lisa took that fateful night. It doesn't, actually, not according to what Mrs. Ricci told us, but I doubt the exact details are in the archives, and it hardly matters what route the tour took or what stops it hit. The important part comes at the theater.

Ms. Dowling—a mousy young woman about Kennedy's age —does an admirable job of explaining the problems the Lake family had with Unstable and the difficulties they caused. She gives us a more thorough picture of the family than I encountered in my online research.

Apparently, while the Lakes passed themselves off as average Christians, they'd been church-hopping for years, each new congregation lacking the requisite fire-and-brimstone. They'd ended up in a very fundamentalist church and, once the girls hit puberty, switched to home schooling, in the belief that the public school system would destroy any hope of a virgin marriage.

The girls led a very cloistered existence, and for them, coming to Unstable was like going to Disney World. Later in life, the younger sister confessed in an interview that she was the one who brought the festival to their parents' attention . . . and pretended to have heard it was a Christian gathering, intentionally manipulating the word "spiritualism." Had she blamed herself then, later in life, for the weekend that led to her sister's disappearance? I hope not. She was a normal teenage girl, desperate for a bit of fun.

It was the younger sister, as I'd learned, who also got them onto the tour. Yet another bit of teenage sleight of hand. Emphasizing the historical elements to her parents and glossing over any of the ghostly bits.

As much as I appreciate Ms. Dowling's research, she does too much, mingling the original tour with the story of Lisa Lake. Whenever she valiantly attempts to recreate the original tour her audience's attention wanes. While a few people will appreciate that, most are just here for Lisa Lake.

That goes double for our group. When Ms. Dowling launches into a bit of local lore, Kennedy shoulders Aiden to the back, where they whisper together, earning stern looks from Ani. I move between the sisters to divert Ani's attention and let Kennedy and Aiden have their moment.

I'm leaning toward Jonathan, about to ask whether Ms. Dowling's version of this local lore is true, when Hope lets out a yelp. The entire tour group turns to see Rian behind Hope, his hands over her eyes.

Ms. Dowling clears her throat.

"Sorry!" Rian calls. "She's really jumpy." He tickles her, and she swats at him, earning an even more severe look from Ms. Dowling and a warning glance from Ani.

Rian straightens. "Sorry. Again. I'll keep her in line." He walks beside Hope and stage-whispers. "Quiet, trouble-maker."

"This is a private tour," Ms. Dowling says.

"I know." He reaches for his wallet. "How much?"

"It's sold out."

"He has a ticket," Hope says, taking out her phone. "I bought seven in case he could make it." She holds up her phone. "See? Seven adults."

Ms. Dowling doesn't let it go that easily, making Hope point out everyone in our group to confirm there really are only seven. Then we're on the move again, Rian with his arm casually slung over Hope's shoulders, Hope chattering away as we walk.

I glance at Marius. He mouths "Do you want me to do something about it?" I consider and decide no. Not now. Everyone had been looking forward to this tour, and I won't spoil it. I won't let Rian spoil it either. If he causes trouble, I'll take care of it myself. After the initial disruption, though, he settles in, listening to the guide and behaving himself as we slowly make our way toward the theater.

WE'RE FINALLY at the theater complex. We aren't allowed inside yet. Chief Salazar had mentioned extra security. What she meant is that we'd have a police escort through the theater portions of the tour.

We're now waiting outside for that escort. I'm with Marius, Jonathan, Ani, Kennedy and Aiden, discussing theories about Lisa Lake.

"Does anyone have one?" I ask.

"If you're looking for a wild theory, I'm your girl," Kennedy says. "Real ones, though?" She shrugs and looks at Aiden. "We're working on it."

To cover my delight, I turn to Marius. "And you, former spymaster. You must have a theory. You just aren't sharing it."

"Oh, I have one. It's written in a sealed envelope that I gave to Jonathan."

"Seriously?" I say.

"Seriously," Jonathan says. "I have the envelope in a secure place."

"In other words," Kennedy says. "You don't want to spoil our fun by telling us what happened to Lisa, but you *do* want to be able to prove you had the answer all along."

"Yep, and if I'm wrong, Jonathan is under strict orders to forget where he hid that envelope."

As everyone laughs and teases, I realize two members of our party are missing. I glance around to see Hope and Rian disappear together behind a row of shrubs.

I murmur something about using the ladies' room and slip away. I stride in the proper direction, and then sneak back around to follow Hope and Rian. Their voices waft from a shadowy corner, tucked between two flowering shrubs. I can't see them, but I have a very good idea what they're up to, and I'm about to "accidentally" stumble on them when Hope says,

"You need to tell Aiden."

Rian sighs. "And here I thought you wanted to make out."

Silence.

"I was kidding, Hope."

"No, you were diverting and distracting, and I'd like you to stop it. I'd like you to treat me like a friend, not some girl you're trying to impress."

He exhales. "I don't mean it that way. I'm just . . ."

"Diverting and distracting. You need to tell Aiden the real reason you blew off that meeting. Tell him you don't agree with the new project. That you have ethical issues with using government loopholes and bribes to kick people off their land."

"Aiden won't care."

"Then why not tell him? Because you think he *will* care. You're afraid that if you tell him the problem, and he gives your parents shit, they'll listen to him where they ignored you, and that hurts."

He snorts. "I stopped caring what my parents thought years ago."

"No, you didn't. You should, but you can't. You need to get away from them."

"Sure, go into business for myself again. Look how well *that* worked out. Nothing more humiliating then being taken hostage because the Connolly they really wanted was Aiden. Everyone wants Aiden."

"Everyone except me."

A few murmurs, as if they're embracing. Then Rian gives a long, drawn-out sigh. "You can say that now, Hope, but trust me, by next Memorial Day, you'll be wondering what the hell you ever saw in me. You deserve better than a uptown party boy who can't get his shit together."

"And maybe you deserve better than a small-town girl who can't get *her* shit together."

"Your parents *died*. You have a reason for derailing, and you're already back on track, heading to college in the fall."

"Maybe. I can get accepted. If I can figure out what I even want to do with my life. All I know right now is that I want to be with you. You want to get your shit together. I want to get my shit together. I propose we make it a joint project. Every-thing's better with friends."

He chuckles. "Everything?"

"Everything. Especially this . . ."

The distinct sound of a kiss. I pause only a heartbeat, and then I back away and leave them alone.

CHAPTER ELEVEN

The security detail has finally joined us. As we start forward, Marius puts his arm around my waist and leans down to my ear.

"Hope and Rian?" he whispers.

I sigh.

"Not quite what you figured, hmm?" he murmurs. "Fancy that."

"If the words 'I told you so' leave your lips . . ."

"Do they ever?" he says, and I acknowledge that with a nod and briefly lean my head against his shoulder. When we stop outside the smaller theater, his arm falls from my waist. I lean against him as we listen to Ms. Dowling tell the tale of the poor younger Lake sister's gastrointestinal distress. That gets a few jokes from the crowd. "Please don't tell me it was the corn-dogs," etcetera as people clutch their stomachs. Then we head into the main theater.

The first room is a small lounge, with benches and restrooms and a portable bar. For pre-show and intermission sipping and mingling. The original tour had then headed backstage for a bit of theater history and the story of the milk-maid ghost.

"You never did get a chance to finish that story," Aiden whispers to Kennedy.

"I'm sure this version will be better."

It is not better. In the hands of Ms. Dowling, the story becomes a very generic missing girl story. The milk maid realizes she forgot something and slips out into the barn at night, never to be seen again.

"Tell me there's more to it than that," Rian whispers.

"Not really," Kennedy says. "I just add more flavor."

"So should she." Rian pantomimes a yawn, and Hope tells him to behave.

"If you want to tell a story yourself," Hope says. "I think you have one for Aiden."

Rian grimaces as Aiden tenses, clearly expecting the worst. Then Rian meets Hope's eyes and nods. He leans over to Aiden and whispers, "Can we talk later? I didn't screw up anything else. Promise."

"Of course," Aiden says. "After the tour?"

Rian nods. "Sure."

Ani motions everyone to silence, and we obey as the story continues. Or most of us do. Kennedy and Aiden step farther away, heads bent as they discuss something. Rian shoots them a worried look, but Hope shakes her head. She's closer to her sister, and she can tell that whatever they're discussing, it doesn't involve him.

Ms. Dowling moves into the Lisa Lake story. This is the point, she says, where the younger sister tore off to use the lounge restroom.

At that, Kennedy glances over and frowns. She looks around before leaning in and whispering more to Aiden, while gesturing. I don't see what she does. It's a small backstage area, poorly lit, with costumes and boxes and clutter.

Ms. Dowling motions for us to follow her through the curtains onto the stage. Kennedy and Aiden bring up the rear, and when I glance back, Aiden is stepping through before Kennedy grabs him and pulls him backstage.

"Finally," Hope whispers, shooting a gaze their way.

Rian chuckles. "Let's hope so."

I stay back near the curtain with Marius, the two of us blocking the way, in case anyone looks for Aiden and Kennedy. As much as I'd love to think they've snuck off for a romantic rendezvous, I suspect it's all about the mystery. Either way, they are together, and that's what counts.

Ms. Dowling leads us to the spot where Lisa Lake disappeared. I follow the group while keeping my eye on Ani and Jonathan, ready to distract them if they notice Kennedy and Aiden are missing. They're busy pointing out something to each other inside the auditorium.

As we assemble, the two police officers move into the aisles and begin sweeping the theater. In other words, the chief knows perfectly well that last night was a setup, and her officers are making sure no "ghosts" are crouched between the seats.

Only when they give the "all clear" signal does Ms. Dowling begin.

"The group stood right where you are," she says. "The same spot where every group stood for this tour. There was even a mark on the carpet to show the guides where to stop. While the carpet has long since been replaced, you can see a replica of the mark there."

She points, and everyone cranes to see it.

"Of the Lake family, only Lisa was with the group. Her parents remained backstage, arguing over how to proceed. Mrs. Lake wanted to go after her younger daughter, while Mr. Lake wanted to continue on and hope no one noticed her absence. He was embarrassed by her outburst and the fact that it concerned a bodily function."

Ms. Dowling turns to the right and waves at the wall. "The guide would have steered gazes to that wall, allegedly pointing out an architectural detail but really drawing their attention in preparation for the power outage and the shadow play. He had done that when—"

The lights go out. Ms. Dowling sucks in breath. She says something, but it's drowned out by the murmur of the tour group—a cacophony of yelps and titters and excited whispers. A light flickers and someone shouts "There!"

I follow the light to see someone on the catwalk. It's a light-haired young woman in a plaid dress. It's still too dark down here to see, and I'm easing back to take Marius's arm when my hip bumps a hand. As I pull away, murmuring an apology, I feel a tug on my purse strap. I wheel, grabbing my bag, and there's a hand inside it. The hand withdraws fast. A yelp. Light flashes. It's Marius, raising his cell phone. His other hand encircles the wrist of a young man with my credit cards pinched between his fingers.

"Officers!" Marius calls.

The young man lashes out, punching at Marius with his free hand. Marius doesn't even stumble. He gives one twist and pins the pickpocket's arm behind his back.

"And where do you think you're going?" one of the officers calls as she steps into the path of a young woman edging toward the exit.

"Uh-uh," says a voice, and I glance to see Jonathan grabbing another man by the wrist. He lifts the man's arm and plucks out a cell phone in a flowered case.

"Hey!" a woman says. "That's mine."

Jonathan passes over the phone.

"What's going on here?" Ms. Dowling says.

"Seems you had some pickpockets in your tour group," Rian says as he checks his own pockets, everyone else doing the same. A few exclamations ring out—someone missing a cell phone, a few others missing cash or cards.

"Oh my goodness," Ms. Dowling says. "Thank you for catching them, officers. I can't believe anyone would do such a thing."

"Oh, I think you can believe it," Jonathan says. "Considering I saw you with this guy." He waggles the arm of the man he's restraining.

Ms. Dowling blinks. "Because he was asking about the tour. Which he joined with two friends."

Jonathan lifts his cell phone, showing a photo of Ms. Dowling and the guy he's holding. They're getting out of a car together. In the next photo, she's giving him a kiss before they presumably went their separate ways.

"I got suspicious this afternoon when someone told me you weren't following the old tour properly," Jonathan says. "That seems odd, since I presumed you'd borrowed our archives, which included a resident's full accounting of the tour—she'd been the assistant guide that night. But it turns out those archives have been missing for years. That got me digging. You didn't quite represent yourself accurately on your application, Ms. Dowling. You're not a historian, and you never went to Columbia. You run a vlog on ghost stories."

She bristles. "It's a history vlog. My angle may be ghosts, but I run an academic site specializing in the history surrounding ghost stories."

"Well, this isn't an actual ghost story," Hope says, waving at the rafters where Ms. Dowling's accomplice had appeared. "You faked it, together with your pickpocket boyfriend and his buddies."

Ms. Dowling continues to protest, but the police are already calling in backups, who are apparently just outside waiting.

"This was a sting, wasn't it?" I say to Jonathan as I walk over to him. "You knew."

"Ani and I figured it out. We told Chief Salazar, who'd already had her suspicions."

"There were reports of thefts last night," Ani says. "Coinciding with both the tour and the chaos afterward. Chief Salazar downplayed it so she wouldn't spook Ms. Dowling and her gang."

"That's the real reason they shut down stores last night," Jonathan says. "A would-be thief set off a security alarm at the jewelry store, and the police were worried it wasn't just a crime of opportunity."

Ani nods. "They thought it might have been orchestrated. They just didn't believe Ms. Dowling was involved."

"They thought someone was taking advantage of her tour, because she seemed legitimately startled," I say. "Who else knew about this?"

"Not me," Hope says.

Rian raises his hands.

I turn a narrow-eyed look on Marius.

"Yes, Jonathan asked me to keep an eye out," he says. "Though I would love to pretend it was my superior wits and reflexes that let me catch that guy with his hand in your purse."

"Wait," Ani says. "Where are Kennedy and Aiden?"

"They slipped out," Hope says, waggling her brows.

"I think it was more about sleuthing than smooching, sadly," I say. "They must have been trying to figure out the thefts."

"They're going to be disappointed," Hope says. "I know I am. It's such a Scooby-Doo solution. I'm still waiting for them to pull the mask off Ms. Dowling."

"Yep," Jonathan says. "Not exactly world-class thieves. Someone should go find Kennedy and Aiden, though. I suspect the police will want a head count."

"I will," I say. "Marius? May I get a little help with my escape?"

"One luck roll coming up."

CHAPTER TWELVE

I manage to sneak out of the auditorium by way of the backstage. I'm slipping through when there's a soft thump, followed by an oath. I break into a jog and find Kennedy standing in the entranceway of a dressing room, the door hidden behind a curtain. Inside, Aiden blocks someone trying to leave.

It's Mitch Keeling—Kennedy's IT guy. Also the person who'd wanted to stop tonight's tour.

"What's going on?" I whisper.

Kennedy starts to answer in a normal voice, and I wave her to silence and then bustle her inside and shut the door behind us.

"There was another fake ghost," I say. "The police are taking care of it." I leave off the part about the thefts. If Mitch is involved, I don't want him knowing his partners-in-crime have been apprehended. "Now, what's going on?"

"I spotted Mitch sneaking in," Kennedy says. "That's why we backed out of the tour. To see what he was up to. We caught him climbing into the rafters. Then we heard that fake ghost —*in* the rafters. Mitch ran down and tried hiding in here."

"It's not what you think," Mitch says.

"What do we think?" Kennedy asks.

"That I had something to do with the hauntings. I didn't. Last night's was obviously fake, and I wanted to prove it. I was hiding down here when I caught a glimpse of a young woman in a plaid dress heading up the ladder to the rafters. I took photos."

He pulls out his phone and shows us. "What I hoped to prove was *who* was behind it. I'm sure it's the tour guide."

"And your concern with that?" Aiden says.

"You've been awfully concerned with all of it," Kennedy muses. "Your family wasn't even here when it happened. I remember when you moved to Unstable and met Jackie. So why all the fuss about protecting the victim of a fifty-year-old local crime?"

"I might not be from Unstable originally, but I've made it my hometown. I didn't like this young woman taking advantage of our legends and our reputation. How will it affect our ghost tours if one is proven to be fake? How will it affect our entire town ethos? Unstable is built on the belief in the paranormal. One debunking, and the entire economy could collapse."

"Yeah, not quite," Kennedy says. "We've dealt with skeptics and debunkers for years, and Ms. Dowling is an outsider. No one would blame us." She steps closer to him. "I think your concern is more personal. You don't want the mystery solved because it would affect you."

"Affect me?" he sputters. "I wasn't even born yet. I couldn't have had anything to do with Lisa Lake's disappearance."

"Oh, I don't mean you directly. I mean someone in your family. Someone connected with the disappearance. Someone who knows exactly what happened."

Mitch blusters, but color rises in his face.

"A parent, maybe?" Kennedy says.

"If you're suggesting my father had anything to do with Lisa Lake's disappearance—"

"But he did, didn't he?" She takes out her phone and flips to a photo. "I found this online. A YouTube true-crime show covered Lisa's disappearance a few years back. They had a photo of her enhanced to show what she'd look like today."

She shows a photo of an elderly woman and continues, "I dug through my old picture files. This one's from five years ago. The annual Labor Day picnic. I was taking photos for Jonathan —the library wanted them for the archives." She lifts her phone, showing an elderly woman beside Mitch and his wife, his arms over both their shoulders.

Kennedy zooms in on the elderly woman and flips back to the age-enhanced shot of Lisa Lake. "It's not perfect, but it's a damn good likeness." She looks at him. "That's Lisa Lake. Your mother."

He opens his mouth to protest. A long pause. Then he deflates with a sigh. "Yes."

"I also tracked down your birthday," she says. "You were born six months after Lisa disappeared. Which is why I said her disappearance is kind of your dad's fault. She was pregnant with you, and so she staged her disappearance."

"Nice sleuthing," he says with a wry half-smile. "Yes, Mom was pregnant. She'd met a boy at bible camp. He asked if she was on the pill, and she had no idea what that meant. She didn't know what sex was or how babies were made either. That's what happens when your parents refuse you even the most basic sex ed. Mom really liked the boy—and she liked what they were doing—so she lied and said she was on the pill."

"And got pregnant."

He nods. "She was terrified of what her parents would do. Even before that, though, she wanted out. The pregnancy gave her an excuse to escape. My father helped her do that. They staged her disappearance, and his family took her in. My father's parents helped her to start over under a new name."

"She married your dad and took *his* name," I say. "They lived happily ever after."

He quirks a smile. "Not exactly. They became lifelong friends, but it wasn't the marrying kind of love. She actually married one of his college buddies, years later. I had a great biological father and a great stepdad. Also an amazing mother." He looks at us. "Whose legacy I want to protect."

"Legacy?" Aiden says.

"Mom passed away two years ago. She was so damned proud of her mystery." He chuckles. "She loved coming to Unstable and hearing people talk about it. She'd even ask about it, just for fun. She *adored* being the local unsolved mystery. There was no harm in it. No crime she was covering up. It made her happy, and yes, it's her legacy, as odd as that might sound."

"You're the one who removed the archives, aren't you," I say.

He sighs. "Yes. I'll return them. It was shortly after her death. I was still grieving, and I got a little overprotective."

"Which is why you tried to stop the tours?" Kennedy says.

"I didn't like the way Ms. Dowling was operating. Jackie's aunt reached out, and she ignored her. It was a cash grab in my mother's memory, and if I could stop her—legitimately—I wanted to. I wasn't going to do anything underhanded."

Mitch looks at us. "So I've confirmed your theory. Is there any way I can ask you to keep it between us? I honestly don't see how solving the mystery helps anyone."

"It doesn't," Kennedy says. "Your family secret is yours."

Aiden clears his throat. "On one condition."

We look at him.

He nods toward Kennedy. "You want to know how Lisa did it. You have a theory. Perhaps Mr. Keeling can confirm it."

"*We* have a theory," she says. "We think it was a switcheroo and that your aunt was in on it."

His lips twitch. "Go on."

"Your mom was only a year older than her sister. They looked similar enough to fool people who didn't know them. Backstage, they slipped behind the curtain and switched dresses. Your mom's dress was simple and loose-fitting. I presume your aunt's was, too. It'd take ten seconds to trade dresses. Maybe a quick hairstyle change to match—your aunt taking out a ponytail and your mom putting one in. Then your mom—pretending to be her sister—runs out complaining of stomach problems. All your parents see is her back. She flees into the bathroom, where she's probably stashed clothing. Your aunt proceeds into the theater with the group. Lights go out—as anyone familiar with the tour would expect—and she darts into the seating, leaving behind the ashes. Maybe she has a second dress there, similar to her original one. Change into that and, in the commotion, pretends to return as herself. Her parents return to the auditorium, and Lisa slips from the bathroom and out the main doors. She meets your dad outside, and they ride into the sunset together."

Kennedy looks at Mitch. "Close?"

"Close enough. Yes, my aunt helped. Most of it was her idea. She hoped if they came to Unstable's anniversary celebration, it'd be so busy that Mom could sneak away. But their parents weren't letting them out of their sight. So my aunt heard about the tour—and the lights going out—and devised plan B. Afterward, she stayed in touch with Mom, and they reunited the day she turned eighteen. So I had my aunt in my life, too. Still do. She lives in Seattle, gets over now and then."

"I'd love to meet her next time she visits," Kennedy says.

"She'd like that, too. A chance to share her grand adventure. Now, may I make my escape before anyone finds me here?"

"We'll help with that," I say, and I head out to make sure the path is clear.

CHAPTER THIRTEEN

We sneak Mitch out, and then we slip into the auditorium. Here again I acknowledge advantages to a small and tight-knit community. When Aiden and Kennedy return after being gone for the entire pickpocketing situation, the police do not for one second wonder whether they were involved. Kennedy is a Bennett, and Aiden is a family friend, and so they are above suspicion. I tell the officers that I found them in the change room, and all they get is a few knowing looks and chuckles, and then it's back to business.

Being from a leading local family, however, does not exempt you from having to stick around and answer the same questions as everyone else. In Kennedy's case, the police want to know if they saw anything backstage, and they mention the young woman—very much not a ghost—they spotted climbing into the rafters. That's it, and then we're all asked what we saw in the theater before being released to enjoy our evening.

Once we're outside, Rian murmurs, "Can we talk?" to Aiden, and they split off from the group. Ani and Jonathan decide they're in the mood for a patio cocktail. Kennedy wants to show Aiden the sights once he's done with Rian. Marius

CHAPTER 13 • 91

declares he absolutely requires that damned elephant ear, and Hope joins him, the two heading off to a booth.

Kennedy and I stroll along Bishop Street, slowly enough for the others to catch up. It's Saturday night, and the festival is in full swing. There are the usual carnival booths—corn dogs and elephant ears and deep-fried candy bars. But being Unstable, there's more. Some paranormal shtick, like a coffee pop-up specializing in "witches brew." There are also the more serious stalls and businesses, promising to read everything from your aura to your astrological chart. We pause at one specializing in palmistry, with a white owl perched outside. Kennedy waves to the owner—her neighbor, apparently—and pets the owl. Then we check on the rest of our group, with Marius and Hope still getting their fried-dough treats, and Aiden and Rian talking under a tree.

"You two seem to be getting on," I say. "You and Aiden."

"We are." She glances at me. "And if that's a nudge for us to 'get on' even better . . ."

"Mind my own business?" I say.

"I'd say it nicer, but yes, please." She steps to a booth and fingers a scarf decorated with mythical creatures. "I want to take my time. Get to know each other. 'Leap before you look' is my life's motto, and I don't want to do that this time. This is too important to jump in."

She looks toward Aiden. "Maybe it's just friendship. Maybe it's more. But whatever it is, I don't want to jeopardize what we have in hopes of getting more. If that makes sense."

I turn to watch Marius, coming back now, waving his elephant ear and saying something that makes Hope laugh.

"It makes perfect sense to me," I say.

OF COURSE MARIUS insists on the damnable Ferris wheel. It's not as if he was going to forget that, however chaotic the weekend has been. I roll my eyes and grumble and insist on checking the safety certificate, but that's all for show. He knows I'm going on it with him, and he knows I'll love it.

The others are also going, but it's a busy night, and the wheel is full when we get on, leaving them standing in line.

As we whoosh up, I gaze out over the town, with all its glittering lights, laughter bubbling up, the smell of popcorn making my stomach growl. Marius passes me his elephant ear, and I pull off a piece, and we enjoy the first revolution in silence.

Then I say, "I was wrong."

"What? You? Never."

"In the long term, I still suspect I'm right. Ani and Jonathan belong together. So do Kennedy and Aiden. I'm also not convinced Hope and Rian do. But for now, they are all where they want to be. Where they need to be."

Marius only nods, the wheel revolves again before I speak.

"I also realize this wasn't about them," I say. "I was projecting. Or transferring. Or whatever a therapist might call it. It was about me. What I need. What I'm not sure how to get. I was meddling in their love lives when the one I'm really worried about is my own."

I glance over at him. "I need to know if getting back together is off the table. Kennedy said she doesn't want to risk her friendship with Aiden by pushing for more. I feel the same, and I need to know if you've had enough."

"Enough of what? Of *you*?"

"I know I'm difficult. I'm dramatic, and I'm demanding, and it can be too much. Far too much."

"No," he says, meeting my gaze. "It can never be too much, Vess. Not for me. I wish you'd stop feeling as if you're—" He inhales, cutting that short. "You left because of Havoc, and that hurt. Of everyone, I expected you to understand. When you left, I felt abandoned. But I came to realize I'd abandoned *you*. You were concerned about me, and I couldn't see that."

He's quiet. That silence might seem as if it's waiting to be filled, but I know it's not, and I wait it out.

He continues. "I pushed Havoc out on her own, as gently as I could, but that didn't fix things between us. So I decided I needed to make a grand gesture."

"The necklace."

"Yep, which went horribly awry. You had to deal with Havoc, which reminded me how she treated you, how unfair it'd been to inflict her on you. I always feel as if I know you best and see through your walls, but with that, I didn't. You said Havoc's bullshit didn't bother you, and I stupidly believed it. Then there was Hector."

I grumble under my breath.

"Yep, he never quite goes away, does he? But seeing again how he treats you reminded me that I can never *be* like him. In any way. I can't push. I need to wait for you to come to me."

"I handled the Havoc situation badly. I should have been honest, but I was mostly upset about what she put *you* through. As for Hector, I would never make that mistake. I know if you want to get back together, I can always say I'm not ready, and you always respect that."

His eyes meet mine. "So are you ready?"

"Beyond ready."

As the wheel swings up, he leans over, hand behind my head and pulls me into a kiss. A whoop sounds below us, and I look down to see Hope bouncing and giving us a high five, Kennedy and Rian cheering, even Aiden clapping.

"Well," Marius says. "One match was made this weekend, and everyone seems happy about that. I call it a win."

"The biggest win," I say, and I kiss him again.

DAIQUIRIS & DAGGERS

A Faery Bargains Novella

By

Melissa Marr

"Come down here!" I stalked around the edges of the mausoleum. Some enterprising soul had festooned the edges of the mausoleum roof with concertina wire. The deadly décor glittered right now thanks to the mix of torrential rain and the glowing streetlights.

Millicent Johnson, eighteen and dead, was supposed to be in her grave. When her mother came to weep at her daughter's grave, she found the ground disturbed. Millie had crawled out of the earth, infected with *draugr* venom. That or necromancy were the only ways to walk after death.

With much wailing and angst, the Johnsons hired me to retrieve her and deliver her to a T-Cell House. After a number of years in containment, Millie would be as rational as any teen. She'd need blood, and never physically age, but short of beheading, nothing would end Millie's un-life.

For that un-life to progress, I had to capture Millie tonight. I'm a necromancer, sometimes freelancer for NOPD, and I do the occasional job for the queen of the *draugr* in this region of the world. All that considered, capturing one dead teenager ought to be easy.

It wasn't.

If she went on an indiscriminate murder spree, typical of the newly dead, she'd be beheaded post-haste. When the *draugr* were revealed, Icelandic folklore revealed to be fact, laws had been made. Walls had been built. Panic had fed a sort of societal shift. According to those laws the Johnsons ought to have observed the required waiting period instead of burying the girl. They'd have saved themselves a pile of cash and saved me a long, wet evening.

"Come on, Millie." I held out my arm, not beckoning exactly her but as if I was holding kibble out toward a cat in a tree.

As rain continued to soak me to the bone, I decided I was willing to pretend to be kibble if it meant she came down easily. This was to be a simple bag and tag, the sort of recovery that I'd been able to pull off even as a teenager still trying to get comfortable with a sword.

"So help me, if I have to crawl up there . . ." I circled again, not entirely sure how to manage this. "Get *down* here, Millie!"

Millie growled at me, glaring at the sword in my hand. She was hunched over, balancing on her hands and feet like she was imitating a less verbal primate. I'd nudge her ass-over-tea-kettle if I could, but the height of the mausoleum meant she was out of reach. And the concertina wire meant that I couldn't vault up there without spilling my blood—which, as a necromancer, I wasn't keen to do in a cemetery.

"If I can't contain you, I *will* chop that pretty head off," I threatened, stalking her from the sopping wet ground. At least if she leaped down, I could catch her. "I mean it, Millicent, pop goes the weasel! Off with your head!"

Millie paused, but unfortunately, she couldn't actually be threatened into clarity. *Draugr* didn't start their "second lives" terribly coherent. They were akin to toddlers, all instinct and drool. Again-walkers grew in clarity and strength after they were transfused, but the newly risen were far from clarity. By about a decade—if they weren't beheaded before that—*draugr* would be nearly indistinguishable from humans most of the time. They were stronger, faster, hard to kill, and mostly allergic to sunlight.

My job was stopping them before they went around New Orleans ripping throats out. Or, in cases like this, I was hired for bagging and tagging so they could be warehoused.

I pointed at the muddy wet ground. "Down, Millie!"

She plopped down on the roof of the mausoleum—looking like a dripping-wet, dead princess—and stared at me.

"Not what I meant!" I swiped at the water sluicing down my face.

Millicent was very obviously *not* coming down. I wasn't an archer, so I had no projectiles other than bullets. That left me with the choice of either waiting until she eventually came down or leaving a confused *draugr* perched on top of a grave. Both options sucked.

I shoved my hair out of my face, flinging water. "Damn it."

I hated bag and tag jobs. Killing was easier than capturing, but that wasn't my objective tonight.

"Millie?" I beckoned. "*Please?*"

I was a witch, born and raised as one. It was a part of my maternal lineage, along with Jewish faith. My paternal genes were more complicated. The sperm-donor was already a walking corpse when he impregnated my mother, so I was the world only living dead woman. Half dead. Half witch. Between the two sides of my heritage, capturing Millie ought to be easy.

Until recently, it *was*. In fact, I was the only haman *draugr* in existence as far as I knew. I had counted on that aspect of my heritage to be enough to handle a simple job. For most of my life, I could summon the dead from their graves to help me in whatever I needed. It made for an awkward childhood, but it was the basis of my career. I was the witch to call for beheadings, summoning the dead, or capturing the walking dead.

However, a few weeks ago, I'd summoned so very many corpses that I'd accidentally restored a dead man to life. Since then, my necromancy was . . . sluggish. Apparently, if I drained my magical reserves, I needed time to recharge.

Who knew?

"Damn it, Millicent. Get your dead ass down here. Right this moment . . . or else!"

"Bonbon?" Eli's laughing voice behind me had me spinning around too quickly.

My feet went out from under me, and I landed flat on my back. Now I was not just soaked but muddy, too. Slimy ooze coated my back, squishing into the neck of my jacket. "Ugh."

My husband held out a hand, as if to help me from a carriage not a muddy mess. I accepted, letting him tug me to my feet, but I dug my feet into the ground, stopping him from embracing me. "What are you doing here?"

"You were late, so . . ." Eli gave an elegant half-shrug that pretended the act was nonchalant. It wasn't. He worried since my magical depletion, balancing on a line between infuriating me by hovering and happening to be near when I needed help. It was graceful enough, explainable enough, that I couldn't even yell at him for being smothering.

And truth was that I *needed* the help more than I'd like. The past three months had been rough. My magic was absentee, and I was restless.

"Plus, I missed looking at you," Eli added lightly. The look in his eyes—and the fact that the fae can't lie—made it clear that he somehow found me appealing even spattered in muck.

I tilted my head up, letting the still-pouring rain wash away some of the mud. My hair, more brown than its usual blue thanks to my impromptu mud bath, hung in clumps, and I was doing a great impression of a wet cat. "You, Eli, are a lunatic."

"Perhaps." He shrugged again. Sometimes, I wished he was a little less breathtaking. The combination of the way he looked at me and the way he looked was distracting. From cut glass cheeks to courtesan's lips, Eli was much too beautiful to be in the rain with my muddy self. Even dripping wet, his darker-than-black hair hid glimmers of stars. Entire universes blinked out at me.

"You shouldn't look at me that way when I'm . . ." I gestured at my muddy self.

Eli shrugged in a way that only a man like him could pull off: elegant, careless, and utterly telling all at once. "You would need to pluck my eyes out for me to look at you any other way."

"Fine. You're pretty, too," I muttered.

Eli chuckled before looking up at the dead girl who was watching us with a keen interest. "How's work?"

"Obstinate. Work is obstinate." I swiped mud out of my hair. "Princess Squirrel here won't—"

"I see," he interrupted before I could rant. "Could you summon her? As with proper corpses?"

I sighed and admitted, "If someone gave me an energy boost . . ."

"My damsel in distress," Eli murmured, stepping closer.

I had a sword raised before he could touch me. "Not a fucking damsel."

"*My* damsel." He pushed my sword away. "As you are, undoubtedly, also my knight."

"Sweet talker." I pulled him closer with a muddy hand fisted in his shirt and kissed him. The moment my lips touched his, I felt the wave of faery magic. His magic. I should have been able to draw on it at will since we were wed, but that, too, was beyond me currently.

Eli poured his energy into me, and I could taste fresh water and blossoming trees.

When he pulled away, I had only moments before that surge would resettle itself in me, feed my depleted reserves, and vanish. I needed my magic to return to me.

I stared up at the dead girl. "Get down here, Millicent Leigh Johnson."

This time, my words held a compulsion, a magical command wrought by my necromancy.

The *draugr* girl stood and cartwheeled to the ground. Millie landed with a sploosh of mud, but as I was already filthy, I couldn't object. Quickly, I bound her hands and feet, smacked a bite-proof gag over her mouth, and dropped my magical hold.

Eli waited, not touching me while I did what I must.

"I free you, Millicent Leigh Johnson. Not mine. Not yours." I stepped back just as the light was returning to her eyes.

As soon as I dropped my compulsion over Millie, she flopped around like an angry caterpillar trying to bite me through the gag. No longer calm, she wanted my blood or at least to strike out at her captor.

"Cutting it close, bonbon," Eli murmured.

I nodded. If I was connected to any *draugr* when Eli's magic stopped working for me, the dead would become my responsibility. I was a human, a witch, so it ought not work that way. Unfortunately, the secret that only my closest friends and family knew was that being a witch-*draugr* hybrid meant that my particular magical affinity—necromancy—had combined with my *draugr* genetics. In sum, I could do things that only the oldest *draugr* could do: bind and control. Any *draugr* I bound to me would be coherent as long as she stayed near me, and if that particular information were to be revealed, I would be both a threat to existing *draugr* hierarchy—and sought after by those who wanted to be brought back to a second life.

However, I had no interest in collecting minions. I'd already accidentally bound two *draugr*, and I was fairly sure I'd bound my human assistant, too. I felt responsible for them, which I hated. I was not interested in adding to that list. Some people wanted an army, or a flock to mother, or didn't feel responsible for those who served them. Me? I didn't even want to have houseplants.

Eli called for transport while I hauled Millie to her feet. "Come on. Up you go."

My hand on her bound wrists wasn't enough to keep her standing. Millie jerked out of my hold and fell to the ground. We repeated the process several times, mostly because I was too stubborn to ask Eli to help, and he was adamant that he would not "overstep" unless my life depended on it.

So, I hauled a trussed up dead girl to the gate where a bright purple van with T-CELL TRANSITION HOMES emblazoned on the side waited.

Once they took the growling girl away, I stood there, wet and muddy but victorious.

"Shall I tell Alice to invoice the Johnsons?" Eli's voice was calm enough to make clear that he wasn't sure of my mood.

"Yep. And add ten percent for complications." I met his gaze. "Dead folk are not supposed to perch on any roof."

Eli nodded, his expression unreadable.

"What?"

"Would you object to walking to the bar, Geneviève?" He offered me his arm, chivalrous as always.

"What? No chariot?" I looked around for his little blue convertible.

Eli was silent for a long moment before saying, "You smell rather atrocious, love."

I sniffed. Obviously, someone had been taking Fido on walkies in among the graves and not scooping. The slimy mud in my jacket was not *just* mud from the smell of it. "Ugh. I stink. I need a shower and a vacation."

"As you wish, bonbon."

And then my patient spouse escorted my mud and poo-coated self to Bill's Tavern, where we walked through the bar and into the back. I all but ran to the shower while Eli was still peeling off his soaking clothes. He was polite enough to give me space to get clean before joining me.

CHAPTER TWO

I sat at the breakfast table as the sun started to dim the next evening. Eli was out somewhere, so I woke alone and filled with nervous energy. I couldn't say that anything specific was wrong. No open cases. No recent attacks or threats on my life. No question or doubt in my relationship. I ought to be more relaxed than I felt. Maybe I was simply accustomed to anxiety and worry.

Eli and I were bonded. Together until one of us died. We'd had a month-long honeymoon after our bonding, and although everyone else was nagging me to get on with dress shopping and venue booking, Eli was being absurdly patient about planning wedding ceremonies. *Plural.* I'd have to endure a wedding in *Elphame* as well as in New Orleans—well, in The Outs where I was raised. We were having a wedding on the land where my mother homesteaded not in the city proper.

Wedding talk was as overwhelming as my magical depletion and my newly married status.

My life was out of *my* control lately, and the details of the weddings were more than I could manage. I'd gotten as far as agreeing to two ceremonies. It was either that or only have the fussy future-queen ceremony in *Elphame*. That was a hard pass. Not everyone was able to travel there. The realm of the fae was separate from the human world, and *most* faeries stayed there. The man who'd once been my friend, fight partner, and was now my spouse had failed to mention that he was not only fully fae, but the self-exiled prince. I had no interest in thrones, but if that's what I had to do to be with Eli . . . well, love makes a person do weird things sometimes. In my case, it meant politics, fussy dresses, and several weddings.

I'd decided that if there was going to be a wedding at all, I'd have at least one wedding that was to *my* taste. We started out discussing the two "suitable" places for formal weddings in the city: the Touro Synagogue, one of the oldest synagogues in the nation, and Saint Louis Cathedral in Jackson Square, the oldest church in the nation. They both held the gravitas appropriate for the wedding of the heir to *Elphame* and his bride, but the thought of being a spectacle, of having strangers gawk at us, of the sheer pageantry of it all made me cringe.

And so, I'd been delaying. Avoiding. Eli and I were already married, so who needed a big fancy mess? "Avoid and procrastinate" was still my default setting for emotional things. Weddings, much like funerals, were for the attendees, and so I wanted nothing to do with either. Call me selfish, but I thought that some things, some moments, ought to be reserved for the guest-of-honor. And Eli was simply content to do whatever made me happiest.

So, I stalled.

I pondered it constantly, though.

The door downstairs opened, which meant Eli was here. No one else could enter. Not surprisingly, the home of the one and only fae prince was fairly secure.

I topped off my drink, pouring mead and blood into my glass in equal measures. Think alcohol smoothie. Add a generous splash of blood, and that was my diet. My metabolism was high—and weird. Alcohol fueled me, but I wasn't intoxicated by it. I was basically a fanged hummingbird.

"Bonbon?" Eli paused, frowning at me. "Has something happened?"

"Nope."

"Are you unwell?"

"Nope."

"Are you planning on explaining or saying 'nope' at me until I guess?" He came to the table, took my hand and pulled me to my feet. "Maudlin?"

"I'm sick of my magical depletion," I admitted as I stared at the only person not yet frustrated with my moods lately. "I want to *do* things. I can't raise the dead, and—"

"You brought a man back to life, Geneviève."

"A bad man."

"Iggy hasn't done anything troubling." Eli wrapped his arms around me.

"Yet," I muttered.

"Perhaps you need a get-away. Something to let you relax so your magic can resettle."

"I feel useless. To do basic things, I need to borrow your—"

"Our," he corrected. "*Our* magic."

"Our magic," I repeated, after a scowl. "Fine. Fine. I can work, but . . ." I glanced up at my husband's very emotionless expression.

"You *are* working, then?" he prompted.

"Yes." I moved out of his embrace.

"But you must rely on me to do so, and that is frustrating after being self-reliant since as long as you can recall," Eli explained my work anxiety calmly and succinctly.

I smacked his chest lightly. "Yes, damn it. I feel weak."

"You have faced Death more times than anyone I know, and each time Death runs away like a frightened dog." He caught my chin in his hand and tipped my face up, so I was looking at him before continuing, "You are not weak, Geneviève. You are trying to refill your magical core after managing a god-like feat. You ought to relax rather than trying to force it."

I was about to agree that he had a point.

Then he added, "But you are an absolutely horrible patient, with the serenity of a child who ate a bowl of straight sugar."

"Hey!"

"Am I wrong?" Eli stared at me with the same arrogance that had made him alluring to me when we first met years ago. He was not lacking in confidence.

I deflated. "No."

"So, let us ponder options." Eli walked away, heading into his—*our*—living area. I could ignore the invitation or follow. He'd offered me the control.

And I was reminded for the two million six hundred and eighth time that Eli really was perfect for me. It apparently took the patience of a faery to worm his way into my heart *and* to live with me.

I followed him, marveling over the wonder that he wanted me despite my catalogable list of complications. Not that he was without difficulty. He came with a damned throne, longevity, and traditions I barely understood most of the time.

We compromised *a lot*.

He'd added a fight dummy to the far side of the living room when we got married. To most people, it probably wouldn't seem like a romantic gesture, but I like hitting things. My own apartment had most of the space dedicated to fighting, but now that we were bonded, I preferred to sleep here at least half of the time.

I touched the dummy, Harper, on the way past. Yes, I name all my fight dummies. Elvis, Bruce, and Doris were my first three, and I'd considered each of their names at length. I liked Doris the best for punching. She was on a wheeled mount so she "flinched."

"I have taken the liberty of giving Christy a long weekend off either this week or next," Eli said as I sat next to him on the sofa. It sounded like a non sequitur.

"Okaaaay . . ." I wasn't sure why he'd given his bar manager, who was one of my closest friends, the weekend off.

"I have *also* taken the liberty of asking Sera if she would be free. Her schedule is more complicated, but—"

"I'm going to need more details, Eli. What does any of this have to do with *anything*?" I interrupted.

He held out a shiny laminated card proclaiming me fae royalty. I'd seen his diplomatic card, but this one was mine. My name. My passport.

"You are the future queen of Elphame, Geneviève. You have a diplomatic passport. No questions. No temperature checks."

"I . . ." I blinked at him, too stunned to process. I'd never really been able to travel far or often. Sure, there were cities that were exceptions, but there were a lot more cities that were forbidden to *draugr*. Those were where I wanted to be, cities where I could truly relax. No dead folk to behead. No pressure to patrol. Any gate checks for such cities could expose me, and after my recent injection of draugr venom I was sure I'd fail. I had failed when we tried to go to Houston. If not for Eli pulling his own diplomatic passport, we would've been turned away.

And the fact that there was a *draugr* with a heartbeat? That was the sort of thing that made international news. The reality was that being one of a kind was dangerous.

"There were not insignificant delays." Eli's voice hid an edge that made me realize that he'd been angrier about those delays than he typically got about anything. "But the matter has been resolved."

I clutched the card, staring at it and marveling. I stared at him. "I can travel."

He nodded.

"Holy goat milk! I can *travel*." I hugged Eli. "For real, travel to places."

"Yes." He smiled possibly because it had been a minute since he'd seen me quite this excited about anything that involved both of us wearing clothes.

Eli lifted a thick manilla folder from the side table. "Alice has been researching, and she will be available this weekend."

He slid the folder toward me.

The last time my assistant had researched a trip, I ended up owning far too much frilly lingerie and accidentally marrying Eli. I had no regrets, but sometimes I thought Alice Chaddock had a magical chaos magnet in her body somewhere.

Tentatively, I opened the folder. "Houston?" was written in Ally's handwriting across the top of a print-out of stapled pages. I lifted the sheath of pages. Underneath was "Prague? Probably too far." A fanged frownie face was drawn there. Several other packets were under those two.

"Alice researched options for a 'Girls Weekend,'" Eli said, wincing a bit at the term.

I was across the slight distance between us and in his arms in the next moment. My husband, my perfect faery prince of a spouse, had put the wheels in motion so I could go away with my friends.

"You are the absolute best," I announced before setting out to prove that truth.

CHAPTER THREE

Later that evening I curled up with the travel options. Prague was, regrettably, too far. I'd seen so many pictures and videos of the Czech Republic that I desperately wanted to visit. And Edinburgh. And Amsterdam. And Berlin. So many places, and suddenly I was allowed to go to places that my genetics had forbidden for my whole life.

After narrowing in on three options—beach, beach, or beach—I decided it was time to get outside opinions. I called Allie, Sera, and Christy for a meeting.

Since Christy was visiting her boyfriend Jesse at work at Tomes and Tea, the bookstore I part-owned despite refusing to cash any of my checks, we agreed to meet there. Since the bookshop was in Gentilly, a good five miles away, I texted Allie and asked her to pick up Sera. Jesse was my oldest, dearest friend, but this was a designated *Girls'* Weekend, so we'd be leaving him behind.

I set out on a jog through the city—not that I *wanted* to jog but I was developing a fear that my *draugr* speed would vanish, too.

Maybe it was silly, but then again, my necromancy's absence had seemed impossible before now, too, and yet here I was, unable to raise even a dead rat. My sudden limits had me anxious in ways I couldn't explain. So, I'd started running a few times a week. It's not like it would hurt me to get regular exercise that had nothing to do with weapons.

I fucking hated running, but the part that no one talks about with physical jobs—and beheading the dead was often an exceedingly physical job—was that you had to keep in shape. Not like boxing movie training montages, but everything from push-ups to jogging, yoga to canoeing. Lots of muscles meant that a varied workout was important.

With my magic on the fritz, I was pouring that frustration into exercise.

I paused along the sidewalk for a long pull of vodka with frozen blood cubes from my water bottle. Hydration was *extra* essential. My diet was almost fully liquid. I could—and did—eat solid food, but it wasn't, strictly speaking, necessary. I used to live on liquor and smoothies, but lately my liquid diet included blood, too. It made me feel gross if I thought about it, but if I ignored that element of my nutritional needs, my stomach cramped, my reflexes slowed, and my general well-being suffered. *Draugr*, although once thought to be nothing more than Icelandic folklore, were blood-drinkers. They sustained their organs with the blood of the living, which meant that I, despite being alive, had started to need fresh blood. It was as gross as it sounded, but I had no choice.

So, there were little heart-shaped, frozen blood cubes in my vodka.

Thankfully, I hadn't started sweating or weeping blood like some bad film. However, I did sweat enough tonight that I smelled like I'd been on a bender, but this was New Orleans. Even after the *draugr* were revealed, we were clutching our Sazeracs and Hurricanes on Bourbon Street. Nothing stopped the party that was life in the Crescent City, not even the appearance of the again-walkers. Booze might not literally be the lifeblood of the city, but it was as essential to our locals and our tourists as the history and music that made New Orleans a glimmering light in the world.

Inside Tomes and Tea, business was still hopping. I was pleased to see little group of readers, including the new start-up "book club with car service" I'd proposed last month. People, locals mostly, were less inclined to go out after hours because of the *draugr*, but Jesse's bar was a "no *draugr* territory"—under penalty of death—thanks to a little discussion with my dear dead grandmother, Beatrice. We'd sort of reconnected. Although she was one of the dead creatures I hunted, she was also my ancestor, and she was eager to make me happy.

Ergo, my bestie's bookstore was a secure place for humans.

Once I knew the shop was a safe space, I'd proposed that Jesse start a night owl's bookclub. It was an opportunity for New Orleanians who were pretty much locked in from dusk till dawn to go out somewhere that was guaranteed safe. From the looks of it, the club was already larger than we'd initially dreamed.

When I walked toward the stairs to go up to Jesse's private space, I paused.

Jesse had the frustrated expression everyone who has ever worked in a shop has worn at least a few times. Next to him was an older man pointing at one of the books in the containment boxes.

Jesse had a tight expression. "As I said, that isn't currently available for sale. They're more decorative—"

"Do you have any idea what that *decoration* is worth?" the older man interrupted.

"Since I'm the one who purchased it, I do, in fact," Jesse said.

"Name a price."

"It's not for sale." Jesse stressed each word, attempting to sound more intimidating that he was. Although Jesse was the sort of man who looked like he wasn't afraid of much—muscles, deep eyes, dark skin, assorted tattoos—he was kind to a fault.

I strolled up with the confidence that came of too much comfort with weapons and magic. A quick glance at the book clarified exactly what I needed to know. The tome in question was one darker than Jesse ought to ever touch, so I'd paid for it when it came to the store. I didn't use it, but it was, technically, mine. Being mine didn't mean I wanted the book in my house. Some books ought to be kept in magic-proof cases. This was one of them.

"Mr. Woods is trying to buy a book that's not for sale, sis," Jesse said as he moved back.

Calling me "sis" casually was our way of saying "step in." I'd started it, calling him "little brother" when I wanted him to get out of the way, and "big brother" when I wanted him to chase off a guy who was obnoxious. It was also accurate in all ways that matter. Jesse was family in all ways but blood.

"I believe my little brother has already answered you." I smiled at Jesse as he walked away. Then, I turned to the man. "We aren't interested in selling this book."

"We?"

"It's my store, too." I smiled again, colder now as I was feeling both irritated at the reality that the customer was, in fact, not always right and because this one was screwing up my good mood.

"Perhaps you'll see reason, Miss . . ." The man extended his hand like we should shake.

"Crowe." I ignored the outstretched hand. Magic some-times required touch, and I wasn't in the habit of making that easier for any potential enemies.

I felt tendrils of inquiry, magical questions brush against me, and it irritated me. My own magic was still sleepy, but I felt it stirring in defense. To him, though, I seemed weak.

Slowly and purposefully, I drew a dagger that was almost long enough to be a single-handed sword. At the same time, I used my absolute best customer service voice and said, "Mr. Woods, I am a necromancer. I freelance for NOPD and the queen of the *draugr* in this region. Do you really want to provoke me?"

He pivoted and left without a word.

From behind me, I heard, "You're sort of scary, boss."

Alice Chaddock—thirty, beautiful, and dressed to stun—stood there with a flat of coffee cups from Sera's place. Next to her was Sera. Both were curvy redheads, although Sera was deep rich red and Allie had that just-set-fire red. Honestly, they looked like they could be related. The difference was that Allie was always ready to pull up a chair and have popcorn when I was in a situation, and Sera gave me that look that said she'd seriously been pondering shoving my ass into a tower in a remote forest because she just wanted a break from worrying about me. My near-death event before the holidays had rattled my friends a lot. Okay. So had my brush with death during the holidays.

And it was quite possible that I'd caused a bit of anxiety with my recent necromantic event where I raised an ancient cemetery and brought a dead Hexen back to life. Sera was eying me in ways that made me want to scream. This was me. Who I am. What I chose. It wasn't like I wanted to die, but I was gifted with skills that made me suited for conflict. I felt obliged to do the proverbial "right thing" even though it stressed out my friends.

In my defense, none of the near-death things had been planned. I didn't really *like* being attacked, stabbed, shot, or other things either. It was just a hazard of being me, and for all that my friends loved me, I think my job was exhaustive to them, too.

"Christy's upstairs," Sera said in that tense "not this again" voice. She nudged us that way. "Time for vacation planning."

"Should we relocate that book first?" Allie asked. "He doesn't seem the giving up sort. Should I call Bea—"

"Not tonight." I folded my arms and beamed at Sera, trying to non-verbally let her know everything was just fine. Cheerily, I added, "*We* are planning a trip. The book can wait for tonight. It's been here three months. Three more days will be fine."

"Are you sure?" Allie prompted.

I looked at Sera, and decided that whatever else was going on, we all needed that holiday weekend. "Positive. Let's go."

Jesse waved cheerily as the man stomped out the front door, and then he flipped the sign to closed, locked the door, and went back to his night owls book club.

"Juice in the fridge, Gen!" he called.

"I really have the *best* brother." I flashed him a smile and left him to debate the merits of the latest read.

As I headed up to the apartment with Sera and Allie in tow, Allie quietly murmured, "I think we ought to tell Beatrice."

I sighed. "Agreed. Just . . . not today."

My assistant was a *lot* on her best of days, but I trusted her instincts. Actually, I trusted all of my friends' instincts. That was sort of the point, though. True friends, we'll-move-a-body-for-you friends, were the people who filled in the gaps for one another. We were a family of sorts, a misfit-band who might not look like we were all one unit, but when things were stressful, we were a team.

"Seriously?" Christy's voice came from the kitchen where she was watching one of the security cameras. "I swear that man could be nice to Satan herself—"

"Do you mean Beatrice or real Satan?" Allie paused in her texting to ask. "Ohh, is real Satan like *real?*"

No one answered in the three seconds that followed so Allie kept going: "Can I get a screen shot from the security cams? I took a few pictures, but Lady B's assistant . . . I wonder if there's an official assistant group that—"

"Allie. Focus."

Allie walked up to the monitor in front of Christy and pointed. "Right! So, can I?"

Christy Zehr was both one of the smartest people I knew, and one of those stunning women that pulled off either intimidating or fade into the background depending on which was needed. The towering Black woman looked down at the diminutive chatterbox in front of her and asked, "Gen?"

One syllable was all I needed.

"Alice is coordinating info in case the guy downstairs was a magic worker," I clarified. Then I looked at Allie. "Please, Allie, do not ask my grandmother if she's Satan. She might be a dead woman, but she's a *Jew*."

"So . . . Satan can only torment Christians?" Allie asked in an increasingly twangy voice. In public, she contained her rural roots, but I swore she sounded like this just because it got a rise out of Christy.

Like I said, we were family, and this family's shit-stirrer was Alice. She'd tried to murder me last year, and Christy and Jesse were the hold-outs on the forgiveness front. I understood why. Allie had been in a bad situation, and back then, I was just a stranger. Alice was a lot of things, but she was loyal to a fault. That loyalty was mine now, and honestly, I understood *why* she tried to kill me then. My friends were a lot less accepting.

Silently, I held out my back-up water bottle to Christy. "Vodka, no blood."

Christy took it and walked into the living room. Sera followed.

"Behave or I'll leave you home to babysit the fight dummies," I warned Allie.

She offered a semi-penitent smile. "Yes, boss."

"I mean it."

This time, she straightened up. "Let me send this to Lady B and then I'll be good. Scout's Honor!" She crossed her heart, which even I knew was not the right gesture, but really there was a limit to what was possible where Allie was concerned.

CHAPTER FOUR

"So South Beach? Myrtle Beach? San Diego? Savannah?" Sera knew me well enough that she didn't bother asking about inland options. I'd had dreams of beaches as long as I could recall. New Orleans offered the banks of the Mississippi and a gator-filled bayou. It was lovely in its own way, but not quite the beach of my dreams.

I was trying to be considerate, though, so I said, "I thought maybe some of you might have opinions . . ."

Christy shook her head. "As long as there's liquor, I'm flexible."

I frowned. Christy wasn't a big drinker. She ran Eli's bar, and she'd hustled pool in it for years. Both required sobriety.

"Liquor? *That's* the criteria. Why?" I asked.

"Hangry Gen? No thanks." Christy grinned at me, and then she pointed at Alice. "And dealing with *her* while we're sober?"

Allie, thankfully, had taken my warning seriously. "I swear to be good. If you say 'shut up,' I'll—"

"Shut up," Sera interrupted.

Allie stared at her, but she closed her mouth. After a few moments, she raised her hand like we were in a classroom.

"Yes?" Sera prompted.

"I have a place down on the North Carolina coast, or there's a great spa in San Diego. Either one would be super cheap." Allie plopped down on the sofa, folding her legs up in some sort of yoga-ish way.

We exchanged looks.

"How is the spa cheap? Spas are usually expensive, aren't they?" Christy finally asked.

"Sure, but . . . I sort of bought it when Prince Eli said you wanted to get away," Allie muttered.

"You bought a spa when . . . we . . . seriously? Who *does* that?" I stared at her. My assistant was wealthier than anyone I knew--other than my husband--but sometimes it still made my head hurt that she was so impulsive.

"I didn't buy it *for* you." Allie pouted like the trophy wife she'd been when I met her. "I just thought that it was a way to atone for the SAFARI days. I would run fae specials, witch specials, and maybe *draugr* specials, but only for those Lady B approved."

Alice gave me a look that shouldn't work on me, but still did. I knew she was sincere, trying to atone for her prior hate-group affiliation, and she honestly had the excess money. I just didn't know what to say. "But . . . you *bought* it?"

"Lady Beatrice looked over the investment papers. I even ran it by Prince Eli." Allie looked proud. "We don't need to go there, but at some point, I do. I mean, I bought it. So, I ought to visit and see it."

I exchanged a look with Christy and Sera.

"I'll give you a good discount," Allie added. "Like a package rate! And maybe you can give me business owner tips?" She looked first at Sera and then at Christy. "Or management tips?"

"San Diego, then?" Sera asked.

"San Diego," Christy agreed.

As much as I didn't know how I felt about the spa part, I

couldn't contain the smile on my face. "I'm going to see the Pacific fucking *Ocean*."

WITHIN MOMENTS of deciding where we were going, Allie had whipped out her laptop to book flights.

"We can charter a flight to go direct," Allie suggested. "Or there's coach class with a layover."

"Charter," Christy said. "The boss is covering the flight." She shot me a sympathetic look. "Sorry, Gen. He's worried about too much publicity because of the you're-the-co-heir-to-the faery-throne thing."

I nodded. I was only the heir at all because of marrying Eli. I had zero interest in being royalty—although I was pretty damn stoked by my diplomatic passport.

The reality, however, was that I was remarkably unsuited to any throne. I couldn't quite wrap my head around the idea that anyone would give two shakes of a duck's butt about me. I guess blue-haired necromancers were rare enough, and the thought of a human—and witches were, in fact, considered human—marrying into fae royalty was supremely news-worthy.

Draugr-human, on the other hand, might create a different sort of news. I'd lived most of my entire twenty-nine years so far with a vague fear that I'd end up in a lab, dissected by zealous scientists. Don't get me wrong: I'm very pro-science. I'm also very pro-not-dying. And the fear—the *rightful* fear—humanity had of *draugr* meant that I wasn't sure science would care too much about my death if it resulted in answers that would assuage fears. I was genetically linked to the monsters. I couldn't blame scientists for seeking answers.

But I was hoping to never get exposed for what I was. That meant no travel. My weird genetics would set off alarms. Now, though, my first flight was going to be on a small, chartered plane.

". . . and they specialize in unique clientele," Allie was saying. Obviously, she'd been talking while I was still pondering, so I nodded as if I'd been listening.

"So, you're saying 10 in the *morning* actually works for you?" Christy prompted.

I guess I'd missed that detail.

"Sure!" I said in forced cheer.

"The boss can nap in flight." Allie clicked a few more keys on her laptop with a flourish. "Tomorrow, we head west!"

THE NEXT DAY, hours after our meeting, the four of us were picked up in an extended-length, black SUV. When I climbed in, I had to suppress a wide smile.

"Excited?" Christy prompted.

My attempt to look calm faltered. "You have no idea."

I'd packed light on clothes and modestly on weapons. My sword-and-bikini bag clattered as it was loaded into the rear of the SUV.

"Are you still going to sleep in flight?" Sera shot me a concerned look.

"Cat naps are all I really need since my, err"--I lowered my voice--"accidental marriage."

"Accidental?" Christy scoffed. "Did you trip and land on his dick? While naked? And professing love?"

Allie and Sera both smothered laughs, and I couldn't help but smile, too.

"Tripping over Eli and being naked is not as uncommon in my life as you might think," I faux protested.

"You're so lucky." Allie made a swooning, sighing sound.

"True," I admitted with a smile. I really really was. *Anyone* finding love was lucky.

I had never expected to be married, but Eli was everything I could want. He understood me. He saw me as an equal. And he never tried to change me. Plus, to be fair, he was the single most beautiful person I'd ever met.

Calling my marriage accidental was unfair. True love and sex created an unbreakable marriage bond with the fae, and my suspicions that what Eli and I shared was true love had been confirmed when a moment of perfect unity—a naked and sweaty moment—had resulted in an eternal bond.

I didn't regret it.

Before that, there were loopholes we'd tried to exploit initially—or rather, loopholes I'd tried to exploit. By the time of our naked, only-two-person-in-attendance wedding, I had been ready to try marriage. Magic involved intent, and my magic knew what I wanted before I truly admitted it.

While I was pondering my newly married state, my friends and I were driven to the little airstrip reserved for charter flights and private planes. Our ride was all tinted glass and driven by a man in an expensive suit and shades. When he parked, he began opening doors.

"Ma'am," he said opening the door for Christy. He repeated the word as Sera stepped out. Allie got the same gentlemanly hand and "Ma'am."

I was last.

He bowed before extending his hand. "Your Royal Highness."

I bit back my grumble. In the short time between marrying Eli and now, I'd been letting Eli handle all the etiquette stuff I didn't know. I didn't have that luxury today. I accepted the driver's hand, stepped out of the car, and tried not to trip.

Four similarly suit-and-shades clad people—a man, one nonbinary person, and two women—surrounded us in obvious formation. Guards. It appeared that my car service was not simple luxury.

"Are the windows bullet-proof?" I asked quietly.

"The entire vehicle is," one answered.

"And you are . . .?"

The one woman, who had undeniable fae features, met my gaze unflinchingly. "Fae Royal Service. When His Royal Highness, Prince Eli of Stonecroft said you would be traveling, His Majesty deployed us."

Maybe it was the early hour, but my temper sparked enough that my hair seemed to be lashing around me like silent, blue serpents. I had my phone in hand with the speed usually reserved for weapons.

Eli answered on the first ring. "Are you bleeding?"

"I only left thirty minutes ago. Why do you always think there's trouble?" I teased, but I grinned despite myself.

The sound of his chuckle drew my sour mood closer to level. "Because you are never predictable, bonbon."

"Did you know the car was bulletproof, Eli?"

"Of course. Aren't all car services?" He sounded perplexed.

I watched as one of the Fae Guard went onto the plane, checking for whatever he felt necessary. The others stood around us as our luggage was loaded.

"I don't want guards," I grumbled into the plane. "I'll accept an armored car, and I'm thrilled by the chartered plane and diplomatic passport, but what sort of fun is a spa weekend with a host of armed guards?"

"Guards?" Eli echoed. "What am I missing, Geneviève?"

"Are they not your guards?" My hand went to my gun. All I'd had was a stranger's word. I was getting sloppy.

"Royal Decree 312," one of the guards said loudly.

I flicked the phone to speaker and slid into the holster that had been holding my preferred revolver. Two birds. One holster.

The Fae Guard continued, "In the interim between bonding and anchoring, the non-fae spouse shall be kept secure and uninjured if said spouse separates from the fae spouse for any length of time longer than thirty-three minutes."

"Legit?" I asked Eli over the phone. My gun was still loose in my hand.

To my left I saw Allie pull her far-too-large .45 from her purse.

Christy pulled out one slick 9mm and one near machete-sized knife.

Sera simply stepped behind Allie, but she accepted the knife from Christy. She wasn't a weapons person, but she could be as fierce as an angry raccoon if necessary.

The Fae Guards eyed us all curiously.

Eli's sigh was loud. The word he said sounded like "row sheen," but I realized it was a name when one of the female guards said, "This is Roisin, Your Royal Highness."

"I assume my uncle sent you," Eli said.

"He did." Roisin watched us, looking almost fascinated. Her gaze lingered on Sera, and I hoped it was only a flicker of interest as opposed to not selecting a target.

"Stand down, Roisin." Eli's voice was deep with anger, and I knew that if I could see him right now, his normally calm façade would have slipped.

The Fae Guard grinned. "You're not king yet, Prince Eli, and I'm no longer your training mate. Unless my king orders me to do so, my squad will be with Her Royal Highness."

"Can I shoot them?" Allie loudly whispered. "I bet we could stop them from getting on the plane."

Roisin and the other guards all flinched, but Roisin was the one who replied, "We don't ride in metal tubes. We will meet you upon arrival."

"How . . ." Sera started.

"Plane. Now." Christy motioned Sera forward, and Allie followed.

"I'll speak to my uncle," Eli said before the phone went silent.

Once I boarded the plane, the steps were raised. The Fae

Guard watched. Once we started taxiing, I looked through the window again.

I could see one of the guards rip a slice in the air. In a moment, they'd all stepped through the shimmering veil. They'd travel into *Elphame* and then re-appear in San Diego. The land of the fae was not beholden to normal laws of science; time, distance, and space were different there. The fae could hop anywhere in the world of humans by crossing through their homeland. My mind boggled at the possibilities—and the speed. It was the next best thing to the *draugr* ability to *flow*— their travel was faster than mortal sight could follow.

Despite the other options available to the fae and the *draugr* —options I could use, too--I was excited to be in the air. The other ways might be faster, but flying felt like a magic all its own. No feathers, no hollow bones, and yet humanity had found a way to hurtle themselves into the sky.

I watched the ground seem to drop from under us as the plane launched into the air. Every bit of logic I had said it ought not work, but there we were, escaping gravity, escaping the very ground, and racing through air. It might not be the sort of magic witches knew, but it left me exhilarated all the same.

CHAPTER FIVE

"We could land in Long Beach," Allie said, jarring me to wakefulness.

I blinked up at her. Apparently, I had dozed off in the comforting fluttering movements of the plane. The pilot had called it turbulence, but it felt a bit like the few times I'd been on a small boat in the Mississippi River, rolling and jolting. It had lulled me to sleep the same as the river's waves had done.

"Context?" I asked.

Allie held out a cocktail with a proud flourish. "Spicy breakfast."

My assistant had a fondness for naming the blood concoctions that she procured. I sipped, paused, and sipped again. "Not Allie juice. Whose blood is this?"

She sighed. "I told her you'd know!"

I sipped again. "Not my grandmother either. Not Eli . . . not human, though."

"Lady B's assistant." Alice patted her purse, where I knew a large handgun and lipstick and itinerary were stored. "I added cayenne, cumin, tomato juice, vodka, probiotics, garlic; it's, sort of like a Tex-Mex Bloody Mary, heavy on the blood. I *told* them you'd know it wasn't my blood."

"Why?" I sipped. Tomato, contrary to many opinions, was a kind of fruit. I knew that with certainty because I was getting a breakfast-drink buzz.

"Oh, well, in case you needed more blood than I have." Allie was chipper as she announced this as if my leechlike appetite wasn't exhausting. Before I could object, apologize, or lament, she patted her giant handbag. "It's like preparation for if I ever need to carry baby formula. I mean, except for the vodka . . . and the blood . . . and—"

"Long Beach?" Sera interrupted. She did not look like she'd slept, more like she'd developed a distinct case of air sickness.

"So, the guards will be at San Diego Airport, but *we* could land at Long Beach—like an hour on the freeway this time of day—and drive there. No guards. No armored cars. Just us." Allie grinned.

"Do it." I didn't even pause. Maybe Eli could call off the guards, but if not, the fact was that an armed entourage drew attention, and I was not interested in that. I wanted to lose myself with my friends and sit on a beach.

"They'll still meet us at the spa," Sera pointed out.

"*My* spa." Allie rummaged in her purse and held up a little packet. "Electrolytes. Great for hangovers and flights."

Sera gratefully accepted, and then Allie went off to talk to captain.

"She's terrifying," Sera muttered.

"You're not wrong." I sipped my breakfast. The fruit would leave me vaguely tipsy, but wasn't that the point of the weekend? Girls' Weekend. Fun, freedom, and frolicking.

By the time we'd landed, I was both excited and tipsy. Sera was even more motion sick. That left Christy and Allie in charge of decisions for car rental, luggage gathering, and navigating. We all showed travel cards—and everyone except me had a temperature and pulse check.

"Would you like to *volunteer* to have yours recorded?" the man asked.

I laughed. "Witch melded with a faery. My readings would be too weird. Plus, I have this." I shook my diplomatic passport. "Wouldn't want to anger the faeries, would we?"

He walked away quickly, much to our relief. I had no idea what readings I'd get. I was not just witch and fae, so I'd register in potentially dangerous ways.

Allie swept away to get a car, and Christy stared after her, frowning.

"What's wrong?" I prompted.

"I may like Alice if she keeps being so . . ." Christy waved her hand in the direction of my cheerful assistant who was clapping her hands at something the rental car agent said.

I nodded. "That's what happens. You're going along minding your business, used to finding chirpy women irritating, and then she pulls out a gun or stocks your drawers with really useful lingerie, or runs over a *draugr* with her car. Then you realize you actually like her."

"Lingerie?" Christy echoed.

"Or she sings," Sera said. "Honestly, if she sang all her prattling answers, I'd listen to whatever she was going on about."

I patted Christy's shoulder and offered her my drink, forgetting the blood part until Christy winced. "Strictly non-blood, Gen."

"Sorry." I fired off a quick text to Eli, letting him know our changed plans.

When Allie returned, she refused to tell us what she'd rented until we rolled our bags to the car. There, gleaming like a bright, beautiful bad idea was a cherry-red Mustang convertible.

"Seriously?" Christy looked at Allie.

"Yep." Allie popped her "p" like it was bubble gum. Then she tossed the keys to Christy. "You said you loved convertibles, and"—she motioned around us—"ocean."

"Damn it." Christy looked at me. "I'm done for."

Sera and I laughed, and we all stowed the luggage and clambered into the car. No guards. No work. Four women in a convertible at the beach.

What could possibly go wrong?

BY THE TIME we reached the spa, things were so ideal that I expected the spa itself to be a dump. However, it was anything but low-brow. Christy pulled the car up to the lobby area, and bellmen swooped out to collect our bags and open our doors.

"I didn't tell them I was coming," Allie whispered quickly. "It's like a stealth inspection." Then she raised her voice and said, "Reservation for Zehr, party of four. Full deluxe package."

"Of course. Right this way."

We were ushered to the front desk, and I was glad I was sober enough to take in the lobby. A massive pedestal fountain, surrounded by tiers of flowers, dominated the high-ceilinged space. Some sort of soothing music, acoustic and earthy, filtered into the room. And the entire space was perfumed with some sort of—lavender? vanilla?-- earthy fragrance. I couldn't identify it, but it was very relaxing.

A uniformed man approached with glasses of what looked like pink champagne, despite the early hour. Apparently, they took relaxation very seriously here.

I accepted a glass and glanced at my phone.

"We have no cell signal on the main grounds," the man said in a low soothing voice. "Jarring things are not permitted, out of respect for the other guests. Phones will not work here."

I expected a reply from Eli, but nothing came up. I frowned and tapped off another text to Eli. Sooner or later, he'd get the message when we hit a hotspot or I caught the wifi in the room.

At the desk, Christy was filling out paperwork. She paused, glanced at me, and slid a black credit card over to the woman. "For all expenses."

The young woman took the card, ran it, and in short order, we were being whisked away through a maze of halls and across courtyards, each with burbling fountains and flowers. A young man with the sort of timeless beauty that spoke well of the spa's service strolled through the grounds, leading us. It felt a bit like we were walking in circles, a labyrinth of landscaped beauty that I presumed he was showing off.

The group of us exchanged a few looks, pointing at flowers —especially the sheer number of Birds of Paradise. They could grow in New Orleans, but here they were seemingly cropping up like bright flocks around fountains.

"Through the statuary garden, you will find trails." Our bell-man--staff guide, whatever he was--motioned. "Beyond the spa rooms you can reach the ocean. Our facilities offer the best of Southern California without the inconvenience of driving or ever leaving the estate grounds."

"It's beautiful," Allie said with a grin.

The bellman finally stopped beside a building. "Your casita."

Sera stepped forward, but he put his hand up.

He slipped off his shoes, standing barefoot inside the door. No, at closer look, he had on what looked like thick gauze socks. "We want nothing outside to contaminate the cleansing energy of the casita."

When none of us reacted, he added, "We don't wear shoes inside."

Once we all took off our shoes, he opened the door for us to walk inside. It felt a bit like the home I shared with Eli, as if nature had come inside. Another fountain. More scented air. This time, the earthy fragrance reminded me of jasmine.

Our guide walked to a large dinning table. On it were several carafes of chilled water condensation trickling down the bottles. And at the head of the table were four folders.

"Each client has a spa rejuvenation and detoxification schedule," he explained. "This schedule will enable you to purify your body and soul."

He pointed to wall where a color-coded "group schedule" was written out in lovely penmanship. "As you can see, meals are also scheduled. Your optimal nutrition for your age and fitness will be provided. No sharing of entrees, please, as it complicates the chef's creative process."

At that, Sera snorted.

"Can anyone enter the facility who isn't a registered guest?" Allie prompted.

"Absolutely not," he said sounding aghast at the thought. "We are an *exclusive, private* spa."

"Excellent." I wandered toward the kitchen, and then the living room, and finding nothing, paused. "Where is the bar here?"

"The casita is not stocked with alcohol." Again with the appalled tone. "It's dulling."

Allie scowled. "So, it's only served at the restaurant?"

"Restaurant?" The man pressed his lips together briefly. "Each guest will have a personally selected meal. We do not burden our guests with making decisions on meals that they may not enjoy."

I exchanged a tense look with Allie. Somehow, I doubted that they'd have my preferred meals available, but we could always go out into San Diego and shop.

Christy shooed the man out. Once he was gone, she met my gaze, "Plan?"

I shrugged, determined not to let a teetotaling stance at the spa ruin my weekend. It was a minor inconvenience, but the resort was lovely, and the spa experience sounded destressing. "Spa visits, and then we can go out in the morning to grab my food."

CHAPTER SIX

L unch arrived a while later. The waiter placed each tray in front of a seat. Our napkins were color-coordinated with our spa charts.

"Your needs are specific to your person," the waiter said. "Your meals fulfill your particular needs in the best way. You will eat the meal provided."

It felt like a threat, which didn't do much for my already agitated mood. Then, I looked at my meal. It was a far cry from fulfilling my needs—and it was bleh. I wasn't expecting quesadillas or loaded fries, but I expected a *few* goodies. My plate was carrot sticks and hummus, and with it was cucumber water and a "dessert plate" of berries and cheese.

The waiter left, and the four of us looked at the plates.

I was seriously starting to question our decision to stay here at the spa. It was bad enough that I'd starve, but the meals were depressing, too. Allie ended up with what looked like raw steak with a raw egg and onions draped over. That was it. Raw steak and cucumber water.

"Steak tartare," Allie offered with a grimace. "Good for iron and protein. . . I guess. I need that to recover from the extra I'll need to feed you, boss."

"Blanched chicken, broccoli, and spinach," Christy offered gesturing at her plate. "And a cheese plate."

"Four bean salad." Sera smiled at her heaping plate. "Did you tell them I was a vegetarian?"

Allie shook her head, poking a fork at her raw meat as if she could threaten it into being edible. "So, everyone is getting iron-rich, high protein meals?"

"Everyone but me. I got *carrots*," I muttered. "Why carrots? Do I look like a bunny?"

"I'll take them!" Allie offered. "You can have this bloody mess . . ."

I winced. I might drink blood in my breakfast smoothies, but I wasn't going to eat raw meat. "Hard pass."

"Maybe they expect us to collect nuts and berries or catch a lobster at the beach," Allie muttered before pushing away from the table.

"Not going to do much for my 'specific nutritional needs,' but I could certainly catch food for the rest of you," I offered. "I'm more than fast enough to—"

"This will not do!" Allie interrupted. "I *own* this place. I *will* have real food and liquor, damn it. And so will you."

The next thing I knew Allie tossed me a blood slushy from her carry-on and ripped open a candy bar she'd stashed in there. That bag was a veritable cornucopia of surprises.

"Either of you need anything?" Allie looked at Sera and Christy.

They shook their heads and dug into their dinners.

After a moment, Christy swallowed the first bite and asked hopefully, "Salt? Hot sauce?"

Ally pulled out a tiny restaurant packet of salt and a little jar of hot sauce. Then she withdrew a small airplane bottle of brown liquor of some sort. Rum? Whiskey? Bourbon? I had no idea. Mostly, we were all just marveling at the variety.

"I just need to grab a few things," she muttered, pulling out a pair of tweezers, a jar of moisturizer, and a fig bar. She set them all aside. Finally, she pulled out a roll of duct tape with a victorious, "A-ha!"

"Do you want me to go with you?"

"Eat." Alice plopped an airplane bottle of bourbon beside the slushy bag of blood. "Get a facial. I'm going up to the office to explain the errors of their ways. I'll be back before"—she glanced at the wall schedule—"our scheduled 'relaxing group beach walk.'"

After Allie marched out, duct tape in hand, Christy whistled. "Man, if Lady B ever transfuses *that* one, Allie could run the whole hemisphere."

We observed a moment of quiet while I searched for a tumbler to use for my blood and bourbon slushy. Honestly, I thought Alice had every right to be pissed off. It was a spa. *Her* spa. She came stealthily to investigate, and what she'd learned was worth a bit of yelling.

"Should we go after her?" I asked, thinking about the no cell phones policy. I had figured the phones would work in the rooms, but so far, I had no signal here either.

"She'll come get us if there's trouble." Sera pointed out.

It wasn't as if we lived in a city that lacked trouble, and Alice Chaddock was not a stranger to conflict, handguns, or pushy people. She was fierce and smart—and armed. I trusted her, but I was used to being the one marching into conflict.

"One hour," Christy suggested. "She'll yell. They'll fix it. She *bought* this place, so they'll get a quick lecture. If she's not back after our 'whirlpool or sauna session,' we go after her. Her idea of waiting until the beach walk . . ."

"Three hours is way too long," Sera agreed.

I wasn't sure if it was paranoia, but I suggested, "Do you

mind if I put all of our things—including shoes and keys—under a stasis spell?"

The relief in their expressions told me that I wasn't the only person with a sliver of paranoia. I didn't want to tote our belongings everywhere, but I was starting to have doubts about the staff.

"Please do! No shoes. No cell signal. No booze." Christy met my gaze. "I'd feel better knowing our weapons were secure."

I pulled on the magic that I could summon. I might not be able to raise the dead, but the *draugr*-blood made for a nourishing slushie. It was one of the more rejuvenating things I'd tried. I made a mental note to pay a visit to my grandmother to thank her for sending blood once we all returned to New Orleans, and then I heaped all of our things in one corner. I placed both a security layer—strong electrical charges on anyone my magic didn't recognize—and a concealment layer over the luggage, weapons, and shoes.

Plan and spells in place, we finished our odd lunch, although I skipped the berries this time. I had a prickling feeling that being tipsy wasn't ideal. Maybe I was overreacting. Allie was probably just dressing down her staff, possibly firing people or explaining that we needed proper meals. I was so used to threats that I saw danger everywhere. Sure, the spa was a little weird, but that wasn't *dangerous*.

Twenty minutes later, Allie wasn't back, but a guide with a satchel popped into the casita without so much as a knock or word.

Christy and I already had weapons drawn.

"Knock first." I pointed my sword tip at him. "Make a note. What if we'd been changing or . . ."

"This is a *spa*, madam. You will be unclothed quite often. The staff is unaware of nakedness." He sounded like he was mocking me, but not in any overt way that I could address. It was that passive-aggressive thing that always made me want to jab people the way Allie had with her raw meat meal.

"Knock," I repeated. "Because I'm not always quick to ask questions before shooting."

At first, he said nothing in reply, merely gestured toward the door with a calm, "I am here to escort you for the scheduled soothing spa or sauna session. Please join me."

As we approached him, he offered us each a bundle with beige robes and some sort of woven thong-sandal things. "We are without shoes or wear *only* these on this ground in order to respect the soil."

"Let us grab our suits, and we'll be right with you." Christy turned to walk into her bedroom.

"That won't be necessary. Material has chemicals, and chemicals could create imbalance in the hot spring that we draw our water from." The guide smiled beatifically. "Simply unburden yourselves of clothing, and we can depart."

Silently, I sent a little magical buzz his way, just to "taste test" to see what he was. If he were a regular human, he wouldn't react. If he was something else, I'd know—at least I would if my magic answered.

It fizzled before I could read him. Still no reliable access to my magic.

"Are there other people there?" I asked, worrying about my friends' privacy. I was a witch, so being skyclad—naked—was as comfortable for me as dressed. But I wasn't sure Christy was entirely at ease with walking around naked, and *that* was enough of a reason for me to object.

"You will have a towel for the sauna if you opt for steam over the hot pools. The spa is heated with the same water, so you will be purified either way." He smiled again, and I was tempted to ask what he'd been smoking. The man was too damned chill.

Shoes left behind, wearing the least comfortable woven

footwear I'd ever put on, we hobbled through the garden toward the spa. Weirdly, this was our second time walking outside, and we still hadn't seen another soul.

"Is the spa always this empty?" I asked.

"Empty?"

"You know, no guests. *Empty*."

He gave us another vacant smile. "We are at capacity, madam. Our guests are simply enjoying the benefits of a peaceful existence."

"Okaaaay." I glanced at my friends. They weren't buying it either.

We walked in silence that felt eerie now, and that creeping feeling of dread didn't relax when we stepped into a vacant spa.

"I'll leave you in the care of your personal spa guide." The man turned and left—after collecting our footwear.

"Select a pair of spa shoes," the vacant-eyed spa guide said as she approached. "They are separated into size bins."

We looked at each other as we collected our shoes. This time, we were given what appeared to be pea-soup green, tissue-paper "shoes." They would do exactly nothing to protect our feet.

"Seriously?" Christy whispered.

"They're crafted of pressed leaves," the vacant-eyed spa guide said. "They'll melt into the pools or protect your feet at the spa. When they fully vanish, it's time to step out of the steam." She gave us a wide-eyed smile. "Isn't that clever? You don't even need to watch the time. We like our guests to be freed of all responsibility."

I'd never wanted a sturdy pair of sandals as much as I did today.

"They *melt*?" Sera echoed.

"It opens your pores, so when you depart the spa center you can absorb the earth," the smiling woman added.

"So, we'll be naked, wet, and barefoot?" Christy prompted.

"Isn't it wonderful?" the woman said.

I think we were all too horrified to answer. This was turning into a vacation focused more on torture than relaxation.

"I'm Misty, your spa guide." She smiled at each of us. "Let us begin."

CHAPTER SEVEN

A fter Misty, the vacant-eyed spa guide watched us put on our shoes, she announced in an unsettlingly calm voice, "Who will be steaming?"

"Steaming?" Sera echoed.

"Hot steam will open your pores and soul," Misty explained. "Calming scents will add to the rejuvenation."

"And we keep a towel?" Christy clarified.

"Oh yes, you can sit on it or cover the softer parts from steam." The young woman looked so earnest that I wanted to ask if they were steaming high grade marijuana or something else in the vents, but I was *really* trying to believe that this place was just extra-eco, extra-earthy, not corrupt. It was San Diego, for goodness' sake! They didn't even have *draugr* here.

"I'll do the hot springs," I said. "See you two after."

Sera and Christy opted for the sauna, but I felt relatively certain that one of us ought to investigate the hot pool. I hoped I was being paranoid, but I was starting to have a strong suspicion that the employees were all high or drugged. I kept trying to explain it away as hippie-dom gone wild. But . . . Maybe it wasn't simply *extra.* Maybe something was actually off here, and although I had no idea what it was, I wanted to ease my potential paranoia.

I waited in my robe and tissue paper shoes until Misty returned. Then, I followed her through a pair of wooden doors into a freezing cold room with a burbling steamy pool about the size of an extended, rectangular dining room table. The room was absent of plants, but the scent of something sweet was just this side of nauseating. Was *that* the drug? It was so sugary that I could taste it in the humidity.

I walked over to the hot spring and dropped my robe.

The smiling spa guide said, "When your shoes fully melt, you are allowed to exit."

"Allowed?" I echoed.

She just nodded, even as I gave her a questioning look. Paper shoes in near-boiling water? They'd melt as soon as I entered the pool. But whatever. There was a hot spring, and flaky spa staff or not, the feeling of sinking into that hot water was like dropping into peace.

Within moments my muscles relaxed, and I sighed.

For the first time since we left the resort lobby, I felt truly relaxed. The extra-hot, bubbling water seemed to sluice in and out around me like waves. Giant rocks rimmed the pool like strange seats. And whatever that scent was, it was calming. Not too sweet. Not too anything. It was like inhaling peace.

I stayed like that, submerged up to my shoulders and feeling calm enough to nap, right up to the moment that my head slipped under water and hit a rock hard. The shock and pain of it jolted me upright and out of the stone tub.

Why was I here? Why was I relaxing so much? Something was definitely wrong. Whatever peace I'd felt quickly vanished.

Naked as the day I was born, shoeless and dripping wet, I walked out of the hot springs room and to the front desk. As I did, I saw an older suit-clad man dart away.

No. Not dart. I saw a man *flow.* Only one creature did that.

Draugr. There was a *draugr* here.

My peace was all sorts of gone.

Misty the spa guide stepped up to me in a flurry. "Are you unwell? Would you like a soothing glass of cucumber water?"

"Who was that?" I asked, nodding toward the doorway where the man had vanished.

"There was no one here." Misty frowned, giving me a baffled look that seemed genuine. Had she not seen him?

"Dead guy in a suit," I clarified. "*Draugr*. Right here, plain as murder."

"No. There are no *draugr* in San Diego." Misty shook her head. "How could there be? We check everyone at the gates."

"I saw him."

"No." She glared at me and repeated, "There are no *draugr* in San Diego."

I couldn't tell if she was afraid or angry. Either way, she obviously wasn't a fan of questions.

I looked around, cursing my continued lack of necromancy. I wanted my magic back. All of it. It shouldn't still be an empty reserve inside me. Weeks of this had worn on me—enough that I was apparently on a hell-vacation.

"There was a *draugr* here. Just now," I said calmly. "You were *just* talking to him."

"*Draugr* don't live in San Diego." This time, Misty laughed like I'd told a joke, but then she said, "Were you in the spring too long, ma'am? Oh no! Let's get you hydrated, mmm?"

She tried to reach out to check my temperature, like a mother putting a wrist to a child's fevered forehead.

I swatted her away. "Stop that."

"You must have been faint. Drink this!" She poured a tall glass of that now-tepid water.

"You drink it." I stepped back.

And she did. She blinked. Then she lifted the glass and drained the whole thing. Then she re-filled it and held it out.

"Cucumber mint water?" She gave me another beatific smile. "Or I have celery if you're hungry."

"Hop."

Still holding the glass of tepid water, Misty started hopping. "Drink the water, ma'am. It'll clear your mind of all troubles."

"Sauna," I managed to say.

Misty scrunched up her face like I'd confused her, and then she started hopping toward the sauna.

"Stop hopping," I whispered.

"I thought . . . weren't you going to the pool?" Misty blinked at me several times before whispering, "You're all wet, you know?"

I bit back my frustrated yell and said, "Misty, I am looking for the sauna. "*Walk* me to the sauna."

"Oh. Are you scheduled for it?"

I paused. I hoped she was drugged, not naturally this daft. I smiled as calmly as I could. "Why yes, I am scheduled for it. I was late. Swimming, you know."

A flicker of terror went over her, and her mouth opened wide like she was going to scream, but then she blinked. The fear and pending scream vanished. The words looked like they were a struggle to get out, but she managed to say, "Stay away from the beach. They'll get you."

There was something wrong here—beyond the celery and carrots and weird-assed shoes.

Just then, Allie burst through the door, purse bulging, a trash bag over her shoulder, and bloody hands gripping what looked like a broom handle. Her feet were bloody, and all she said was, "Boss! Weapon."

She tossed me her back-up gun, a tiny .22 that was perfect for concealing in your cleavage, but not exactly high-powered.

"News?" I gripped the gun, just as Allie swung the broom at Misty, who dropped the syringe she'd had concealed in her hand.

"I'll take that." Allie scooped up the syringe, wrapped it in a couple pairs of the tissue paper shoes, and stuffed it all into what looked like an empty blood bag.

She met my gaze and announced, "*Draugr*. Witches. I don't even *know*, but talking to the staff was like talking to a bunch of drunk bunnies!"

I nodded; not-interrupting was often best with Alice.

"They locked me in a supply cabinet. Can you believe that? As if that would cage me! I whacked my head hard when they shoved me in there. But that meant I was clear-headed long enough to grab some stuff before escaping."

"Are you—"

"I figure I bought the resort already, so I'm not *actually* stealing!" Alice tapped her broom handle on the floor like she was some old, wizard with a staff. "Let's get the others."

"Right." I sort of blinked, realizing that I was still a little woozy from the hot spring. "Get them. Go outside to get fresh air."

We walked through the spa center, guns and broom handle at the ready. No one was there. Anywhere. The first few treatment rooms were empty. As we walked further, we discovered that a few rooms had people—*comatose* people—stretched out on the massage tables. They all seemed alive, but more than a few had been there long enough that their muscles were significantly atrophied.

"They won't wake," Allie said. "I tried to wake one I saw beside the pool on a lounger."

"What in the name of duck gizzards is going on here?" I muttered.

Allie shook her head. "We need to get out of here, and . . . I'll need a well-armed cleaning crew for this place. First, though, it's rescue-and-run time."

After several more minutes, we found Sera and Christy, giggling uproariously in the vanilla and fruit-scented sauna.

"Gen!" Sera yelled cheerily.

We tugged them out of the sauna, but they were giggling like they had been smoking *all* the drugs at the same time.

"Why are you taking out trash?" Christy pointed at Allie's bag. "Are there chores?"

"Pain helps shock you out but . . . I cannot hit *them*," Allie motioned at them.

"Bee!" I yelled. "Get it, Sera! On Christy's cheek."

Sera slapped Christy's face, and Christy shoved Sera backwards. Sera kicked Christy, taking her legs out. I let one friend smash into the wall, and the other crumble to the ground. I felt a flicker of guilt.

Then Sera blinked. "What . . . where? Huh?"

"Why are we naked?" Christy asked, wrapping a towel more firmly around her.

"*Draugr.* Possibly magic. Drugs in the steam, I think . . ." I ticked it off. "The flowery, fruity scent."

Sera grabbed robes and handed one to Christy—and then she started going through cupboards until she found one for me. "Clothes, Gen."

I grinned. Right. Fighting while naked could get super awkward.

Allie had opened the trash bag, although her gun was still in reach if she needed it. She pulled out several cans of aerosol cleaner. "Here. Aim for the eyes."

Sera and Christy each stuffed cans of cleaner into one of their robe pockets. Then Allie pulled out a long-necked lighter. Grinning, she held it up. "Fire balls, anyone?"

She pulled out several glass jars, each filled with a yellow liquid, thumb tacks, nails, and a floating candle. The candles' wicks were sticking out of holes at the top and black electrical tape covered them. "Pull off the tape, light, toss, and *boom*."

Christy shook her head. "You and me need to have a *long* chat, Tennessee."

Allie beamed. "Nicknames imply friendship."

"Give me the bombs, Tennessee. I played softball." Christy held out a hand, and Allie, smiling widely, gave her the three improvised bombs.

"I'd feel a whole lot better with my swords," I admitted.

Allie looked at me. "I can't give you my favorite gun, but you can have my staff."

Now someone who had no martial arts training might not realize that a broom stick—a staff—was a worthy weapon, but a staff was able to execute all the primary blows a sword was. The difference was that the sword would slice flesh, and a staff would pummel the bones and organs.

I twirled my new weapon. Up close, a staff was just as good as a sword. And at a distance, we had improvised bombs, two guns, and homemade fire balls.

"Shall we go get our clothes, and get up out of this place?" Sera asked.

"Sounds like a plan," I agreed.

"But, you know, try not to set it *all* on fire," Allie said. "I *did* buy it."

"Come on, Tennessee. Let's test your bombs." Christy grinned at Allie.

And while it wasn't *exactly* a weekend that matched our plans, I felt good seeing them get along. It was a Girls' Weekend . . . but our way.

CHAPTER EIGHT

We walked out to the lobby, watching for lurking *draugr*, human staff, or witches. Honestly, I had no idea what all sorts of trouble we had to face, and the one certainty was that the air was toxic.

The groggy-but-upright Misty looked horrified to see us—and I was fairly sure it wasn't just the fact that Allie was bloody. She stared at us like she was trying to speak and couldn't. I didn't know if she was drugged or enthralled to the *draugr* I'd seen or maybe just blackmailed. Either way, she stared at us and twisted her hands together.

"Windows," Sera muttered. She was swaying like she'd been on a bourbon tasting marathon.

I stepped around the hand-wringing spa guide and started shattering windows. The staff gave me reach, and there was something satisfying about bashing them. Glass tinkled down around me like a localized ice storm.

"Wait!" Misty suddenly grabbed at me, trying to grab the staff that I was currently using as a baseball bat, and in the process hanging onto me like an angry koala. "The air is deadly!"

Allie stepped back as Christy detached the worried woman from my back and arms. Misty was struggling, though. She was convinced that the air *outside* was deadly, and in her attempts to rescue us, she kept trying to cover our mouths and noses as if to save us.

"Hit . . . her," Sera suggested between clearing breaths of fresh air. "Seriously. . . some . . . one . . . just *hit* her."

Christy was trying to hold the woman while avoiding getting clawed in the face, and Sera was struggling to speak. That left me or Allie.

Before I could figure out how to safely hit Misty, who was clearly drugged, Allie—still holding her gun—punched Misty in the temple.

Misty dropped like dead weight.

We dragged the now-unconscious Misty with us as we went outside. Her legs were being scratched all to hell by plants and rocks as she was half-dragged half-carried across the ground.

An alarm sounded and a series of sprinkler heads shot out of the ground. The misters that were strung through the trees and the sprinklers all started spewing a pinkish mist.

"Cover your mouth!" Sera gasped, putting her robe-covered arm over her mouth and nose.

"Bombs," Allie gasped. "Blow it all up!"

Christy shoved the unconscious spa guide toward Allie, who more or less caught Misty. Within moments, Christy started lighting and launching bomb after bomb as we ran through the garden. Small fires started and flashed to life, burning away the scent of sugary toxic air.

But too soon, the misters were switched to full-on geysers. Pink water fountained upward, putting out fires and creating a tinted floral fog that seemed to linger over everything. Allie's homemade IEDs were overkill on sprinkler heads, and someone was watching closely enough to turn mist into fountains.

I would have loved to take down whatever security system

our unseen assailants had, but for now we had no targets other than mist, and *that* was impossible to counter without a few industrial fans.

We ran toward the casita, slower since Sera was dragging Misty along with us. Christy still tossed the occasional bomb, and I played whack-a-mole with sprinkler heads. Everyone tried to avoid the hot, steaming pink water that spurted up at odd intervals.

"Don't stop running!" Sera ordered. "Almost there. Any corpse armies, Gen?"

"No!" I tried, but I wasn't able to summon anything large. Plus, short of dead crustaceans, I wasn't finding any corpses within range. I felt the edges of my magic flickering like the energy wanted to surface, but that wasn't terribly useful without corpses. Right now, my best options were assorted crustaceans, a few fish, and some jellyfish. Typically, I could summon both human and animal corpses, create an undead fighting force to attack enemies or defend me. Being magically depleted meant that I had no juice to summon much of anything, but even I did . . . well, let's just say that dead fish and invertebrates weren't as helpful as wolves, coyotes, or even the occasional yappy dog.

I had no army to bring to our aid.

We were all stumbling, and when we reached the casita we found several angry spa employees waiting, I wanted to cry. Beyond them were our weapons, keys, and clothes.

Christy tossed two bombs in short order, and as the smoke and fire overpowered the mist, I surged forward with my staff, bashing and shoving them with all my remaining energy.

As they fell, we stumbled into the casita. I watched as my friends stepped over the fallen spa employees. Then I followed, slamming the door as if it would protect us.

"Sewer weasels. . . " I leaned my whole body up against the door. There was no steam here, but the sugared scent was so strong that I wasn't sure if it was in the casita or if it was all over us.

"We need to get out of here." Christy watched the door. "If this place is really run by *draugr* . . . we have until nightfall."

"Weapon check?" I pulled the magic away from our belongings.

"We can't shoot our way through steam, boss." Allie pulled her sopping wet hair into a messy bun. "I can make more Molotov cocktail bombs, but . . . it's not enough."

"So how do we get to the rental car?" Sera was tossing clothes at all of us.

She paused to grimace at our thrashed feet. We weren't exactly used to barefoot living. As a child in the Outs, I had soles as tough as leather, but these days, I lived in the city.

"Beach?" I suggested.

The spa guide blinked up at us. "I was sea kayaking when they caught me."

"What?" Sera asked.

"Tossed a net over me, drugged me, and . . ." Misty touched her temple, wincing. "Thank you for clearing my head."

"So not by sea." Sera paced as Christy watched the door.

"The walked right out of the ocean, set up camp, captured us and drained us." Misty shuddered. "Then they set up here and victims just check in. No one ever leaves."

"You need a *juice,* boss." Allie looked over the woman we'd rescued, and I knew what she was saying.

I couldn't, though. Not her. Not here in front of someone who'd been so victimized by *draugr*. The poor thing had been captured, brainwashed, and undoubtedly used as a walking juice box already.

"What we need," Christy pronounced, "is a way out. I don't think we can reach the lobby, get to the car, and not get drugged up. Maybe Gen can, but not all of us."

I turned my back to Misty and whispered, "I can *flow* with one of you, then come back and—"

"Or you could rip a hole in the air and take us to Elphame," Christy suggested. "Doorway, Gen. We need a door out of here."

"There are a lot of rules," I hedged. "Mortals brought there are required to stay unless they are cleared prior to arrival."

I tried not to look at the stranger in the room. The reality was that if I took her over there, she was staying. No negotiation would change certain laws, not with the fae.

Sera and Christy were pre-cleared because they were in my wedding party. Allie wasn't, not yet.

"Allie . . ." I met her gaze. "You don't currently have clearance."

My fiery assistant gave me a look that could undoubtedly quell small nations. "Darlin, I'm not a person. I'm a *lunchbox*. Call me the red platelet special, but that man—any man—isn't going to keep me from my vow to you. He might be the fae king, but I go where you go, when you go, if you need. I'm like a part of you."

Sera snorted, gathering our bags up and shoving one toward Alice. The thought of Allie facing off against the king of the fae made me wince, but I couldn't image leaving her. Marcus would be reasonable. He *had* to be.

Misty flinched as something broke a skylight.

A cannister of pink smoke clattered from the ceiling.

"Prisoner here or prisoner there," Misty muttered. "Which is worse?"

"Here." I reached out into the air with one hand, pulling on the part of my energy that I thought of as an extension of Eli and seeking a grip. I didn't want to open my mouth and inhale that toxic fruit and flower scent again, but I did yell, "Bags."

Then I found what I was seeking My hands parted the air as if it had become a heavy curtain that I could grab. I wondered briefly if it was easier to tap *this* magic because my life had always been magical. Being a witch-*draugr* meant I'd always had magic. This particular bit was because *all* fae could open a doorway home, though. Now that I'd married Eli, I was included in that tradition.

The air took form and separated at my will.

"Go." I held the intangible curtain aside as if it had actual form, and Christy stepped into the other world with her luggage. Sera followed with her bags. Ally carried my weapons bag, her handbag, and her gun—outstretched as if she might need to shoot her way through enemies. She didn't bother with her suitcase. Priorities.

Misty paused. "Will it be better with the fae?"

I nodded, hoping I wasn't wrong, and she followed my friends in *Elphame*.

Then I stepped through, leaving the pink smell behind.

We all paused, gasping the clean air, and I waited for the inevitable fae assembly to arrive. I wasn't going to take one more step into *Elphame* until traditions were met.

CHAPTER NINE

"Geneviève of Stonehaven," the king of *Elphame* greeted as he stepped into the clearing with a group of fae soldiers.

"Crowe," I corrected. "Greetings to you, Marcus, King of *Elphame*."

The king smiled but it was a tense expression. He was put-together as always. If my husband had an older brother who had just slain an army single-handedly, the king of *Elphame* would be that man. I trusted him as much as I trusted any faery or politician—which is to say that I felt as wary as he looked.

"Be welcome tonight, bride of my nephew." The king met my gaze. The assembled guards, easily fifteen people, kept their silence. Swords were at the ready, and several were looking far too eager to draw them.

I sighed and dropped to a not-awful curtsy; my friends followed suit. Misty looked around like a drunk at an open bar. Allie held her gun loosely, ready but not starting trouble so far. Sera silently dropped our bags and handed me a sword.

"I seek haven for my friends . . . and a victim we rescued. We were attacked." I was suddenly hyper-aware that we were bedraggled and pinkish. "We are safe, but . . . there was no way out."

The assembled guards looked far from calm suddenly. They awaited orders, perhaps a rescue attempt.

"My nephew?" Marcus asked.

"Eli is at home, safe and blissfully unaware. I'd like to keep it that way." I gave him a wry smile.

"Oh, Death Maiden, I think my nephew has more than met his match in you, hasn't he?" The king didn't stifle a smile that looked a lot like a laugh in waiting. "I shan't be the one to tell him."

The king stepped forward as if I wasn't clutching a steel sword, and then the king of all fae in his world or mine kissed my cheeks in what appeared like fondness. I didn't exactly trust that it was. The fae were nothing if not political.

"Welcome home, niece," he whispered.

When he stepped back, I motioned to Sera, Christy, and Allie—naming each as I gestured their way. Then I added, "My friends and I were on holiday at the coast."

"Roisin had mentioned an inability to reach you." Marcus glanced at the fae guards. "There was a failure to update your travel plans for some reason. She was pursuing consent to forcibly enter the buildings where you were housed."

"I told you something was wrong," Roisin grumbled, sounding uncharacteristically human.

"You were correct, Roisin." Marcus grinned. "Shall we prepare for battle, Death Maiden? I've not had a skirmish in quite an age. Let us roust those who have cast insult on my family."

I tried to reply and choked on my words. "Roust?"

"I thought you said he was stuffy," Alice whispered far-too-loudly in the silence.

And the king of *Elphame* laughed as if a grand joke had been shared. Then Marcus looked at Alice and said, "There are quite a few changes in my mood since my nephew has accepted his duty—subsequently marrying the prophesied Death that I thought would steal my throne. As a faery, Alice, I had thought that *my own death* would come if I grew too attached to a woman."

"That's so sad!" Alice stepped forward and hugged him.

As she did so a dozen guards surged toward her, and I stepped forward in answer. I was but one sword against fifteen, though. Rage bubbled in my belly.

"Boss?" Allie called. She was clasped in the king's embrace, watching armed warriors aim weapons at her.

And in that moment, the magic I hadn't been able to access since I'd raised a cemetery to fight woke with a roar.

"*Mine!*" The word echoed across the ground like a quake. A surge of almost maternal affection rose up—as did the very ground around us. The king and Alice were suddenly atop a tall hill where the ground had been flat.

Walls of soil encased Sera and Christy, and by proximity, Misty. They were safe from harm.

And Allie was out of reach of the guards with swords.

From atop the newly formed hill, Marcus stared down at me with a curious expression. He raised his voice and asked, "Yours *how?*"

Allie smacked him. G-d help me, she smacked the king.

"Don't be a perv! She's family," Allie shouted at him. "I wouldn't be fool enough to bed her even if she wasn't twenty-seven kinds of drunk on Prince Eli. She's a lot of work emotionally just being her assistant . . . and platelet supplier."

Marcus made a gesture and stone steps appeared, carved into the soil and sod of the new hill. He offered Alice his elbow.

His words were clear as day as he asked, "Platelet supplier?"

"When boss almost died, she sprouted fangs you know? Lady B—she's like you but fangier and scary but not quite as sexy—she said I need to feed the boss."

They descended the steps as everyone there stared at them in a mix of reactions.

Allie continued, "So, Prince Eli tricked Gen into drinking blood. Not like all throat-bitey, though. That seems . . . intimate, and not really for me. I have a siphon and—"

"Allie, dear? Shut up," Sera said calmly.

Alice snapped her mouth shut and nodded.

"Is she addled?" Roisin asked from my side.

"*Such* a good question," Sera muttered.

Alice rose her hand, the one that was still holding a gun, like a pupil.

"Yes Alice?"

"Can we get a meal and some liquor for you before we go kick in the doors? And can we bring the faery lady who is staring at Sera?" Allie paused and grinned at Roisin. "Was that too blunt? I'm not sure of the etiquette. She's single, though, Miss Faery Lady."

Roisin folded her arms. "Not addled at all, is she? Sly."

Sera grinned. "Try dealing with her regularly."

"Food and refreshment sounds lovely," I said loudly. "Then I will go deal with whatever monsters are there. If I could leave my friends here while I—"

"I go where you go, boss." Allie still had a hand on the king's arm, and he made no move to dislodge her.

"We will bring a squadron or two to handle this, niece of mine." Marcus made eye contact with several guards, and they departed. Whatever orders he passed were handled so subtly that it was as if it hadn't happened.

"Can we message Lady B?" Allie added. "I bet she'd love an excuse to come to San Diego. Plus, she loves a good fight."

Marcus patted Allie's hand. "So do I, my dear. So do I."

I paused. "Alice, did my grandmother know about the spa?"

Alice paused, frowned, and then said, "She's how I discovered it. Her legal team knew a guy, and we bought it from the original owners who had gone missing."

I sighed, suspecting that my dear dead gran knew that there were *draugr* operating in San Diego. She couldn't go there herself, because of the no-*draugr* policy the city had, but I had to wonder if she'd intentionally sent me as her emissary. If so, although I might not have known it, she'd dispatched me like a rabid hunting dog.

The king met my gaze, and I knew he'd made the same connection I had. "I'll be at your side, Geneviève of Stonehaven."

"Crowe," I muttered. Then I added, "I look forward to battle at your side."

By the time I'd taken my friends to Eli's house, which was also mine now that we were married, I felt the awkward need to ask my uncle-by-marriage what his intentions toward Allie were. There was no mistaking that spark of interest in his eye, and I wasn't sure Alice was in the right frame of mind to be seduced by a faery king.

Once the guards had left, and Misty was sent off to wherever mortal who stumbled into *Elphame* went, I was ready to pull the king aside for a little chat.

"Misty will be okay, right?" Allie prompted again.

"I swear she will." I gave Alice a reassuring look. "They treat humans well. She'll have all her needs met, and she'll build a life with the other humans. It's sort of a forever-cosseted thing here. She can work—or not. She can date—or not. The only rule is that she can't leave."

Allie nodded. "Marcus is so sweet. I probably shouldn't worry."

Christy snorted. "Sweet on you is more like it. Human or

fae, people are people, and *that* man was panting at you so hard he was practically tripping on his tongue."

Allie sniffed as if dismissing Christy's words. "He was just kind. Friendly. Being a good host. Right, boss?"

I met her gaze. "Allie, the king wants you. It was as obvious as the way Roisin watched Sera. The fae might not be blunt, but they are believers in enjoying love and sex. So, in that area . . ." I shrugged. "Eli likely slept his way through half the city. Beautiful, eternal, and sexual. It's what they are."

Allie walked over and started to clear the table when we saw trays of food being carried toward the house. "Well, I think you're wrong," she said primly. "I'm a *widow*. He was just being a gentleman."

I exchanged a look with Christy. Clearly, I would be having a super awkward chat with my new uncle. Maybe reaching out to Eli—and asking him to handle it—wasn't such a bad idea after all.

CHAPTER TEN

Once we'd tucked into the sort of meal that vacations actually require—complete with a decadent dessert tray filled with everything from apple pie to crème brûlée to a Chantilly cream cake to a four-layer trifle and a selection of truffles—the dishes simply vanished.

"I'm feeling significantly less sympathy for you today, Gen." Sera stretched. "That was amazing. This place is . . ."

"Gorgeous," Christy finished.

"No *draugr* either," Sera added. "Would it be so bad to live here?"

I shook my head. It was a complicated question, which I wasn't entirely sure I could answer. Being here *was* incredible, and the best part was that it meant that I was now bonded with the only person who had ever made me feel whole. I'd always thought that "you complete me" business was silly, but then I melded with Eli. He *literally* completed me. Our souls were fused; our lifespans now tied together. I would die when he did —or the inverse. It was both terrifying and wonderful.

"It's incredible here, but I have a duty in New Orleans," I started. "Each person should leave the world better than how they came into it. That's my faith. It's as much a fact to me as anything science or magic can prove."

"So basically, you can't let yourself be happy because it's your duty to behead monsters?" Sera gave me the sort of stink eye that highlighted the increasingly difficult issue in our friendship of late. She didn't like what I did. Never had. Never would.

"Yes." I met her gaze head-on. "You don't have to like it—"

"Good. I don't." She folded her arms. "Why can't you just be a faery princess, Gen? You love Eli, and being his wife creates *other* responsibilities that you could spend eternity working on. That would be making *this* world better, and you'd be safer!"

"Eli knew who I was when he chose me, and he accepts it." I tried to keep my temper contained, but this had been the elephant-in-the-room for us for years. "This is me. Warts and all. You don't have to like it, but you need to accept it."

Sera pressed her lips together and walked out.

I sighed, hating the threat of tears I felt in the corner of my eyes. I wasn't a crier, hadn't ever been, but there were moments I wished I could be softer. I was happy with my life, loved my job—or *jobs* as the case now was—and I looked forward to my life with Eli. That didn't erase my identity. That was not the point of marriage, at least not the point of my marriage.

"She just worries," Christy said.

A thousand words wanted to come out, but it wasn't Christy who needed to hear them. And I didn't think Sera could, no matter how many times I tried to explain. Sure, she worried. She didn't see the world as I did—and that was fine. However, it wasn't my responsibility to change her mind.

I shoved the hurt away. It was time to focus on what I could do.

"So, my magic appears to have found its way home," I started. "And the king is kindly offering me a few fighters. I'd like you to stay here. Enjoy *Elphame*. With fae back-up, I'll get things sorted out over in San Diego."

"With minimal damage, please!" Allie interjected. "Maybe I should tell Marcus . . ."

That was that. I was taking the king. The last thing I wanted was to leave him and Allie alone. They were both adults, but Allie was my responsibility.

And, of course, starting a fight with the king of the fae when he broke her heart would be . . . complicated. I wasn't fae by birth, but I was fae enough to open doorways here now that I'd melded with Eli. I was, technically, a subject of *Elphame*. A citizen. Being the wife of the future king didn't change that.

Of course, it also didn't mean that I would stand by and let a friend be hurt.

"Marcus will be with me," I pointed out. "You, Alice Chaddock, will be staying here with Christy and Sera. Relax. Sunbath. Eat desserts."

Allie twisted her hands together. "I hate not being with you. What if you need me?"

"I do need you. Make me a pretty platelet smoothie, Allie, for when I return," I said in my mothering-est voice. "I won't be gone long."

Then I left to find the king and troops. My magic was itching to be used, and I was ready to kick some ass.

WHEN I REACHED the path that led to the palace, Marcus was outside. No crown. No guards. Instead, he was a man with a broadsword and a grin. A chain shirt covered his tunic, and thick leather gloves dangled at his belt like a sporran on a Highland clansman. He wore weathered boots, and his hair was braided back.

"Are we going to a medieval war?" I teased.

Marcus laughed. "I haven't fed my blade for a few decades, Death Maiden. Duty to the crown, to the people. Now if I fall to a foe . . . this"—he gestured around us—"is all Eli's responsibility. It's freeing to have an heir willing to fulfill his duty."

I nodded and drew the blade he'd gifted me when I wed Eli. "Freeing in all sorts of ways, I'd wager. . ."

Marcus bowed and lifted his blade. "Help an old man stretch before battle?"

I snorted. He might be a few centuries old, but the king of the fae looked to be only a few years older than me. This man was not a creaking old grandpa—and I was glad of it. I wanted him to live and age, wed and breed. I wanted him to have an heir, so Eli and I were never required to take the throne.

I bowed my head and waited for his first attack.

"So . . . does this mean you're going to take a bride?" I asked as I parried his *oberhau* strike.

"Indeed."

Since he volunteered nothing, I pushed the topic. "Shouldn't you be casting your eye toward fae maidens? I recall quite a few beautiful women lining up to offer to marry my husband."

Marcus grinned again. "Couldn't wed the prince, so they'll settle for the king. I suppose I could glance that direction."

I decided to be blunt. Time was short when it came to private conversations with the king. "Alice is a widow, Marcus. She loved her husband, and he was murdered last year. That's how we met. She hired me, tried to kill me, and the rest"—I lunged at the king— "is history."

He blocked. "She's a mortal in Elphame, Geneviève of Stonehaven. I am within my rights to keep her here, and I find that I'd like that."

"Crowe." I attacked with a series of *mittelhau* strikes, all of which he deftly parried. "I'd like to see you try. King or not, you don't want me as an enemy. Kidnapping Allie would create a problem for you. Don't do it."

We fought in silence for several moments.

Finally, Marcus offered, "*If* I break this law for you now, you will bring Alice for visits, Geneviève of Stonehaven. I offer you this bargain in kindness and familial regard." The king lowered his blade. "You shall not speak of the terms of this faery bargain to anyone save for your husband."

Unfortunately, I couldn't strike him unless we were exercising—and I couldn't actually refuse his bargain. I might be his niece by matrimony, part-fae because of my meld with Eli, but Marcus was the king of the fae. He was not one to be outwitted or outmaneuvered.

And we both knew it.

"I will only accept this bargain if I have your word that you do not intend to harm or use Alice. Romance? Fine. Seduce her *if* she understands your intentions are temporary? That, too, would be fine, but she's mine to protect as surely as every faery here or in my world."

Marcus looked at me curiously. "What makes you think my intentions are fleeting? My family always knows when we meet our destined bride. I knew she was in *your* world, as did my sibling and my nephew. So, I simply stayed in *Elphame* to avoid meeting her. And yet . . . you brought her to me."

I opened my mouth, but no words came out.

"Alice is beautiful, clever, and charming. Anyone would be lucky to know her." He gazed in the direction of the cottage where she waited. "Your loyalty is admirable, Geneviève, but your opinion of our kind could benefit from a bit less bias."

"Oh."

Marcus sheathed his sword, raised a hand in a gesture, and then added, "I believe mortals speak to the parental figure before beginning a courtship. This I have done with you. Do you accept our bargain?"

He paused until I nodded.

Once I did so, he continued, "I will allow my future bride to depart back to your world, but you are bound by our bargain to bring her here to know this world and people. In due time I shall inform her of our future."

"I don't know whether to feel tricked or simply worried for you," I admitted, thinking about the fury that Alice would direct at the king when she discovered his intentions. She could, of course, refuse him—and it would serve him right. I met his gaze and said only, "So mote it be, Marcus of Stonehaven, King of *Elphame*. This bargain is accepted."

"So mote it be," he repeated with a cheerful grin.

In the next moment, twenty-odd guards joined us. And in another blink Marcus had rent a hole in the air. Unlike mine, his gate was instant, elegant, and shimmering like opals had been drawn from the soil to create a stately archway.

"Together into the battle?" Marcus offered.

"With pleasure," I agreed, but this time I was grinning in anticipation.

I had monsters to slay and magic to use.

CHAPTER ELEVEN

We stepped out of *Elphame* onto the beach in San Diego. The waves slammed against the shore, and birds of some sort seemed to cartwheel through the sky, riding currents in the air. The taste of salt lingered in the air, and a glance at the horizon told me that the ocean truly did seem to end the world. It was a lovely stretch of sand, spotted with large rocks and sprinkled with tidal pools.

"They wouldn't have had to drug me to keep me here if they'd simply showed me this," I murmured, partly to myself.

"We have a sea at home," one of the guards pointed out.

"*Elphame* is still new to me. As a girl, I used to dream of pirate ships and lost islands. Foes to fight and sea creatures to discover." I smiled briefly, thinking back to books I'd devoured. "When both the fae and the *draugr* are normal to you, when magic is in your veins, sometimes it's nature that holds the most allure."

"Indeed," Marcus said in an odd tone. There were secrets hidden in that word that I wanted to ask him to explain, but now was not the time. He added, "This nature has allowed the dead to invade their shore. Man has forgotten to learn his history. The *draugr* do not need air as we do. They can walk out of the sea."

"So the gates . . ."

"Are useless," Marcus finished. He gave me a look. "They do not stop *your* kind, Death Maiden."

"Classy," I muttered. Louder, I added, "I'm not dead, Marcus. Not all *draugr*. I need air, just like you."

Then I turned away from the faery king and let my magic roll out in front of me like a wave, and with disuse or perhaps with the added juice of my new genetics, my wave was neither gentle nor subtle. My magic rolled like a tsunami across the beach, the spa, the city as a whole.

I could summon armies, I thought with a shiver of something that felt more like pleasure than fear.

"Daughter of Mine?" Beatrice's voice filled my mind. *"Are you unwell? Imperiled?"*

"San Diego. Girls' Weekend. Spa is run by draugr *that have magic and drugs."* I continued to walk, feeling the dead in the distance awaiting my summons. *"Got my juice back. Could raise a city . . ."*

"Please do not." My dead grandmother sounded worried. *"Are you alone?"*

"Nope. Uncle Marcus popped out of Elphame *to wage war at my side. Brought a wee army. We're family bonding with swords and violence."* I glanced at the king, who looked at me curiously.

"Fight well. Draugr, even those with magic, are susceptible to your will. Speak if you have need of my aid."

Then I felt her withdraw from my mind. Whatever secrets she had were not ones she was sharing today. Perhaps she was envious. She *did* like a good fight.

Or she might be possessive. My grandmother was not entirely fond of the fae.

Or perhaps she knew what *draugr* were here and intended that I resolve this issue.

I made a mental note to talk to Beatrice. Dear old gran

wasn't above using me as a weapon, and typically I might not object. This time, though, she'd sent me to battle alongside my very human friends and *without* my magic.

I concentrated, sending what I thought of as tendrils of curiosity out toward the spa. Six *draugr* were here. They were old, but not ancient. Two were magical.

"Six dead biters," I said to the fae. "Two work energy."

"You didn't plan to tell us about that until now?" a guard asked.

"Had to be here to feel them." I shrugged. "Death Maiden thing."

We ascended the cliff from sea to spa. My foot slipped a few times on the loose rocks and sand, but no one else seemed to struggle. They lived in nature. I'd spent the last few years on concrete sidewalks or dodging the roots of old oaks in the cemetery.

At the top, a man in a linen suit of some sort, yoga teacher meets lost-in-the-desert prophet, stood waiting.

"Friends," he started. "Such violence is not welcome here."

"Dead," I announced. "Old dead if he's in the sun like this."

The man gave me a pitying smile. "Oh, child. Not at all. I've simply found enlightenment. Breathe peace with me."

"You trap people here. Fruity drugs or whatever." I gestured to the pink-tinted water that sprayed from the misters.

"I encourage peace through natural—"

"Nope." I sent a thought toward the misters, freezing them, stopping the toxins. "Not stalling while you wait for everyone to 'breathe peace.'"

The beatific expression vanished. Fangs dropped. And he charged—toward the king. The dead guy clearly thought he could *flow* and latch onto Marcus' throat before anything happened. No older *draugr* at home would make such a mistake, so it was nice to have my draugr-traits as a surprise for a change.

I *flowed*, almost as fast as the *draugr* yoga-preacher.

My back was to Marcus' chest before anyone could blink. My own fangs were sticking out as my temper sparked. Magic made my bright blue hair shiver as if actual serpents extended from my scalp.

"My family is off limits," I said as I shoved magic into the *draugr*.

I was surprised when he simply blinked at me and said, "Mistress?"

"Not the leader," I explained. "Too weak."

"Mistress, how may I serve your guests?" the now befuddled fanger asked.

With a sigh I stepped away, and in the next heartbeat, Roisin had severed his head. Another guard kicked the head away.

"He attempted injury to the king," Roisin explained with a shrug.

We continued onward, quickly dispatching the next two *draugr*. Marcus and I beheaded one each. He chortled happily when his quarry put up a decent fight. Truthfully, I thought he missed several obvious openings to end the fight, and I said as much.

"Why not extend a fight for your joy if it's not truly dangerous to do so?" he asked.

I couldn't truly fault his logic. My own fight was far easier than I wanted. This entire excursion felt like the proverbial walk in the park—and not just because we traveled with armed fae guards. My magic was back awake inside of me. I felt like I could stay awake for years, take on hordes. I couldn't fault a king who had missed the fields of battle.

We made our way toward the spa building. I felt at least one more *draugr* there, but as we were walking through the garden, I felt multiple new dead signatures. Gaps where there hadn't been any. Early on in my life, I'd thought that meant a new *draugr* had arrived, but now that I was older, I realized it was something worse: new death.

People were dying, murdered. I felt sick enough that I stumbled as the number of gaps continued. I couldn't get to all of them in time, no matter what I did. How was I to choose? All life mattered, and I felt suddenly helpless.

"Niece?" the king prompted.

"Murders," I managed. "Rooms."

"*Draugr?*" Marcus asked, eyes gleaming in anticipation of a fight. "How many?"

"Two *draugr.* Killing." I shook my head, trying to focus. Was it better to go to the rooms? Or the spa? There were three *draugr* on site here, and they all needed to be stopped.

"You know these monsters better than I, Geneviève. What do you need?" Marcus asked.

"Stay."

The king quirked his brow at me, but he gave orders, sending fae guards to the rooms as we continued toward the spa.

Once it was just us, he murmured, "Most fae wouldn't speak to me like a disobedient hound."

I scoffed. He was lucky I could speak at all. My senses were all screaming as body after body died. The spa obviously *had* been at capacity. All of those people gone. All of those lives ended.

I hoped the fae warriors were prepared to handle the *draugr* there. My heart ached at the thought of their deaths, but my magic screamed that the *draugr* at the spa was stronger. They could handle the others. I had to go to the spa. Magic recognized its own, and now that I was back in possession of all of my capacities, I knew this *draugr* was one of my kind: magic and death.

I glanced at Marcus before we entered the lobby. "This is

my fight, uncle. I need you to defend yourself and take the head if you can."

Marcus gave a curt nod. "Why?"

"Death magic." I jerked the door open and let my magic roll out like a hammer seeking a target. No subtlety. "Hey, asshole! I'm here for your head."

At my side, Marcus made a noise that might've been a laugh.

We stalked past the front desk where a man was slumped over, blood not yet congealing on the savaged wound on his neck.

"All I wanted was a relaxing weekend," I called out. "Some fruity drinks and beach time. A massage. But nooooo, you ruined it."

I slammed open the locker room, heading toward the *draugr* with the unerring focus of a bloodhound on a scent trail. I felt his dead presence as surely as any corpse. This one, though, shimmered in a way that only Beatrice did—and my great-times-great grandmother was the only other magical *draugr* I knew.

"Come out, come out, frog nuts!"

I kicked open the door to the spa where I'd been half-high on that fruity fog earlier, and there stood the tallest man I'd ever seen. At almost seven foot and change, the *draugr* standing in the steamy room looked like he'd done a few turns on a medieval torture rack and stepped off. His eyes widened at the site of Marcus, and without using whatever magic he had been utilizing to control the people enslaved at this toxic hell-spa, the lanky *draugr* wrongly assumed that the faery king was the biggest threat.

"You come here, onto my ground, with your fae magic and—"

"Way to be sexist," I interrupted the villain monologue he was about to spout.

"You." The *draugr* studied me. "Why is your heart beating if you are of us?"

"Because I'm alive." I shoved my death magic into my blade . . . accidentally . . . and for a blink I faltered. That hadn't been what I meant to do, but now my fae-wrought sword was glowing like some sort of bad special effect in an 80s movie.

"You're a *draugr*. Submit to my authority. I am William of Diego, regent of this place." The too-tall dead guy flashed fang at me, as if it was some official dead person greeting. Hell, maybe it was, but I wasn't here to chat.

I *flowed*, stopping across the pool from him. "Not really looking for a king, Billy."

"I am the *draugr* ruler of this—"

"I'm a necromantic witch, and I'm full up on regents ordering me around." I flashed my own fangs, though, as if in a reactive response. Behind me I heard Marcus moving, and I knew he was looking for an opening.

"Get rid of the steam, Marcus," I called, hoping fae magic was as powerful here as in *Elphame*.

As I felt magic that felt like summer fill the hot springs room, Tall Bill lunged to try to steal my sword or bite me. I honestly couldn't tell because when he got closer, the magic in my sword flashed out like a shield and enclosed the two of us in a bubble of magic.

I made a mental note to figure out what that was because being trapped with the thing trying to kill me wasn't exactly ideal. For now, I just hoped that the magical bubble wouldn't drop out from under us.

"Okay, Bill, you can either surrender or—"

He snapped again, like a rabid dog who'd forgotten his remaining manners. This time his teeth caught my shoulder and tore into the meat of my arm.

"Or, I can make you," I finished, reaching out mentally to try something that suddenly seemed possible. I shoved life into

Bill, mentally massaging his heat, coaxing it to beat, and filling his lungs with air. I pulled the fae magic into my necromancy, and in that moment, I tugged a half-century old *draugr* into living.

He stepped back, throwing himself at the magical bubble in horror, clutching his chest as he noticed the long-silent heart begin to beat.

"Stop. Stop this," Bill begged me, voice sounding older, weaker by the second.

And something cold inside me smiled. "Certainly."

I tugged all of my magic back, and Bill's centuries of existing as a walking, biting dead man caught up in front of my eyes. Bill aged rapidly, and as mortal men can't live for centuries, Bill withered, died, and floated away in dust.

My magic retracted into my body, dropping the bubble from under my feet, and I fell in an ungraceful crash into the hot spring.

"Son of a monkey!" I stood up, sopping wet and trying to scramble out before the toxins made me high.

"I purified it," Marcus offered as he extended a hand.

Embarrassed, wet, and a little mortified at the joy I felt in ending Dead Bill's un-life, I stepped out of the hot spring and shoved my wet hair back.

We made it as far as the front desk before we were met by the same son-of-a-weasel who had been at Tomes and Tea arguing with Jesse. He was stacking files, shredding some, and singing what sounded like a sea shanty.

"Ms. Crowe," he greeted. "I had thought that the stories were exaggerated."

"What? How?" I blinked at him. Of all the things I'd dealt with of late, this one was the first to surprise me.

Marcus raised his sword. "What are you doing here, Chester?"

"Chester?" I echoed.

The man raised a hand. "Please skip the prurient jokes, Ms. Crowe."

I wanted to object, but I resembled that remark. A lot. So I simply said, "Who are you? Why are you here? And why does he"—I motioned to Marcus—"know you?"

"You are far more adept than anyone had reported." Chester tapped the files in his hands like an orderly office manager. "For an untrained Hexen, you're capable."

I flinched. Capable? That was the sort of flattering that sat next to "nice." And while I didn't think I was the best thing since sliced bread, I was a lot more than merely capable. I was an original. I was a half-*draugr* witch who melded with a faery prince. *The* faery prince, as a matter of fact. I opened my mouth, temper getting ahead of logic.

"You knew about this?" Marcus said, forcing focus back to the matter at hand.

Chester shrugged. "It wasn't sanctioned if that's what you're asking."

I watched him, still fairly in the dark, and realized that the little tiff at the bookstore was an act. He was powerful enough that the King of *Elphame* was being cautious.

"Who are you?" I asked again. "*What* are you?"

Chester straightened his impeccable suit before he smiled. "I maintain balances, educate, and sometimes assassinate. You made a mess of this place."

"They were keeping people in . . . vegetative states." I stepped closer. "And they attacked me and mine."

"And yet . . . here you are." Chester made a *tsk*-ing noise. "You seem unharmed." He shoved the files in a drab leather briefcase and snapped it shut. "And you restored a deceased Hexen. Granddaughter to a *draugr*. Niece of a king. That's a lot of influence for one . . . woman."

Marcus put a restraining hand on my arm, which Chester

noted. Then the man—*being?*—departed with a poof of jasmine scented pink smoke.

I looked at Marcus. "He? That? He was involved?"

"Perhaps." Marcus released my arm. "But . . . Geneviève?"

"Hmmm?" I met the king's gaze.

"You're a terrifying being." The king held my hand as he spoke. "Know that if I had knowledge of the power level that you'd achieve by melding with Eli, I'd have killed you. Chester, however, is liable to do so if you provoke him. Be cautious with your choices."

I swallowed. I wasn't sure what Chester was, but I knew I *really* didn't want to fight with the king of *Elphame*. Carefully, I explained, "I had no idea that the trio of . . . heritages? . . . That being this would be so unstable."

Marcus nodded. "I believe you, but know that if you ever try to wrest power from me or threaten my people, you will not survive."

"You think you could kill me?" The question was out before I could think about what I was saying.

"Spouses are bound in life span. To kill my nephew is to kill you." Marcus released my hand finally. "It would be wise to remember that if you face enemies who do not hold him in the same high regard that I do."

And I heard that both as the wisdom it was—that I ought to make sure my spouse knew everything, and so was able to keep himself protected—and as the threat that it was. If he thought it was necessary, the king of *Elphame* would kill his nephew to save his people.

We walked out of the spa building in tense silence, only to be greeted by the rest of the fae soldiers.

They gave reports to the king as we all made our way to a good spot to return to *Elphame*. Only Roisin was bold enough to ask if I was well, but the best I could do was nod. My magic was back, and it had brought new tricks with it. I needed time to think and process—and I needed my husband at my side.

My "Girls Weekend" wasn't anywhere near what I'd expected, but obviously it had achieved the unspoken goal: I had relaxed enough that my magic was back.

CHAPTER TWELVE

When we returned to *Elphame*, my husband was standing there looking far-from- cheerful. His gaze took me in, which was fairly normal. Pre-matrimony, Eli had stitched me up so often that I thought he'd earned an honorary field medicine degree.

"Geneviève." He bowed his head to the king then. "Uncle."

Marcus looked at me. "Someone's apparently in trouble."

"Did no one think it prudent to notify me that my *wife* and my *king* were off in a skirmish?" Eli's formal tone said more about his mood than anything else could. He reverted to increasingly fae mannerisms when he was upset.

"It was *six draugr*." I gave a little twirl. "Barely a scratch."

Marcus met Eli's gaze. "I do not twirl."

Then the king bowed to me. "You are a worthy warrior, Death Maiden." He paused, eyes still holding mine, and added, "Do not forget our conversations."

Without another word, the King of *Elphame* departed, his soldiers dipping their heads to me as they trailed the king.

When it was just the two of us, Eli sighed. "Bonbon. Really? Even at a spa in a *draugr*-free city?"

I shrugged. "They came out of the ocean, apparently."

We walked to the house. *Our* house. And I tried not to smile at the sheer joy I felt. Successful battle. Magic back. Husband here.

"Where are the others?" I asked.

"Sera and Christy are on a beach, and when I left them, Allie was trying to convince a kelpie to give her a ride." Eli sounded amused, so I figured that despite their reputation for being monstrous, the kelpies in *Elphame* were not murderous water horses.

"The king thinks he's going to marry her."

"A kelpie?" Eli stopped mid-step. "Because you certainly cannot mean that he wants to wed the widow Chaddock."

"Destiny," I offered as we reached the cottage. I stripped outside the door, leaving my pile of toxin-covered clothes on the ground to be destroyed. It was a casualty of the job, but I still frowned at losing another pair of reliable boots. "I really liked those boots."

Eli said nothing as we walked to the shower.

"I spend an awful lot of time cleaning away my work," I muttered.

My husband held his words, simply looking me over as if I'd hidden injuries. As the grime washed away, as the flecks of blood washed away, Eli relaxed. "You are uninjured."

"I am." I softened as he visibly relaxed.

"Geneviève . . . you weren't here. You had no magic. And my uncle, who has not left *Elphame* in at least a century and change, was in San Diego. I was . . . alarmed. What foe would be so fierce that the king himself would take up arms? What danger were you, without your fierce magic, facing?"

He stripped as I stared at him, understanding dawning on me. I hadn't realized exactly how serious it was that the king had joined me.

"My magic is back," I whispered, summoning it to my will to

touch him without moving a muscle. The very air stiffened into intangible hands that brushed along his bare chest, marveling that a man like him was mine forever.

"Shouldn't I want you less now that we're an old married couple?" I whispered.

Eli laughed. "Never. I think my need and love grow stronger by the day."

I nodded, words failing as he stepped into the shower with me. His hands were curled around my hips, and finally we were kissing.

It had only been two days, but just then, two days felt like an eternity.

When he pulled back, I teased, "I have it on good authority that Girls' Weekends often include someone 'hooking up' with a gorgeous stranger . . ."

"Hello, I'm Eli. We've never met before, but would you mind if I ravished you now?"

"Yes, please. I'm . . ." I managed to whisper as he parted my legs. My attempt to role play failed instantly as he slid two fingers inside me. "I'm . . . I'm *yours*, Eli."

AFTER OUR NOT-REALLY-MAKE-UP SEX, Eli left me there with my friends for the next two days to enjoy a proper Girls' Weekend. Wined, dined, and sun-soaked, my friends were relaxed. Although after the first twenty-four hours, we'd all given up on convincing Allie that the fact that magical creatures suddenly obeyed her was because Marcus told them to do so.

"Did you know that if a kelpie chooses to do so you can breathe under the sea?" Allie was explaining.

"Yes."

"And did you know that the village for mortals here is just . . . basically . . . like a big artist colony?" Allie was carefully packing a blown-glass kelpie in her luggage.

"Yes."

"And did you know that know that Marcus says I can just pop in here whenever I want?" Allie paused, fidgeting with an embroidered linen dress.

I glanced at her. "Did he offer that to the others?"

She shook her head.

"I see." My faery bargain was making my tongue feel twisted. There were things I wanted to say but couldn't.

"You think he likes me . . . " Allie held my gaze. "Why aren't you saying anything, boss?"

"You're very likeable," I said, sounding as cheery as her.

And the often-underestimated Alice Chaddock crossed her arms and pronounced "You know something."

I'd been thinking on it since the conversation with Marcus. I could not tell her the bargain, his interest, or that he'd made a bargain with me. I could, however, think like the fae and talk around it.

"Do you recall how I ended up married?"

Alice's eyes grew comically wide.

"And do you know how sometimes an eternal being . . . like say my grandmother can be clever and outwit mortals?"

Allie nodded.

With carefully chosen words, I warned, "It's wise to be careful, Alice Chaddock. I am, and yet, I have been *accidentally* married to a faery. . . and probably manipulated into going to San Diego to kill off *draugr* who were behaving badly but out of Beatrice's reach."

Allie looked around as if there were potential spies, and then whispered, "So you think Marcus has plans to manipulate me?"

It was far too direct of a question, so I looked at her, hoping she was clever enough to hear what I was really saying, "I *cannot* say, Alice. I simply *can not say*. But"—I shrugged as if was no big deal—"I know I ended up where I am because I made faery bargains with Eli."

"Well, I won't be doing that." Allie hmphed, and I repressed a sigh. She wasn't getting what I was saying, and the bargain prevented me from outright telling her—or anyone else. It wasn't my future on the line, but I wasn't going to let Allie stumble into something she didn't want.

Later, when I was back in New Orleans, I'd come up with a plan to help her without breaking my faery bargain—right after I went to see my great-times-great grandmother Beatrice and pointed out that I wasn't a hunting dog to be sent out at her will.

"Gen?" Sera called as she came into the room. "Alice, come on! Pack later! Drink now!"

"Coming!" I grabbed a parasol, another of the things Allie had stocked up on, and Allie and I headed outside to join Sera and Christy for a glass of faery-made whisky or two at the firepit. It might not be the spa weekend we'd planned, but we were together, and laughing.

Christy looked up from her lounger. "Fruit bowl for you on the table . . ."

Then Sera added, "And a beautiful shawl for you, Allie." She pointed to the delicate pink thing. "Just you."

The shawl was in a box with a tag in what looked like calligraphy but was probably just Marcus' handwriting. "To Alice, for cold nights when you are far away."

Alice looked at it, looked at me, and said, "He *like* likes me, doesn't he?"

I couldn't reply because of the faery bargain, but Sera and Christy simply said "yes." And I took a long drink to cover for my silence. After all the faery bargains that I'd made, this one was proving more complicated than I expected.

"I made some ice for you." Alice plopped several blood

cubes in my whisky before settling in with her drink in a chair beside Sera.

We weren't living in a perfect world, but I realized I'd lucked out on friends. I lifted my glass and said, "To sisters!"

"To sisters!" Sera, Christy, and Allie echoed back at me.

We drank, relaxing until Alice said, "So is it weird that you and Sera used to boink? But you're like sisters?"

"Not literal sisters, we just—" Sera started.

"Shut up, Allie," Christy interrupted.

And Alice grinned at us as she settled back with her drink.

"I love you people," I added, looking at them one after the other. "Best Girls' Weekend ever because you were with me."

Maybe Alice's influence was wearing off on me because I sat back with my drink and relished the stunned looks on all three faces. I could totally be sappy if I had to, and honestly, if it shocked everyone *that* much, I might just do it more often.

Our weekend was a little off plan, but it truly had been exactly the beach trip I'd needed. I felt ready and able to handle whatever challenges life threw my way next. Good friends, good booze, and the occasional beheading were my sort of weekend.

EPILOGUE

I left *Elphame* and returned to New Orleans with a bounce in my step that I attributed to the holiday as much as the return of my magic. It was evening, so Christy and Sera headed to their jobs.

Allie and I exchanged a look, but she didn't ask any awkward questions.

"Can I borrow a car to go to the Outs?" I asked Allie. My first order of business was visiting my grandmother.

My assistant gave me another odd look, but she handed me her keys. "Try not to break it. I'll get Tres to fetch me so I can go home."

I nodded. I hated keeping the secrets I was—not just about Marcus' interest in her and what that meant, but the Chester situation, too. Hopefully, no one would need to know about the odd man, but if so, I'd tell them when it was necessary. Not today. *This* was my work: figuring out threats and handling them.

As I drove toward what was once called Slidell, I tried to think of ways that the Chester situation wasn't alarming. There weren't many. He was a stranger who knew far more than he ought to about me.

When I arrived at the castle that Beatrice called home, I stepped into the familiar humid air, loud with the chorus of frogs singing and mosquitoes buzzing.

"Lady Beatrice is expecting you," my gran's assistant said, appearing seemingly out of nowhere. Eleanor was maybe fifteen upon her death, and she was dressed in her usual Renaissance garb.

Inside, Eleanor guided me to a library where Beatrice was standing in front of a giant fireplace. She didn't turn to face me even as she greeted me: "Geneviève. Daughter of Mine."

I was usually patient with her, attempting to forge a relationship. She was, after all, my ancestor and one of only two blood relations in my life. Tonight, though, I was tired of etiquette.

"Did you know about the spa?"

Beatrice didn't insult me by pretending not to understand. Her back was still to me. "I did."

"And you didn't think to warn me?" I asked.

The fierce ruler of the fanged monsters that plagued my city—my *world* in fact—finally turned to face me. Her eyes were swollen and blackened. Her lips were bruised and cracked, and her left arm dangled at an angle that was far from natural.

"I could not," she said.

I was across the room in a blink, *flowing* to her. Gently, I steered her to a chair. "Who did this? Did you kill them? If no I w--"

Her hand covered my mouth, stopping the word. "I am fine. Healing. Chester was most upset that I ruined his little seaside venture."

"Who *is* he?"

Beatrice offered me a terrifying smile. "My creator. The one who saw fit to hand me to a group of *draugr* to create a hybrid."

I froze, pondering the appearance of *humanness* in the suit-clad man. He had seemed innocuous. Human. Weak. Uninteresting.

"He did this?"

She gave a single nod. "He's the oldest living human, Daughter of Mine. An alchemist who made a crossroads deal if you ask him. I don't honestly know, but I know you need to stay away from him. If I'd known that it was his business . . . I didn't though." She took my hand in hers. "Please, Geneviève, heed me on this. The last person to cross him was Iggy. And he died for it."

Iggy. The Hexen I'd restored to life.

"Please?" she repeated. "I'm fine. Healing . . . I was simply not expecting him. Chester brings up difficult memories. You must stay away from him, Geneviève."

"I hear you." I felt a wave of tenderness toward her. Sure, she was a monster in her own right, but she was my family, too.

"I've asked Lauren to stay with me," Beatrice mentioned, tone falsely calm. "You and Eli, Alice, you're all welcome here. Tres is watching over Allie for now, but . . ."

"I'll talk to Allie. Is Mama Lauren here?" I sat on the floor at Beatrice's feet.

Beatrice, again, smiled, but this—despite the bloodied mouth—looked happier. "She's working on a hydroponic garden I started. She's been crafting herbal drinks to heal me."

I nodded. If there was a garden, it was because Beatrice knew it would entertain my mother. And if there were herbs to heal the already-dead, my mother would find them.

"So . . . aside from the Chester issue, tell me about the trip," Beatrice invited.

"Worst. Spa. *Ever*," I started, offering her the distraction we both needed. "Shoes made of leaves. Pink mist. No booze."

"I'd heard it was hellish, but it was a *dry* spa?" Beatrice grimaced.

"Completely."

"Eleanor!" Beatrice called out. "Daiquiris? And the gifts?"

I regaled my great-times-great grandmother with tales from my trip as her assistant brought in a tray of Blood Daiquiris. Alongside them were two daggers that looked to be the length of my forearm.

"Magic imbued," Beatrice said as if such gifts were minor. "For any future needs. One for you. One for Eli."

I accepted them with the same casual tone. "Daiquiris and daggers? Maybe I ought to visit more often."

"I'd like that," she said, and we left it at that. I may have no choice. For now though, we did as one must when disasters always lurked: we shelved it and shared a drink.

Later we could figure out the looming disasters, but for the moment, I was rejuvenated, magic-wielding, and my friends and family were secure. All was as well in the world as it could get.

The End

A GRAVE GIRLS GETAWAY

A Night Huntress Novella

By

Jeaniene Frost

CHAPTER ONE

I was *not* spying on my daughter. I wasn't.

Sure, I was flying to the spot in the woods where Katie was, but that wasn't to avoid her hearing my footsteps. It was just...convenience. If you came from a line of flight-capable Master vamps like I did, would you dirty your shoes by trudging through the dirt and leaves?

And sure, I was avoiding branches that would snap in a telltale way if I got too close, but that didn't prove anything. Why ruin the natural sounds of the forest?

Okay, fine, my slowing down and ducking behind a tree when I glimpsed Katie was incriminating, but why couldn't a mother enjoy a few private moments admiring her recently discovered daughter? Katie was lovely, with auburn-colored hair, the same dark gray eyes as mine, skin like sunlight on snow, and an uncommon gracefulness that was on full display as she danced among the trees.

If I still breathed, my breath would have caught as I watched her. I'd had her in my life less than three years, so I didn't have the memories most parents had of watching their babies coo in the crib, or laugh for the first time, or take their first steps, but I could watch Katie dance now, and it was indescribably beautiful. No prima ballerina had Katie's grace, precision, or speed.

And that was why we still had to keep her hidden. Those traits would reveal that Katie wasn't fully human. Mixed species people might be legal now, but Katie's particular blend of species had almost caused two undead wars before.

I was about to call out to her when she suddenly turned a pirouette into a roundhouse kick that leveled a nearby birch tree. Another spinning combination took out a larger spruce to her left, and then a ferocious roll-and-kick combo felled three evergreens in a row. As the coup de grâce, she ripped the stump of the nearest toppled evergreen out of the ground, and then held it up by its roots as if the stump were a decapitated head.

Dammit! Katie wasn't out here secretly dancing. She was practicing killing. Again.

I knew something was up with all her recent "walks." That's why I was spying on her—and yes, I had known all along that I was spying. Don't judge; motherhood was still very new and overwhelming to me. Hell, I hadn't even known I was a mother until a few years ago, when I found out that—while I was unconscious—my eggs had been harvested, fertilized, and implanted into a surrogate. Sound impossible? So does a half-vampire working for a secret branch of Homeland Security that polices murderously misbehaving members of the undead society, but that was my old job. Unbeknownst to me, I'd also been a guinea pig for a shadowy government official who'd been trying to create a paranormal super soldier. He'd succeeded with Katie, and though she was only ten years old, all the growth hormones they'd pumped into her meant that she looked several years older. The worst part, though, was by the time I found her she'd already racked up a body count that would do a hardened mercenary proud.

I'd spent the last few years trying to undo the brutal tutelage Katie had received when she was the government's secret weapon, hoping that with time, she would forget much of her early years. My husband, Bones, and I had given Katie as normal a life as we could, especially considering that we were both vampires hiding out from the vampire world because of Katie's unique combination of species.

We thought we'd been making progress with Katie, yet here she was practicing killing people again despite being told that killing was wrong. Did she think I couldn't protect her? Or did...did she *miss* killing people?

If she were human, I could read her mind and know the answer, but Katie was inhuman enough for her thoughts to be locked away. That left me guessing, and I couldn't come up with any innocent reason for what she was doing. Despair pricked me. Maybe I hadn't given Katie enough normal to help undo the massive psychological damage done to her. Was that why she was reverting back to her old behaviors?

My lips tightened as I shoved my despair aside. If my daughter needed more normal in order to break free from her horrifying past, then fine. I'd deliver an ass-ton of it.

———

LATER, I gripped my knife so hard that my knuckles whitened. I'd been in many battles before, but seldom had my nerves been stretched this tight.

"You'd better be worth it," I said to my prey.

One hard slice later, my hopes shattered. "Mother...fudger!" I swore, altering the curse just in time.

A stifled laugh behind me increased my ire. I whirled to see my mother turning away with her hand covering her traitorously twitching lips.

"I told you to take the turkey out half an hour ago," Justina murmured.

Yes, well, the meat thermometer hadn't registered 165 degrees then, and the recipe said poultry *had* to be cooked to at least 165 degrees. I gave the meat thermometer an evil look. Either it was broken, or it was possessed by the spirit of a vengeful chef bent on destroying my attempts at a nice family dinner. Hey, stranger things had happened.

"Sorry. Dinner's going to suck, but on the bright side, no one's getting salmonella from *this* burnt offering."

"You're all vampires, and I'm not fully human, so salmonella can't harm any of us," Katie replied. Her tone was faintly quizzical, as if she was trying to hide her surprise that I hadn't figured that out for myself.

"I know, honey," I said gently. "I was making a joke."

"Ah," she said. Then, she smiled a little too wide. "Of course. Your joke was very entertaining!"

Now I was the one smiling. Despite Katie's many skills, she had yet to master lying. It was almost comforting.

"Don't fret," Bones replied, getting up and moving into the kitchen. "That bird will do nicely with the right roux. Give me a few minutes, Kitten."

I left the kitchen, defeated by it once again. No matter how many recipes I tried, I still couldn't cook to save my life.

Bones began whisking the pan drippings while adding wine, spices, flour, and other ingredients. Soon, the aroma was heavenly. His roux, or gravy, as we Americans called it, was so good that it made even the overcooked turkey delicious.

By the end of dinner, I would have called tonight a success, except for what Katie said after taking her plate to the sink: "I'm going for a walk in the woods."

Granted, ten o'clock at night might be well past bedtime for a human child, but for a household of vampires, it was barely evening. Also, our nearest neighbor was several acres away in this stretch of forested land in Mission, British Columbia, Canada, so she was safe. Still, I tensed.

Going for a walk, my ass!

I had to handle this. I just wasn't sure how to do so yet.

"Fine, but don't be gone too long."

CHAPTER TWO

I waited until I couldn't hear Katie's footsteps anymore before I said, "She's up to no good out there."

My mother's eyes widened. "She isn't smoking, is she?"

"I wish," I replied with feeling.

Justina gave me an appalled glance. My wave dismissed it.

"That would at least be an expected form of pre-teen rebellion. She's sneaking off to practice killing."

Saying it out loud made it more real. Guilt, grief, and rage scalded me with its usual toxic mixture. I saved Katie from the human monsters that had held her captive, so why couldn't I save her from the horrible things she'd learned from them?

"You've been spying on her?" Bones sounded more surprised by that than he was by hearing of Katie's activities.

"I prefer 'practicing attentive parenting,'" I muttered.

His look plainly said, *Who are you bullshitting?*

I threw up my hands. "Fine! Spying on her is messed up, but that's hardly our main concern, is it?"

"Kitten, we told Katie it was wrong to kill anyone who wasn't trying to harm her, but we never told her that she couldn't still train."

My eyes widened. "Isn't that focusing on the letter of the law while ignoring the *intent*?"

"Maybe training is just familiar to her?" my mother said.

Justina, the excuse-making, indulgent grandmother? Never would've pegged her for that, but here she was, showing Katie more understanding for her trial slaughters than she'd shown me my entire childhood.

"She wasn't just shadowboxing, Mom. She was kicking trees in half and then decapitating their fallen stumps."

And appearing to enjoy it. That worried me the most. Had she *enjoyed* killing people in her former life?

Bones didn't look concerned. For a second, something flashed across his face that looked traitorously like approval.

"Oh, come on," I snapped. "She's just a child!"

His dark brown eyes seemed to stare into my soul. "Yes, but she's no ordinary child, and you know it. So, what's really bothering you about this, Kitten?"

"I keep screwing things up with her!"

The words burst from me while emotions that I tried not to think about, let alone show, exploded free like a cork shooting out of a shaken-up champagne bottle.

"I wasn't there for the first seven years of her life when she was experimented on and forced into becoming a killer," I said, trying to regain control. "Now? What sort of mother am I? I can't cook, I keep dropping f-bombs, I could barely stitch the tear in her favorite pants, and, oh yeah, I'm spying on her."

My mother stood, not appearing to notice that she upended her chair with her fast, jerky movements.

"You love your daughter as she is." Her voice vibrated, and I was shocked to see her eyes shine with unshed tears. I could count on one hand the number of times I'd seen my mother cry.

"I failed to do that with you when you were growing up, and it almost killed you. Don't worry about the other stuff. Keep

196 • A GRAVE GIRLS GETAWAY

loving your daughter unconditionally, Catherine, and unlike me, you'll always be a *wonderful* mother."

With that, she left. Moments later, I heard her car start, and then the spin of gravel as she pulled away.

"Your mum is right."

Bones's statement broke the silence. I turned toward him, a humorless smile tugging my mouth.

"You and my mom agreeing? Is it the apocalypse again?"

He smiled back although his gaze was serious. "Hope not, but still, she's right. You'd see it, too, if you weren't so busy punishing yourself for what happened to Katie before we found her."

Damn Bones. He always cut to the heart of matters, and worse, he frequently used logic as his scalpel.

"I know I'm not responsible for what was done to Katie, but I *feel* like I am," I admitted. "Maybe, deep down, Katie feels that way, too? Maybe that's why she's acting out this way?"

Bones let out a soft snort. "Kitten, Katie isn't doing this because she blames you for what happened to her."

"Why, then?"

Bones gave me an unfathomable look. "Ask her, but not now. Ask her after you've had a mental break from trying to make up for every evil deed that someone else committed against her. That way, you'll be able to truly hear her answer."

"How do you propose I get this cleansing mental break?" I said with a wry scoff. "Give myself a lobotomy?"

His lip curled. "Those don't work on vampires, so we'll go with the more effective option of going on a getaway."

I waited, but he didn't follow up with 'just kidding!' "You think I'll stop worrying about Katie if we're off somewhere where neither of us can make sure that she's okay?"

"'Course not," he replied in an easygoing tone. "That's why I'll be staying behind, and you'll go."

I laughed. He only arched a brow.

"I'm quite serious. Denise was just saying it's been too long since she's seen you. I'm sure she'd love the chance to catch up, and Charles can certainly spare her for a week."

Charles was Bones's best friend, just like Denise was mine. I hadn't seen her in several months, and I missed her, but...

"I can't just up and leave. Katie—"

"We will be fine," Bones interrupted. "I'll be here, your mum and Tate are right down the road, and your uncle still floats by frequently though the spectral sod thinks I don't know it."

"That sounds great, but...uh..."

"Can't imagine doing something solely for yourself?" Bones let out a knowing grunt. "Like most good mums, you're too focused on everyone else, and now you're burnt out from taking on too much. Time to recharge, luv. You deserve it. I'll miss you, but we both know you won't relax unless I'm here with Katie, so ring Denise and tell her you're inviting her to a girls-only getaway. She'll love it."

I had no doubt. I kind of loved it, too, even if I had already started to think of a hundred reasons why I shouldn't do it. Still, I hadn't had a vacation in...God, several years.

"Fine. I'll call Denise."

"Call her later. Now, we're making the most of Katie being out of the house. Have to give you a good reason to miss me, don't I?"

He gave me a heated glance while a far hotter emotion slid through my subconscious, suffusing me with tantalizing sensations. He'd changed me into a full vampire, and that bond meant I felt his emotions as if they were my own—if he wanted me to. He wanted me to now, and when he grabbed me, his low laugh teased my lips before his mouth covered mine.

I barely noticed the blur of household fixtures as Bones flew us out of the kitchen and up the stairs. When we reached our bedroom, the door closed behind us on its own, and my clothes came off without either of us touching them.

Cooking wasn't the only thing Bones excelled at. He'd also become a fairly powerful telekinetic, and he'd expanded his abilities far beyond moving simple objects with his mind. My moan turned into a gasp as both his hands and his power slid over me, caressing and teasing with knowing, skillful touches. Then my gasps turned into cries when his mouth replaced his hands, and his tongue shot honeyed fire through my veins.

I writhed beneath him, too caught up to say more than a panted "Now!" as I tried to pull him up from between my thighs.

His laugh hit my flesh like an erotic brush of feathers.

"Not yet, Kitten. I did say you needed some 'you' time, didn't I? Let me get back to work on that..."

CHAPTER THREE

B y the time I left on my trip, I was feeling far less guilty. Katie seemed to look forward to having some one-on-one time with Bones. In fact, they'd both all but shoved me out the door. I mused on that as I waited for Denise. Maybe in my attempt to be an attentive mom, I'd been smothering Katie? How did anyone manage to raise a kid without constantly screwing up?

"Cat!"

I turned to see a beautiful woman with long, mahogany-colored hair and hazel eyes running across the hotel lobby toward me. I barely had a second to brace myself before Denise launched herself at me. Her momentum swung us in a circle, and I found myself breathing in her familiar scent of honey and jasmine as I hugged her back.

She caught what I was doing and laughed. "You're smelling me, aren't you?"

I grinned, sheepish. "Sorry, but hey, at least I didn't give you an exploratory bite, too."

She snorted. "I'm not your brand, remember?"

No, she wasn't. Because of my funky half-breed lineage, I

was the only vampire who didn't drink human blood. Instead, I fed from other vampires, not that most of my kind knew that. That's why I had a couple bags of Bones's blood packed in with my clothes. Sure, I could eat real food, but it didn't nourish or strengthen me the way vampire blood did.

Denise gave me a wide grin. "I'm so glad you're really here! I kept thinking some emergency would make you cancel."

I fought a wince. I'd cancelled lots of plans with her in the past several years. Guess that made me a bad friend in addition to my questionable mothering abilities. In my defense, someone had usually been trying to kill me during all the times I'd cancelled. Fighting off an attempted murderer was hardly a "the more, the merrier!" type of occasion.

"Nope. I'm here, and we're going to have so much fun."

"You bet, and look at this place!"

She waved at the sumptuous lobby, where the huge domed ceiling hung like a crown over the ornately designed floor. All that paled next to the magnificent views of the Pacific Ocean through the many windows. The Ritz Carlton at Half Moon Bay sprawled on top of steep bluffs like a modern version of a medieval castle. Only a narrow strip of beach ran between those bluffs and the surf, and further up that sandy stretch, there were tide pools that would soon be swallowed up by the incoming high tide.

"The ocean in front of us, and redwood forests behind us," Denise continued. "Plus, the clubs in San Francisco are only half an hour away. This is perfect! I wasn't expecting this, to be honest." She paused to grin again when I squirmed, and then teased, "Bones picked this place out, didn't he?"

Denise knew my thriftiness would never allow me to splurge like this, even if I thought it was perfect, too.

"Of course he did."

She laughed. "I'll compliment him on his taste later. Now, let's get dressed in something fabulous. Tomorrow, we're hiking in the redwoods or going horseback riding on the beach, but tonight, we're shutting down the clubs."

I couldn't remember the last time I'd gone to a club just to have fun. Mostly, I went clubbing to hunt and kill vampires. Tonight, though, all I'd be a danger to were gin and tonics.

"Sounds great, and if you like this, wait until you see our rooms. We have our own mini cottage on the beach."

Denise groaned in mock ecstasy. I grinned as I made a mental note to call Bones later and thank him. Maybe he was right, and this break was just what I needed. I already felt better, and the night hadn't even begun yet.

———

SEVERAL HOURS LATER, Denise and I walked down the beach, both of us holding our shoes instead of wearing them. The foamy surf came closer, threatening to soak our feet. Our hotel was still a few miles ahead, but we'd chosen to walk since it was such a lovely night. Still, the incoming tide might force us to change that plan.

It wouldn't be the first time we'd changed our plans tonight. So much for shutting down the clubs. We hadn't even lasted until midnight before both of us decided to head back. Even now, Denise shook her head, bemused.

"Were clubs always that loud? I could hardly hear a word you said, and damn, were we the only ones *not* high? I swear, I saw twenty pill handoffs at that last place, and some of those kids looked like teenagers!"

I let out an amused sniff. "They weren't. They only looked that young because we're getting older."

"Thirties is *not* old," she said at once.

"Of course it isn't, but it's old enough to admit when we're not having a good time versus staying and faking it."

She shook her head. "I don't get it. I used to love dancing all night. Now? My feet hurt, my ears are ringing, and I want to curl up on the couch and order dessert from room service."

I laughed. "That sounds great to me, too."

Denise gave me a wry grin. "I'm still kinda human, but you're a vampire. What's your excuse for crapping out early?"

"Spending time with you," I replied. "Like you said, it was too loud to talk before, and I've missed you."

"I've missed you, too."

We kept walking, chatting with an openness we hadn't managed in a while. Calls, texts, and video chats were great, but they didn't beat the joy of being together.

Soon, we reached what was left of the tide pools. I slowed my stride to avoid slipping, and then caught Denise's shoulder when she almost stumbled on the uneven rock.

"Want to head back to the street and call a Lyft?" I asked.

"Or you could fly us over these," she pointed out.

I could, but vampires had kept their existence hidden from humanity because we avoided public displays of power. Still, it was pitch dark, and the nearest hotel was a good mile away. I sent my senses outward. Nope, I didn't hear anyone else along the beach...Wait. I strained my senses more.

There. Someone was in the caves tucked into the bluffs bordering the beach and the sea. If I were human, I wouldn't have heard the low murmur of voices that almost blended with the sounds of the surf, and I *really* wouldn't have caught the new tang to the air before the sea spray snatched it away.

Still, that brief, sharp, new scent was unmistakable, *especially* to a vampire.

Blood.

"Earth to Cat," Denise began.

I pressed a finger to my lips in the universal gesture for silence. Then, I leaned in and whispered, "Stay here. Something's wrong," against her ear.

Maybe that blood was from a normal crime, or maybe I

wasn't the only person out here with supernaturally great hearing.

I flew toward the sounds and the smell of blood.

At first, I was confused when I reached the spot where the scent and sounds were strongest. Nothing but smooth, unbroken cliff wall met my gaze. Where was the entrance? There had to be one, and...what was that? A new, stronger wave had swept seawater all the way up to the cliff. It stopped everywhere except in one spot, where the water somehow disappeared into the rock.

I tried to touch that spot, and like the water, my hand vanished as it appeared to go through the wall of stone. I pulled it out and did it again. Same result, only this time, I concentrated and felt cool air coming from the side where I could no longer see my hand.

This part of the wall wasn't real. It was glamour, the term for a magical mirage. To use this, someone really didn't want their bloodletting interrupted.

Too bad.

I felt around until I found the rest of the entrance. Then, I squeezed into the hidden cave. Once inside, the glamour disappeared, revealing a narrow passageway. The smell of blood pointed my way, as did the sounds that I realized were chants in an unfamiliar language. Now, I caught snatches of thoughts, too.

...can't be happening...oh God, no...no, please, stop!

Chanting, pleas, magic, and blood—never a good combination.

I kept going, ducking when a new, flickering light appeared after a sharp bend in the tunnel. I could pick out several voices from the chants, and underneath them, the ominous sounds of grunts, as if someone was trying to scream and couldn't.

I pulled a knife from its sheath beneath my skirt. Since I found out at sixteen that silver through the heart killed vampires, I'd never left home without one. I'd barely palmed the silver blade when icy water soaked me to the ankles.

The incoming tide had reached the cave. This whole place would be underwater soon. I might be beyond drowning, but whoever was bleeding wasn't.

Fuck being stealthy. It wasn't my style, anyway.

"Housekeeping!" I sang out, and flew around the corner.

Nine hooded heads jerked up. The robed figures all appeared to be women, and four of them were vampires. Weak ones, if their auras could be trusted. Must be why I hadn't felt their energy before now. Strong vampires usually gave off vibes like an electrical current.

"Get out," a vampire with hair as red as my own snapped.

Torchlight revealed runes and other ancient markings drawn onto the cave walls. The women were standing around a pentagram that had a gagged, panicked boy inside it. He couldn't have been more than seventeen, and runes had been carved onto his chest, leaving bloody trails running down his body. No surprise, the mental pleas I'd overhead were coming from him.

"Hell no," I said, pissed for more reasons than their clear intention to murder this kid. "Less than a year after magic's been declared legal, you bitches are doing a ritual sacrifice of a teenager? First, that's evil, and second, are you *trying* to give the vampire council a reason to ban magic again? Innocent witches did not fight so hard for freedom from persecution for you selfish schmucks to fuck it up this way!"

The redhead wasn't the only one giving me an incredulous look. Guess the last thing they expected was a lecture, but magic wasn't the only thing that the vampire council had recently declared to be legal. Mixed species people like Katie were now legal, too, and it wasn't a stretch to assume that if one law got overturned because of assholes like these witches, the other law would get overturned, too.

"We obey no earthly council," the redheaded vampire

hissed. "And you have sealed your fate, intruder. Now, we will have two sacrifices to give our goddess instead of one."

Oh, she'd picked the wrong girl on the wrong night. Anticipation thrummed through me. Hiding with Katie had retired me from my former ass-kicking lifestyle, and I hadn't realized how much I missed it until now.

More water rushed around my ankles. It was now up to the bloody boy's cheek since they had him restrained to the cave floor. He flailed, the stench of his fear almost choking.

Don't worry, kid. You're not dying on my watch.

I snapped his restraints with a single, concentrated thought. One perk of being a freaky vampire who fed from other vampires was that I temporarily absorbed any powers the other vampire had. Bones was my favorite food, and since he was telekinetic, I had some of that power, too. I wasn't nearly as good at it as he was, but small, inanimate objects were easy.

"What?" the redheaded leader said in shock.

I gave her a nasty smile. "Yeah, and that's not all I've got."

Silver flashed in their hands as her three vampire minions lunged at me. I flew straight up, causing them to smack into each other instead of me. Then, I flung my silver knife.

It landed in the blonde vampire's heart. With another concentrated thought, I gave it a hard twist while using my body's downward momentum to slam the other two vampires against the cave walls. One vampire's head hit the wall so hard that she instantly went down, but the black-haired one screamed as she raised her knife and aimed for my unprotected back.

With a focused thought, I yanked the knife from her hand and sent it into her chest with another hard twist. Now two of the vampires were dead.

This was too easy. If they hadn't been about to murder a teenager, I might've felt bad about slaughtering them this way.

"Stop!"

I whirled to see that the redheaded witch now had the boy up against her chest while her back was to the cave's wall.

Smart. Now her heart was protected from both sides. She also had an ancient-looking knife pressed against his throat, and her eyes glowed with a vampire's trademark bright emerald light.

"One more move and he dies," she swore.

"Hurt him and I'll rip your head off right now," I countered.

Her smile showed her newly extended fangs. "No, you won't. If your powers were that great, I'd already be dead."

Ooh, a thinker. She was right, too. I hadn't mastered the ability to use my borrowed telekinesis on people yet, especially people with supernatural energy like vampires. But I didn't need to be able to control her to stop her.

I focused on her knife, and then yanked with all the mental strength I had. To my shock, the blade didn't even budge.

If snakes could grin, their smiles would look just like the one the redhead flashed me. "Your impressive abilities are useless against enchanted objects, intruder."

Inwardly, I cursed, but all I said was, "Really? Guess life's a bitch until one kills you."

"You *will* die," she said flatly. "Pity. With your abilities, you would have been an asset to our coven."

Her human acolytes started to chant in the strange language again. From their thoughts, this spell would end with my death. So much for thinking this was too easy. I'd seen how nasty magic could get in the hands of a skilled practitioner, and if the redhead had an enchanted weapon, she wasn't a poser or an amateur.

That's why I couldn't let her minions finish their incantation. The humans might be easy to incapacitate, but if I went for the last two vampires, I risked the boy's life. How to stop the chants without endangering him?

I glanced above the redhead. Yes. That could work.

I put my hands up in an "I surrender" pose. "Maybe we can come to an agreement—"

The redhead's scoff cut me off. "After you killed two members of my coven? Our only agreement is your death."

I readied my power, careful to look only at her. "You don't want to do that."

She scoffed again. "Oh, but I do."

Just a few moments more... "Not if you don't want a shitload of trouble. I'm Cat Crawfield Russell, and if you don't know that name, does the term 'Red Reaper' ring a bell?"

From her widened gaze, it did. "Wife of Bones, and friend of Vlad Dracul," she whispered.

I'd earned my nickname after cutting a bloody swath through the undead world when I was still half human, and she was defining me only by my relationships with the *men* in my life?

"You don't deserve a vagina," I muttered, and finished wrapping my power around the thin slice of protruding rock above her. With a mental yank, I tore the rock free.

The narrow slice of ledge slammed into her hard enough to take off her head. I lunged at the same moment, pulling the boy down so he was out of the rock's deadly, slicing path. Then, I took advantage of the other witches' shock to rip my knife through the nearest one's heart.

My head exploded with pain. I turned, seeing the formerly unconscious vampire through a haze of red as blood dripped into my eyes. At some point during my exchange with her leader, she'd woken up. Now, she held a piece of debris in her hands, its tip stained with scarlet. I was so dazed that it took a second to figure out what it was.

Bitch had brained me with the rock ledge I'd just used to kill her coven leader. Admirable, really.

I ducked under her next swing and managed a sideways kick that knocked her briefly unconscious again. I tried to use my abilities to send a silver knife flying into her heart, but though I concentrated, nothing happened. Guess the decent-sized piece of my skull on the ground meant my telekinesis was temporarily out of order.

The boy stared at me in horror.

"Run!" I said, fumbling around to grab one of the silver knives from the dead vampires.

He did, and after my second try, I had a knife. My head felt a little better, too. God bless vampire healing abilities.

Problem was, I wasn't the only one healing. The final vampire jumped up, giving me an evil glare. She didn't lunge at me, though. She stayed back, making me come to her.

I did until my legs suddenly had trouble working. *What the hell?* She'd whacked my head before, not my legs...

The spell, I realized. Shit. Not amateurs *at all*.

I changed course and flew at the chanting witches. This area of the cave was so small, it didn't matter that my power failed halfway through my flight. I still barreled into them, slashing as I went. Blood coated me in a hot spray, and two of the human witches fell. What I'd lacked in coordination, I'd made up for in strength. The other two witches screamed as their friend's head bobbed up and down in the water next to them.

Then they ran. Or tried to. The seawater hampered their strides since it was now up to our waists.

But one of the running witches was still chanting, and pain blasted through me as the remaining vampire slammed my head against the cave wall. I tried to block her next blow but ended up only swatting at her hands. *Damn that spell!* I felt like I'd been dropped into a cylinder of quick-dry cement.

The witch's chant grew until she was screaming. My vampire attacker smirked as my legs suddenly couldn't hold me up. Water went over my head as I collapsed beneath the waves and the weight of the spell. Through the haze of the sea, I saw the vampire walk away, presumably to fetch a silver knife. If vampire bodies floated, she'd have her pick of knives from the ones sticking out of her dead friends, but vampires lacked air in our lungs, so her dead friends had sunk straight to the cave's bottom. Just like I had.

I tried to force my body free of the invisible hold over it. Nothing happened, not even a twitch. *Fucking hell!* Why hadn't I learned any defensive magic? I'd learned every which way to fight, but only physically. Not mystically.

The vampire hauled me up from the water so I could see her smile as she raised a silver knife. For some reason, I found myself taking in every detail of her appearance. Cornsilk blonde hair, sky-blue eyes, skin as pale as a porcelain doll, and a near flawless complexion, except for a little scar near her eyebrow that she must have gotten when she was human.

Was this what people who were about to die did? Memorize the last face they saw, even if that face belonged to their killer?

Anger surged, so hot and fierce, I half expected the water around me to start boiling. Fuck her, I was *not* going to die this way! I might not be able to move, and my borrowed telekinetic powers might not work on vampires, but I wasn't totally help-less. She still needed that knife to kill me.

I focused on it with everything I had. Just as she slammed the blade home, it shattered into a thousand pieces, leaving only her hand to hit my chest. She stared at it in disbelief, and then stared at the roiling water that swallowed up the now-tiny silver shards that used to be the knife.

I kept my mind wrapped around a few of those shards as the vampire screamed and began bashing my head against the cave wall. Guess she'd decided on decapitation by battery since she could no longer stab me to death.

My vision went red, and not in a rage sort of way. In the *oh shit, I have massive cranial hemorrhaging* way. Acid being poured into my brain likely would've hurt less, and I could do nothing to defend myself. I only had one shot to survive, so I used the last of my quickly fading mental power to form those silver shards into a long point.

Then, right as an ominous ringing overshadowed the sickening crash-crunch-repeat sounds of my head being pulverized, I sent the combined shards toward her heart and twisted.

The next instant, everything went dark.

CHAPTER FIVE

Ow.

No, really, *owwww!* If anything hurt more than a mostly-shattered head knitting itself back together, I hadn't felt it yet. I puked three times inside my mouth before I had enough coherence to try spitting it out, and then I was frustrated and furious when I couldn't move enough to do that.

Damn that spell! No wonder some vampires had been so afraid of magic that they'd convinced the ruling council to outlaw it for thousands of years. I was normally strong enough to bench press a car, and now I couldn't so much as spit.

But, spitless or no, and collapsed in an underwater cave or no, I was still alive. *Thank you, freaky power-absorbing abilities. I couldn't have done this without you.*

Something hard hit me, interrupting my gratitude. Great, was it the final vampire? I thought I'd twisted that blade and killed her, but maybe I hadn't. Everything had gone black before I could be sure she was dead.

Another hard thump, and then I felt a leg. A warm one.

Not the vampire then. Our species was room temperature,

and in this cold water, we'd feel downright chilly. Whoever this leg belonged to was human.

Was it the boy? I'd told him to run, dammit. Or was it the final chanting witch? I hadn't heard her during those last moments before I passed out, but that didn't mean it was because she'd left the cave. More likely, it was because I couldn't hear anything beyond my skull being beaten in.

If it was her, she could be trying to finish me off. Normally, a human wouldn't stand a chance against a vampire, but in my condition, she'd have reason to feel confident.

Whoever it was yanked on my arm. I tried to shake off the mental fog that made me feel like cotton had replaced my brain.

Focus, Cat! You probably have to mind-smash one more knife!

She yanked harder, and my head cleared the surface. The first thing I saw was mahogany-colored hair plastered to a familiar face before that face broke into a smile.

"Thank God, I found you!"

I was shocked. What was Denise doing here? The water was so high, she barely had any room to breathe.

"Are you hurt? Why aren't you moving?" she asked me.

I couldn't answer, of course. I could only stare at her.

"What's wrong with you?" Now she sounded scared.

She should be. I found that I could move my eyes, and I glanced at the ceiling, the water level only inches below it, and back at her.

Get it, Denise? You're the one in danger!

"Yeah, I know," she muttered, and then relief suffused her features. "If you can manage to show your annoyance despite not being able to move or speak, then you're still in there. Good. I was afraid you might be dead."

She'd been married to a vampire for years; didn't she remember that we shriveled back to our true age when we bit the dust? Some vamps looked like old-school mummies after they died. Then again, I hadn't been changed into a full vampire that long ago, so I guess Denise had had reason to be unsure.

"Gotta get out of here, but I don't have your vision, and the torches are all out," she said, more to herself than me.

She was right. It was almost pitch-black in here, and with the cave's bends and turns now hidden underwater, it would be easy to get lost. And trapped. At least the part of Denise that wasn't human protected her from all but one form of death, and drowning wasn't it.

Still, drowning and coming back only to drown again and again would be horrible until low tide came and took the water away. Besides, who's to say the two witches who'd escaped wouldn't be back with reinforcements before then?

"Do your eyes still work?" Denise suddenly asked.

What did she mean by...? Oh, right.

I let out the green glow in my gaze. An emerald light instantly illuminated a couple feet of the cave. Denise gave the light a critical look, and then hefted me over her shoulders.

"Ugh, you're really heavy."

There goes your Hanukkah present, I thought irreverently.

"This isn't going to work," she said after dragging me a few feet. "The water's hampering me, and you're dead weight."

Go, I tried to tell her with my gaze.

She'd done everything she could. I'd have to wait for the spell to wear off.

Denise glanced up again. The ceiling was now brushing the top of her head. Soon, there wouldn't be enough room for her to breathe at all. She barely had time to get herself out of the cave even if she left me right now.

Go! I thought again, my gaze brightening with urgency.

A look of obstinance crossed her features, and she hauled my face close to hers. "I know what you're thinking, and no, I'm not leaving you behind. You'd never do that to me—"

A new surge from the tide swept water into her mouth. She

spat it out, coughed, and tilted her head all the way back. It was the only angle she could now use to get a breath in.

Just go! I mentally roared. *Both of us don't need to be stuck here, and I'm the only one who doesn't need to breathe!*

"That hurt," she said in a hoarse voice, and then choked out a laugh. "Don't know how fish stand breathing that..."

She stopped speaking. I was terrified that she'd lost the remaining scant space she needed to breathe, and I couldn't angle my head in order to see. Her grip had loosened, and the currents from the incoming tide now had me facing away from her.

"This'll be weird," I thought I heard her say, and then her grip on me vanished completely.

Without it, I sank to the bottom of the cave. I tried to see where Denise was, but the green glow from my gaze barely cut through the water. Then, a tremendous thrashing turned my limited vision into nothing but movement and bubbles.

Pain ripped at me. That must be Denise, drowning. Oh, God, she'd suffer that horrible death over and over because she'd refused to leave me, and there was nothing I could do to help her! How many hours until low tide...?

A large shark suddenly filled my vision, mouth open as if grinning while it swam straight at me. Jesus, Mary, and Joseph! I'd never wanted to move so much in my life, but I could do nothing but stare as rows of knifelike teeth sank into my arm.

Agony shot through me, and inwardly, I screamed. In my darkest wonderings about how I'd die, and I'd had many of those, getting eaten by a shark had never made my list. Guess I hadn't given Fate enough credit. *Good one, you sick bitch!*

The shark bit me again, this time catching my upper shoulder. Amidst the new burst of pain, an image of the last time I had seen Bones flashed in my mind: his deep brown hair, creamy alabaster skin, high cheekbones, winged brows, full mouth, and eyes so dark brown they could have been black.

And Katie, my beautiful little girl, standing next to him, watching me solemnly as I promised that I'd be back soon—

Red light suddenly suffused the shark's black eyes. Shock numbed me for a few seconds as to what that meant. In that short amount of time, the shark swam us out of the sacrificial chamber and into the cave's winding tunnels. There, its sleek body easily maneuvered around the bends and turns. I was the one who hit every protruding wall. Those hard jostles caused the shark's serrated teeth to tear deeper, but aside from holding me in its jaws, the shark didn't bite me again.

Red eyes. Only demons had those...or people whom demons had branded with their power, thus transferring some of their supernatural abilities to the branded person.

Jesus, Mary, and Joseph, I thought with awe this time. *You have outdone yourself, Denise!*

CHAPTER SIX

If the shark's new red eyes weren't proof enough that this was Denise, the fact that it was carrying me out of the cave instead of eating me did. Sure, I knew that being branded by a shapeshifting demon years ago had given Denise the ability to transform into anything she wanted to, but I'd forgotten that anything meant, well, *anything*. I'd also forgotten that in many ways, the transformation was literal. Unlike the glamour used to cover the cave entrance, this wasn't a magical mirage. Denise didn't just look like a shark; she was one, as the water rushing through her gills and her toothy grip attested.

Don't know how fish stand breathing that, she'd said when she choked on the water, followed by a muttered, *this'll be weird.*

She must have realized the only way she'd get out of this unscathed was to breathe water like a fish, and not just any fish. The most badass fish in the sea. I might have been too heavy for her to carry before, but now? She glided us both through the waves like a hot knife through butter. If not for the searing pain in my shoulder, this would almost be fun.

In minutes, we were out of the cave. I expected Denise to drop me now that we were free of that labyrinth, but she kept swimming parallel to shore, adjusting her bite every so often when her many rows of teeth nearly severed my shoulder and almost sent me tumbling out of her mouth.

Each new bite had me mentally gritting me teeth. *How did you spend your girls' getaway, Cat? Oh, getting eaten by my best friend. No, not in the fun way. In the wow-that-hurts! way.*

I was starting to worry that Denise had taken her transformation a little too literally when she suddenly beached herself and spat me out with a painful rip. I lay there healing while the shark next to me shuddered several times before skin replaced scales and then Denise rose naked from the sand.

"Weird as fuck," she pronounced, spitting what was probably little bits of my flesh out of her mouth. "But it did the trick. There's the hotel, and unless I'm wrong, there's our cottage."

I had to take her word for it since I couldn't angle my head to look. Denise gave me a sympathetic glance, and then dragged me by the shoulders up the beach. I saw the steps of our cottage moments later, and then felt a hard thump from each of them as Denise dragged me up the stairs.

Once inside, she positioned me so I was sitting on the floor with my back braced against the couch. Then, she left my line of sight. Moments later, she was back, wearing a robe and a contemplative expression.

"Can you blink?" she asked me.

I tried and found that I could. She made a relieved noise.

"Okay, blink once for yes, twice for no."

I blinked once to show I understood.

"I saw a naked kid run out of what looked like a solid wall in the bluffs. He was cut up and screaming about witches and monsters, so I gave him my jacket, helped him up the incline, and told him to head for the hotel. While I was going back down, two women ran out of that 'solid' wall as well. So, I knew it was fake, and since you hadn't come out yet, I went in to find you. Were those women really witches?"

I blinked once.

"What about monsters? Were those real, too?"

I blinked twice.

"Guess that's good," she said in a weary tone. "So, if they were witches, a spell did this to you?"

I blinked once.

"Fuuuuck," she breathed out.

My thoughts exactly.

"I'll call Bones," she said.

I blinked twice in rapid succession. I couldn't wait to see him again after coming so close to death, but Bones wasn't an expert on magic, and we needed someone who was. Before I worried him halfway to his grave with my condition, I at least wanted some facts about it first.

Denise sighed. "I get it. You don't want him to see you like this until you know if it can be fixed."

I blinked once while fighting back tears.

Yes, exactly.

"Ian, then," she said. "Between him and Veritas, they've forgotten more magic than these witches probably ever learned in the first place."

I blinked once, hard. Yes, Bones's rebellious vampire sire, Ian, had been illegally practicing magic for centuries, and his several-millennia-old new wife, Veritas, was half-vampire, half demigod, so she almost had magic coming out of her pores.

Denise left. When she came back, she had her cell phone. "Calling and texting both of them now."

They must not have answered because she left two voice-mails. Then, over the next few hours, she kept calling and leaving more voicemails and text messages. I was disappointed that she couldn't reach them, but I couldn't say I was shocked. Ian and Veritas had taken an extended honeymoon to parts unknown these past several months. Even Bones hadn't talked to them in a while, and he was Ian's only living family member.

"I'm sure they'll call back," Denise said, trying and failing to sound optimistic. She was married to a vampire, so she knew they didn't measure time the way humans did. It could take them days to check their messages, at least.

"In the meantime, let's get you cleaned up—"

"Don't bother."

The words came out of me, shocking us both. I'd thought them, but hadn't expected my mouth to form the words.

"Testing, one, two, three," I found myself saying.

Denise leapt forward and hugged me. "You can talk!"

"Seems so," I said, now trying to move, too. Still no motion in the limbs, but were my toes and fingers wiggling? With Denise blocking my view, I couldn't tell.

"Off," I said, and Denise jumped back.

"Sorry, did I hurt you?"

I could laugh, too, apparently. "Not then, but can we never play 'shark and chew toy' again, even if that was a great way to get us out of there?"

"Don't worry," she said, shuddering even though she was smiling. "It's been killing me not to leave you so I could brush my teeth, like, a thousand times."

I laughed again, and then gasped when I saw my hands and feet. Yes, my fingers and toes *were* moving. The spell was finally starting to wear off!

Denise's face suddenly drained of color, and she stared at something behind me.

"What?" I said, trying to turn around and failing. All I could do was crane my neck a little, and it wasn't enough to see what was behind me.

"Company," Denise said in a strained tone.

"Yes, company," an unknown female voice replied, followed

by a wave of supernatural power that almost knocked me over even though I was still braced against the couch.

From the power stinging me like dozens of angry hornets, our "company" wasn't human, and she also wasn't alone.

Denise visibly tensed, but she planted her feet and didn't move. "All of you, don't come any closer."

"Begone, mortal," a new voice said, and Denise was suddenly yanked up by an invisible force and hurled out of the cottage.

I was strafed with broken glass before I tried and failed to stand. My feet and hands only made weird, jerking movements while the rest of my body stayed put.

Dammit, the spell wasn't wearing off fast enough!

"Don't get up," said yet another new voice, with an undercurrent that was more ominous than seeing how Denise had been magically swatted away as if she were a pesky fly. "I promise you that this won't take a moment."

CHAPTER SEVEN

At least a dozen vampires wearing the same style of blue robes as the witches I'd killed earlier came into my line of sight. Good lord, of all the places to vacation in, we had to pick the one that was apparently a hotbed of witches!

One of the robed figures stepped forward and tilted her head. Her hood fell back, revealing hair the color of dark umber, deep brown eyes, and lovely sepia-and-cream skin.

"I am Morgana," she said.

"How unoriginal," I replied.

Okay, antagonizing a vampire witch while I was still mostly paralyzed wasn't my smartest move, but come on! Naming yourself after the sorceress who trapped the famed wizard Merlin from the King Arthur stories? She was asking for that sort of clapback.

Morgana glanced at my hands and feet with a smirk. "You must be very strong to have such motion. That spell doesn't expire until sunrise, but it matters not. Your death is sure."

I couldn't move enough to get away, but my hand worked

well enough to give her my one-fingered opinion about that threat.

"Heard that from the other witches," I replied while focusing my energy on the silver knives I had stored in the bedroom. Even now, I was using my borrowed telekinetic ability to quietly pull back the zipper on the knapsack they were in.

Angry emerald light flashed in Morgana's eyes. "Do you have any idea what you did tonight?"

"Stopped an innocent kid from getting murdered," I said while thinking, *Keep talking. Your friend made that mistake, too.*

Now her brown gaze was all green, and fangs peeked out from her lips. "You interrupted a sacred ritual and killed seven of our newest coven sisters. Half of them weren't even vampires yet! Then, we had to sacrifice one of our sisters who survived your butchery because our goddess had already been summoned, and lifeblood is required after a summoning. At least our surviving sister gave us the means to avenge ourselves. We found you by following the magic in the spell they had left on you."

Some days, I really hated magic. Today was one of them.

"We'd kill you now, while you're still helpless," Morgana went on, almost hissing with rage, "but you don't deserve a quick, merciful death. So, we are giving you to our goddess."

With that, Morgana said something in an unknown language and drew her finger across my forehead. Everywhere she touched burned as if a hot poker was scorching me.

I quit being subtle and ripped open the satchel with my mind. Several silver knives flew out of the bedroom, but though they hit their targets, none of the vampires dropped the way they should have with silver in their hearts.

Morgana bared her fangs in a smile. "Before we had to sacrifice our coven sister in place of the boy you freed, she told us of your abilities. That's why we're wearing these."

With that, the vampires drew open their ceremonial robes

to reveal that they were all wearing Kevlar vests. Murderous they might be, but dumb they were not.

Morgana traced my face with her finger again. This time, it didn't burn.

"Don't worry; you won't die tonight. I want you to think about what awaits you first. So, you have until the moon is full and the tide is high before our goddess comes for you."

I took it back—they *were* dumb. If they didn't kill me now, I would find a way out of this.

Morgana must have read some of that from my expression because she gave me a nasty smile. "Go ahead, let your loved ones gather around you trying to save you. You will only doom them, too. Everyone who spends so much as five minutes in your presence will be marked as a sacrifice, too, because this"— her finger traced my forehead—"is contagious. That's why we'll be leaving, but in case you're capable of surprising us with your abilities again..."

She said something else in that strange language. All of a sudden, I couldn't move a muscle. What had taken the other vampire several minutes with a supporting group chant to accomplish, Morgana had done by herself in seconds.

Maybe she'd chosen her name aptly after all.

The front door burst open, revealing Denise. She had cuts in several places and she was soaking wet...and furious.

"Back away from her, or I swear I will turn into a dragon and eat every last fucking one of you!"

The other vampires laughed. Morgana's brows rose, and she gave Denise an amused look.

"For the most entertaining threat I've heard in a while, you may live. For now," she added, with a sly glance at me.

I seethed, but I couldn't tell Denise to stay away from me. I couldn't so much as blink anymore.

Morgana gave me a final smile. Then, with a poof of smoke

worthy of a B-grade horror movie, she and the other vampires disappeared.

Denise rushed over to me.

"Bitches knocked me all the way out to sea," she said while running her hands over me to check for injuries. "Sorry it took so long to get back. Are you hurt?"

I only stared, hoping that Morgana's threat was bogus. Maybe she'd only told me the mark was contagious because she wanted me to be too afraid to ask for help getting rid of it, assuming I could find a way to do that.

Denise made a sympathetic sound. "They hit you with another immobility spell, hmm?"

When I didn't blink or speak, she said, "Guess so. This one's stronger, if you can't even blink now."

God, what a cruel curse, forcing someone to be trapped in their own body while also dooming everyone around them. If I found a way out of this, I'd make those bitches pay.

"Something's on your forehead," Denise said, using the hem of her wet robe to wipe it. Then she frowned, rubbing harder.

"Sorry. It's not coming off."

No, it's not because it's a frigging contagious curse! I wanted to scream, but I could do nothing to warn her, and my helplessness burned more than the scorch of the mark.

Denise sighed and gave up trying to rub it off. "At least we know your paralysis is temporary, although it doesn't make sense that they'd find you, paralyze you again, and then *not* kill you. Yes, I threatened to eat them, but they don't know that I could really change into a dragon and do it."

Hope perked in me. *That's right, Denise, figure out that there's more going on here!*

"Something's up, isn't it?"

I stared at her as emphatically as I could.

"Thought so." She sounded resigned but not scared. "I'm calling Ian again. He can't ignore a ringing phone forever."

She spent the next ten minutes calling Ian and Veritas over and over. I swung back and forth between hope and terror as the time ticked by. Morgana had said anyone who spent more than five minutes in my presence would be cursed, too, but so far, Denise seemed fine. Maybe the witch *had* lied...

Denise suddenly dropped the phone. "I don't feel so good..."

Horror pierced me when a line appeared on her forehead. Then another one slowly snaked its way above her brows. Then another. Denise grabbed her forehead while, inwardly, I screamed.

No, no, no!

Denise walked toward the mirror above the bar, touching her forehead as her reflection showed more marks appearing. After a few steps, she staggered and almost fell.

No! I mentally roared again. *Please, God, no!*

"Shit," she murmured. "This is...bad, isn't it?"

Her words slurred, as if she were having trouble speaking. My God, it wasn't just the "sacrifice" curse that was contagious. The immobilization spell must have been, too!

And I could only watch, tears trickling out of my eyes. *Oh, Denise. I'm so, so sorry...*

She suddenly grabbed a bottle and a glass from the bar. Both almost fell from her hands, but she held on, and managed to spill some of the dark amber liquid into the glass.

What was she doing? I loved liquor as much as the next person, but this was hardly the time to drink!

She sank to her knees, yet one hand remained raised, holding up the glass. "Ashael," she rasped out, and then swallowed some of the liquor.

Ashael? The mostly not evil demon who was Veritas's brother? Sure, if anyone knew about magic, it was demons since their kind invented magic, but didn't demons require specific symbols drawn with virgin blood plus their true names in order to be summoned? That's the complicated ritual I'd had to do the one time I'd needed to summon a demon.

"Ashael, it's Denise," she went on, slurring her words so much that it was getting harder to understand her. "Come...*now*."

With that, Denise swallowed again. Then, the glass fell from her hand, and she collapsed onto the floor.

CHAPTER EIGHT

I had to do something! Maybe I could use my powers to send out a text message to get Denise some help?

As quickly as that hope flared, it died. Even if I *could* use enough of my borrowed telekinesis to do that, anyone I called would be stricken by the contagious spell mere minutes after they got here. I might already have condemned Denise. I couldn't condemn anyone else—

Shadows suddenly swirled between me and Denise. In seconds, a tall, extravagantly handsome man with short black curls, deep brown skin, and walnut-colored eyes appeared. Never let it be said that demons failed to make a memorable entrance.

I stared at Ashael as he brushed imaginary lint from an expensive-looking peacock-blue suit. Then, red lit up his dark brown gaze as he glanced at Denise, at me, and then back at Denise.

"Got into a bit of trouble, haven't you?" he said with an appreciative whistle.

Denise groaned and sat up.

I was so shocked that I barely noticed Ashael pull out his cell phone and say, "Don't wait up," to whoever was on the line.

Had Ashael done something to Denise so she could move again? If so, thank God! Or thank...whoever, since he was a demon.

"Whole...body's...stiff," Denise said with a moan.

Ashael's snort managed to be elegant. "Of course. From what I see, you've been doused with a powerful immobility spell. You wouldn't be able to move at all, except for those brands. Magic doesn't work on demons, and you have enough of our power in you to avoid being a living mannequin like your friend over there."

I wasn't even insulted. I was more stunned that Ashael knew that Denise was demon-branded. That was a closely guarded secret. Only me, Bones, Ian, Denise's husband Spade, and Denise's relative Nathanial knew about it, or so I'd thought. And how had Ashael known we'd been hit with a spell?

"Good thing both my natures protect me," Ashael went on. "Now I know why you sounded so desperate. Anyone else you called would only end up stricken by the contagion in that spell."

How could he know any of this? I mentally raged. *How?*

"Can you get...this spell...off us?" Denise ground out.

He paused. "Yes and no."

Always a bargain with demons, and those bargains rarely ended without a lot of regret on the bargainee's part.

Denise gave him a baleful look. "Do the...yes part."

Ashael came closer. "Are you sure? Neither of you will enjoy what it takes."

That sounded ominous. Maybe this wasn't a good idea.

Denise must have read my reluctance from my expression because she said, "Do me first, then."

Wait! That wasn't what I meant at all!

Ashael's lips twitched. "If only I had a dollar for every time I heard a woman say that..."

"You'd be rich?" Denise finished, managing an eye roll.

His grin widened. "Rich*er*."

With his sin-wrapped-in-seduction looks, I didn't doubt it, but that wasn't what grabbed my attention. It was the haze of light that now glowed from Ashael's hands, and how his gaze had gone from red highlights to twin beams of silver.

Holy shit. This must be Ashael's *other* side. I'd never seen it before, our previous contact being very brief, but I'd seen it from his half-sister, Veritas. And she'd almost leveled a house with that *otherness* after a mere mood swing.

"If you consent," he said to Denise while power thickened the air, "give me your hands."

Denise stretched out her hands. As soon as Ashael clasped them, that glow from his hands increased, and Denise screamed.

I didn't even have to concentrate. Every single bottle from the bar suddenly slammed into Ashael. Glass, alcohol, and then blood covered him from all the flying, cutting shards.

His gaze slanted my way in annoyance, but he didn't let go, and the glow from his hands only intensified. Denise screamed again, and then bit her lips as if to hold back another scream.

"I'm okay," she gritted out. "I know what he's doing."

Her words were no longer garbled from a half-paralyzed tongue. She also wasn't slouched over anymore. Now, she was sitting upright, even if her face was pinched with pain.

"How much more?" she asked with a gasp.

"Just a bit," he replied as more light poured from his hands. That light began to absorb into Denise's skin, until her whole body started to glow.

"Almost done," Ashael said in a soothing way.

White sparks came off their joined hands. Denise squeezed her eyes shut, breathing hard while the air filled with the strangest power. Not the skin-tingling energy that marked the auras of strong vampires, or the icy brushes of power that heralded grave magic. This was something I'd never felt before.

Ashael released her hands. Denise fell back. He caught her, lowering her to the floor across from where I was positioned. For a moment, our eyes met, and I stared at her in disbelief.

Were those flashes of *silver* in Denise's gaze now?

Then she blinked, and all I saw was Denise's normal hazel eyes. "Wow, that feels weird," she murmured.

With that, she stood up, moving as normally as she had before the spell had infected her.

Ashael scanned Denise and then nodded as if satisfied.

"That should hold you, but this power upload is only temporary. To make it permanent, we'd need to strike a deal, and despite what you know, I doubt you'd want to go that route."

"I don't," Denise said, adding "no offense," with a wry smile at him. Then, she glanced at me. "Don't worry, Cat. His power upload only hurts for a few minutes—"

"I'm not doing that with her," Ashael interrupted. "She has nothing in her to increase the way you did."

That sounded insulting, but more importantly, did it mean I was beyond help even from a half demon, half demigod like Ashael?

"I can, however, give her something to weaken the immobility spell so she can move again," he went on.

If my hands could have shot out to indicate consent, they would have. *Do it! Whatever it is, bring it on!*

"But she won't be good for much after that, and it's very important that you kill whoever hexed you both," he finished.

"Why won't Cat be good for much?" Denise asked, echoing my own thought.

His smile was as bright as sunshine. "She'll be too high."

I stared at the demon. Now I knew what he intended to give me to counter the spell. His blood.

Demons weren't just the inventors of magic; they were the walking embodiment of it. That's why spells didn't work on them. Their blood also had a unique effect on vampires, and by unique, I mean that vamps who drank demon blood ended up more wasted than a frat boy after a drinking contest.

Still, being wasted would be an improvement over my current state. Besides, Ashael was only half demon. His other side was of an indeterminate celestial nature, so maybe his mixed blood wouldn't get me as trashed as straight demon blood would. Even if it did, Bones had once managed to win a fight to the death while sky-high on demon blood.

If he could do it, I could do it.

I stared at Denise, hoping she could intuit my answer.

She sighed. "I don't like this, but...Cat says yes."

Ashael rolled up his sleeve while grabbing one of the broken bottles I'd telekinetically hurled at him. Then, he came toward me with a wolfish smile.

"In that case, my lovely redhead, I hope you're thirsty."

CHAPTER NINE

Being born half vampire meant that I'd only been drunk once, after a ghost had tricked me into chugging an entire bottle of uncut moonshine. Not even my half-vampire nature had been enough to make me immune to half a gallon of 180 proof "white lightning," as it turned out. Still, despite my relative inexperience with being intoxicated, I felt prepared to deal with the wonky side effects of Ashael's blood.

Oh, what a sweet summer child I was!

The first splash shot past my lips and went right down my throat. If my muscles still worked, I would've gagged.

Be a little more gentlemanly when shooting your load, Ashael!

At least I didn't need to worry about my lack of ability to swallow. With how forcefully his blood came out, it felt like it went straight into my stomach, and...wow, this rug was so thick. And *lush*. Had it always felt like this? And the colors in this room were so vivid, especially when reflected in the lights from all the broken glass.

"Beautiful," I sighed, and then squealed in delight.

I was talking again! Sure, I'd dribbled blood to say the words, but who cared? I wasn't wearing this dress again anyway.

"More," I said next, and grabbed Ashael's wrist.

"Uh, if she's moving now, is that enough?" Denise asked.

"No," I garbled out before Ashael could answer. Every swallow made the world more beautiful, warm, and glorious.

"Slow down, Cat," I heard Denise say.

I loved her, but she seriously needed to shut up.

Ashael's dark curls brushed my face as he bent near my ear. Even that slight touch felt like silk trailing over my skin.

"Last swallow, little vampire," he murmured, his voice curling around me like warm, dark waters.

"No," I said, my inhibitions drowned. "Eat you...all night."

Ashael's laugh was more decadent than the richest dessert. "If circumstances were different, I'd let you, but alas."

Then, his wrist was gone, and that addictive flow stopped.

I tried to yank his wrist back and ended up only grasping air. I leapt up to see Ashael on the other side of the room, wagging a finger at me.

"Ah ah ah, my lovely one. You're cut off."

I lunged at him, and then staggered in surprise when the floor rose up to trip me.

"Stop it," I snapped at the floor.

It undulated in response, taunting me. I stomped on it, and it surged up with an abrupt wave that knocked me flat.

Asshole.

Denise rushed over. "Cat! Are you okay?"

"Fine," I said, brushing her aside. This was between me and the floor, and I was kicking its polished driftwood *ass.*

I stomped up and down on it with all my strength. Planks cracked and gave way. When I was ankle-deep in the floor's wreckage, I howled in victory.

Take that, motherfucker!

"Cat..." Denise sounded worried, but she shouldn't be. I'd beaten the floor, so it couldn't attack her next.

"Don't bother trying to reason with her," Ashael said. "She's too high. Give her a few minutes to adjust to the effects of my blood. She'll be better by then."

"I'm fine," I told Ashael. "In fact, I'm *fabulous*."

His grin was annoying in its smugness. Should teach him a lesson. Make him bleed a little...and then lick it.

"She's, ah, growling," Denise said with concern.

Ashael waved. "Pay it no mind. Now, care to tell what happened that caused you two to run afoul of a sea god?"

"A sea god?" Denise repeated.

"You're both infected with contagious sea god magic, so you must have run afoul of one," Ashael said.

I was going to answer, but suddenly, the whole room tipped. Fucking floor was at it again! I grabbed the wall to stay upright, confused to see that Ashael and Denise were still standing without help. Why wasn't the floor attacking them, too?

Denise sighed. "I couldn't see most of what went down, but from what I know, Cat pissed off a bunch of witches, and they hit her with an immobility spell. They must have hit me with it, too, although mine didn't take effect until after they left."

"They didn't spell you. Cat did," Ashael said. At Denise's shocked look, he continued, "Not on purpose. You know I can see magic as easily as you see colors. That's how I saw that the magic on Cat is contagious. Once she was infected, she infected you. You would've infected me, too, if I wasn't a demon. This type of magic is very rare, so what did Cat do to anger those witches?"

"She stopped them from killing a kid," Denise said, sounding a bit dazed now.

Ashael whistled. "Ah. That'll do it. Ancient gods have *no* sense of humor when it comes to someone interfering with their sacrifices, and that child must have been the god's sacrifice."

"That's what they said," I filled in, no longer needing to hug the wall to stand. My head felt a little clearer, too, although I still thought the floor was daring me to a fight.

Ashael's dark gaze fixed on me. "That's why the sea god gave its acolytes the power to hex you with contagious magic."

"Goddess," I corrected him.

"Goddess, then. Did her acolytes tell you about the other spell they sealed onto you?"

"What other spell?" Denise asked, sounding surprised.

That's right, she didn't know. All of a sudden, I felt a lot more sober. "The one that makes me the goddess' new sacrifice on the full moon." Then, my voice hitched from more than the room-tilting effects of Ashael's blood as I added, "And anyone I've infected with the spell is her sacrifice, too."

"But you're a vampire," Denise sputtered. "Only decapitation or silver through the heart can kill you, and *nothing* can kill me except demon bone through both my eyes."

Ashael looked thoughtful. "Under normal circumstances, that's true, but with ancient gods, all bets are off. You have until the full moon, hmm? That gives you two nights."

"So, how do we kill this goddess?" Denise demanded.

Ashael snorted. "You don't. The sea is older than anything on this planet, so the gods it produced are among the most ancient and powerful. You can't kill her. Neither can I."

I started to speak, and then burped with such force that it rustled the hair around my face. I clapped a hand over my mouth, aghast. Then, despite our very serious circumstances, all of a sudden, I couldn't stop laughing.

"I haven't burped since I was human! Wow. That *sounded* like years of trapped air ripping out of me, didn't it?"

"There must be a way to stop this," Denise said, ignoring my comment.

Ashael gave her a level look. "Most spells die with their caster, so kill the witch that hexed Cat, and that should do it. I warn you, though: a witch powerful enough to channel sea-god magic won't die easily, and my race has a truce with other gods, so I can't help you. The sea goddess would consider my killing her acolytes a violation of that truce. But vampires and humans have no such truce, so as long as you offer the sea goddess a substitutional sacrifice, she shouldn't avenge her acolytes if you kill them to break the spells."

Really? That was some bullshit.

"Bad goddess," I said.

Denise didn't seem to care about the sea goddess's refusal to avenge her acolytes. "How do we find the witch who hexed Cat in order to kill her?"

I waved my arms. "I know this one! The same way they tracked me, through the magic in their spell. Right?"

Ashael inclined his head. "That, I could do for you, but aside from that, and from leaving you more of my blood to stave off Cat's immobility spell, I must remain out of this."

"You've already done so much," Denise said, touching his shoulder. "I don't know how to thank you."

Ashael's smile was half sardonic, half wistful. "You already did when you and your husband claimed me as family last year. You both had reason to hate demons, and Veritas had only demanded you show me respect, yet you called me family while expecting nothing in return." He touched the hand she'd placed on his shoulder. "You don't know how rare that is, but I do."

"I meant it," Denise said softly.

He gave her hand a light squeeze. "I know. It's why I came at once when you called."

"Aww," I said, coming over to them. "So sweet. Group hug!"

Denise let me hug her, but Ashael teleported away right as I got close enough to snap my fangs at his neck.

"Too slow," he said, laughing as I cursed him in frustration. "And too obvious. You need to be much stealthier if you're trying to steal some of *my* blood."

Denise gave me a cagey look, and then turned to Ashael.

"How long before your blood stops giving her immunity from the immobilization spell?"

He rubbed his jaw. "A few hours, probably. That's why I'll leave more blood for you. She'll need it so you can get her somewhere safe before you go after the witch who hexed her and, by extension, you."

"Denise isn't doing that alone," I protested.

Ashael's brows rose. "You think you can help her in your condition?"

"Fuck yeah," I said, incensed at the scorn in his voice.

"Cat." Denise's carefully neutral tone made me swing around to stare at her. "Maybe it's better if you sit this one out."

She didn't think I could help either? Doubt frothed up, covering my anger. Were they right?

Was I...useless again?

Fuck that! "Come at me," I said to Ashael, decision made. "No demon tricks. You'll play the evil vampire witch, I'll be me, and if you stop me from skewering you through the heart with silver, I'll stay behind."

Ashael sighed. "You can't fight. You can barely stand—"

"Then this won't take long." I waved at him in the universal gesture for 'bring it on.'

Ashael just stood there and stared at me.

"Lazy demon," I muttered, and charged him.

He sidestepped with an ease that made me so angry, I didn't notice the wall until I hit it. Then, a smack on the back of my head gave me another face full of plaster. When I spun around, Ashael was studying his nails as if his swat hadn't given me a second face plant into the now-dented wall.

"We finished?" he asked in a light tone.

Anger burned like someone had detonated a flare inside me. "Not nearly."

I charged him again, this time swerving into his sidestep. His overconfidence cost him, and I landed a punch that rocked his head back. When I went for another, he pivoted and swept my legs out from under me. My head cracked against the floor as I fell, hard.

Dammit! I should've anticipated the leg sweep. That was Fighting 101, and I'd fallen for it. I was still too sloppy, and he was taking full advantage, as any opponent would.

Ashael's sigh as he stood over me stung more than my hitting the floor had. "I'm only fighting as if I'm a mere vampire, and you're still unable to best me. Stop now, Cat. This is getting embarrassing."

Rage briefly cleared the fog in my head. I'd been trained by the toughest, dirtiest fighter in the vampire world! Drunk and sloppy I might be, but I was *not* going down this easily.

I got up and lunged at him, not fighting my sloppiness this time. He saw it and went for the leg sweep again. Right before I reached him, I dropped low and slid beneath his kick while punching his other knee with everything I had.

It fractured with an audible crack. At once, I yanked at his still uplifted leg, throwing him off balance. His broken knee crumbled when his weight shifted onto it, and he crashed down on top of me hard enough for me to briefly see stars.

No problem. I didn't need to see. All I had to do was think. *Now, knife! Now!*

An instant later, I felt a thud as something hit Ashael's back. Denise gasped, and Ashael rolled onto his side, showing the knife handle now sticking out of his back. Thank God my fledgling telekinesis wasn't sloppy drunk like the rest of me.

"Who's embarrassed now?" I ground out.

Ashael threw back his head and laughed.

"By the gods, even high, you're as vicious as you are beautiful. Are you certain you love your husband, my feisty little redhead? You and I could have such fun."

His voice deepened until it felt like an acoustic caress at that last word.

I got up with a snort. "Not a chance, and believe me, I have *plenty* of fun. Bones isn't just my husband's name, it's practically his life motto."

"TMI," Denise muttered, but Ashael laughed again.

"Then I'll take my defeat with grace, if I must."

He vanished, leaving the knife to land on the floor now that it no longer had a back to stick into. The blade was still coated with his blood, and I'd snatched it and licked it before it occurred to me how crass I was being. Then, I didn't care as his blood lit my senses up even more.

Oh, that felt so good!

"Should I be worried about her new...enthusiasm for demon blood?" Denise asked Ashael when he reappeared next to her.

"Only if she seeks it out after you've defeated the witches," Ashael replied. "Otherwise, this is only a temporary craving while she's under the influence, although I strongly advise that you don't let her drive."

Denise gave him a look that said, *Do you think I'm stupid?*

Ashael grinned before his expression became serious.

"I'll return later with more blood, and later again once I've found your witches. In the meantime, let Cat teach you how to fight. You have powerful abilities, but those witches have powerful magic, so if you're going to survive, you need more than your shapeshifting skills."

"I can fight," Denise sputtered.

"Done!" I said with a jaunty wave at Ashael.

He nodded at me, and then vanished with a swirl of shadows that were much more impressive than the witches' smoke trick.

Denise sighed and then turned to me. "There's too many people who could get close enough for us to infect them if we stay here, so we need to leave."

I nodded, trying to ignore how the simple gesture made the room swim. I'd felt much more focused while fighting with Ashael, but that must have been rage combined with muscle memory from all my years of fighting. Now, however, I felt downright woozy. Had that little amount of blood I'd licked off the knife made me so much worse? Or was I truly feeling how high I was, now that I didn't have anything left to prove?

Either way, Denise was right. We had to leave before we infected anyone else.

"Yes, and once we're somewhere safe, I'm going to turn you into a world-class ass-kicker."

CHAPTER TEN

Okay, so I might have been overambitious when I said I could turn Denise into a world-class fighter. Even under the best of circumstances, doing that in less than two days would be hard. Trying to do that while supernaturally sloshed? That was next to impossible.

It wasn't easy on Denise, either. Imagine trying to learn to fight from a sky-high teacher. If Denise took a shot every time I said "See what I did there? *Don't* do that," I wouldn't be the only one so intoxicated that I had to incorporate tripping into our fighting routine.

Still, we muddled through, after we found an Airbnb cottage up the coast near Dogtown; an unincorporated community in Marin County that used to be called Woodville. The place lacked every amenity we'd enjoyed at the Ritz's beach house, and that was fine. It also lacked neighbors for at least a mile in every direction. The population of Dogtown was only thirty people, so the owner was all too happy to make the unexpected reservation, even at that pre-dawn hour.

The small, one-bedroom cottage had a fine layer of dust over the scant furnishings, plus the only scents I caught were must and mildew, but its neglect suited me. No one being here recently meant that no one would come into contact with our contagious magic. Also on the plus side, the little cottage had a flat yard bordered by the nearby forest. That's where I trained Denise until I felt a lot more sober, which coincided with it being harder for me to move as the effects of Ashael's blood wore off.

Denise helped me back into the house. I could still walk, but if I thought I was staggering before, it was nothing compared to how my muscles were seizing up now.

"Put me on the couch," I said. "You take the bed. You need the sleep, and it won't matter where I am once I freeze up."

She gave me a pitying look, though thankfully, she didn't argue. She just helped me onto the sofa.

"I'll put your knives and your phone next to you," she said, and briefly disappeared into the bedroom. When she came back, she set my knapsack near my feet.

"Thanks. I want to use my cell to record a message, while I can still speak enough to do it."

Her expression clouded as she sat next to me. "You're recording a message for Bones?"

"Yeah," was all I said.

She was silent. Then, she said, "I suppose I should do the same for Spade," in a tone much thicker from emotion.

I felt so awful, it took me a moment to reply. "I'm sorry, Denise. If I hadn't gone after that scent of blood—"

"Then you wouldn't be the person who saved my life the night we met," she interrupted, her tone turning hard despite her eyes brightening with unshed tears. "If you remember, a vampire was turning my neck into an all-you-could-eat buffet. You heard my scream, came running, killed him, and saved me. So no, I won't let you apologize for saving that boy tonight, either. Saving people is what you *do*, and I'm glad because I wouldn't be here now if it wasn't."

Now I was the one fighting back tears. "I was the lucky one that night. Your friendship has saved me so many times."

"Metaphorically, maybe," Denise allowed, with a little smile. "Especially when you were so miserable while you were hiding from Bones. But that wasn't the only time you saved my life. You also did it when a horde of zombie-like things attacked that New Year's Eve, and you did it when a vampire drug dealer was trying to turn me into his latest sellable product."

"I wasn't alone any of those other times," I protested.

She took my hand. "You're not alone now either, Cat."

My throat closed up. Not from the spell overcoming me. From all the emotions welling up to take away my voice.

"Thank you," I finally managed to say.

She squeezed my hand. "You're welcome."

We sat in silence for a few minutes. Then she said, "You shouldn't just leave a recorded message. You should call Bones."

Oh, how I wanted to! I'd give anything to hear his voice right now, but if I did, I knew how it would end.

"I can't. No matter how I pretend, Bones will know something's wrong, and if he knows that, he'll track me down. Then, he'll get infected, too. I can't let him do that. If things go south, one of us needs to be there for Katie."

Denise gave me a sad smile. "That's why I'm not calling Spade. He'd insist on coming, too. We don't have a child to worry about raising, but regardless, I don't want him getting infected. Ashael's power upgrade to my demon brands might protect me from the immobilization spell, but I'm still marked as a sea goddess sacrifice, and I'm still contagious, too."

I squeezed her hand. "We'll kill the witch who hexed us. That'll reverse both spells, and we'll both be okay."

She squeezed back. "I know we will. And, hey, in the meantime," her tone brightened, "I get to learn how to fight. I've wanted to do that for years, but Spade kept brushing me off when I'd ask him to teach me."

"Why?" Her husband was notoriously overprotective, and the vampire world was frequently violent. Because of both, I would've thought Spade would be all over teaching Denise how to defend herself if she asked him.

"I think he...took it personally." Denise sounded bemused. "Like I was implying that he wasn't doing a good job protecting me when it wasn't that at all. I wanted to learn how to fight for *me*. It had nothing to do with him or his abilities."

I found myself scrunching into a smaller shape even though it was hard for me to move. Wow. This was hitting close to home.

"Well, you're learning now," I said while wondering if I owed Katie an apology for how I might have misinterpreted her reasons for training. "And you'll learn again tomorrow, once Ashael drops off more blood."

Denise rose. "Speaking of that, I'll go summon him so he knows where we are. I'll do it outside so you have some privacy while you record your message for Bones."

She left, taking a bottle and a glass with her. I waited until I couldn't hear her anymore, and then I placed my cell in front of me and hit *record*.

Or I tried to. It took two attempts before I pressed the right button. I didn't have long before I froze up like a mythical gargoyle turning to stone in the sunlight.

"Hey, Bones," I said when it was finally recording. Then, I forced a smile. "If you're watching this, things didn't go as planned, but I want you to know that I love you. So, so much. That's why I couldn't tell you what happened until now..."

Fifteen minutes later, Denise returned. I was still recording, but I'd stopped speaking. I couldn't talk anymore. I couldn't even move to shut off the phone. At least I'd said what needed to be said, even if it felt woefully inadequate. The truth was, I'd never be ready to say goodbye to Bones, even if I had over a thousand years with him. And Katie...How did you begin to say goodbye to your child?

Denise shut off the recording. Then, she swung my legs up over the side of the couch until I was lying on it instead of sitting. Finally, she tucked a blanket over me.

"Ashael didn't answer, but I'm sure he'll be here soon. In the meantime, try to sleep. There's nothing else to do anyway."

There wasn't at the moment, but I doubted I'd sleep. I had too much on my mind.

We just have to kill one vampire, and this will be over, I reminded myself. *Just one. Easy-peasy.*

Except this vampire was also a powerful witch, so it wouldn't be easy. She also probably wouldn't be alone, so we'd have more than her to contend with. Plus, we had no guarantee that killing her would nullify our spells. Ashael had said that it should. What he didn't say—what he couldn't say—was that it *would.* Sometimes, killing the spellcaster didn't end a spell. Only the spell's completion did, and our spells would only be complete when we were sacrificed to the sea goddess.

"You know what I'm going to do, once this is over and we've won?" Denise said in an admirably confident tone. "I'm going to start the adoption process."

If I had any movement, my eyes would have widened. Denise must have sensed my surprise because she let out a soft laugh.

"I know, I didn't tell you that Spade and I have been talking about adopting. It was too serious to discuss over the phone, and I was still undecided. Sure, I could technically have a baby since I still get my period, but Spade's sperm has been dead for centuries, and I didn't want to go the in vitro route. I'm demon-branded. What if the kid came out with demon-y powers? Or I miscarried because I accidentally shapeshifted in my sleep? I did that once, you know. I blame you because I was thinking about you when I went to sleep.

Then, a few hours later, Spade woke up to a friggin' *cat* in his bed."

I couldn't laugh out loud, but on the inside, I was wheezing with humor. Poor Spade, and poor Denise! Aside from the obvious issue of suddenly waking up as another species, Denise was also allergic to cats.

"So, no pregnancy for me," she went on. "But I always did want to be a mom, so why not adopt?"

Why not, indeed? She'd make a wonderful mother, and Spade would be a great dad, though he'd probably spoil his kid rotten.

I'm so happy for you, Denise, and we will *win tomorrow,* I wanted to say. *We have so much to live for. No murdering, sea-hag-worshipping bitch is going to take that away from us.*

Shadows suddenly leapt from the corners before stretching into the familiar form of a tall, startlingly handsome man. Ashael wasn't wearing a suit this time. He was in a fluffy white robe and nothing else, as a breeze revealed when it lifted a corner of his short robe.

"Sorry for the delay," he said. "I didn't expect your summons so soon."

"Sorry if we caught you, ah, entertaining," Denise replied. That's when I noticed the lipstick marks on his neck. Guess he wasn't in a robe because we'd disturbed him from his bath.

He waived. "They'll wait."

They. So, not just one. No wonder he'd taken more than half an hour to respond.

"I brought you more blood," he said, pulling two bags out and handing them to Denise. "Give one to her before training tomorrow, and the other when you leave to meet the witches, but you'll need to hide the second one until then."

As if I would risk our lives by stealing it early! Then again, no sense trusting the willpower of someone trashed. After all, I'd licked a knife coated in his blood mere hours ago.

"I've also found some of the witches," Ashael said, snapping my attention back to him. "They appear to be prepping for a special ritual. There are several covens in one place, yet thus far, I haven't seen the one you described as Morgana."

Bad news on top of more bad news. Our luck this trip wouldn't have it any other way. We couldn't attack until we knew Morgana was there. She was the spellcaster, so she was the one we *had* to kill.

"But don't worry," Ashael went on. "If Morgana is as high-ranking among the coven as you suspect, she wouldn't be involved in the preparations. Royalty never sullies itself with menial labor. She'd wait until the end to appear."

Plausible. Morgana hadn't been at the sea cave, either. Guess some events really were too lowbrow for her. At least this ritual sounded important, if it had multiple covens. She should show up for the end of that.

"Remember, once you attack, any new spells the witches hurl at you shouldn't fully stick while the power in your brands is increased, Denise," Ashael continued. "They also should mostly bounce off Cat because she'll be so newly filled with my blood. The witches won't expect that, so be sure to use it to your advantage."

"Oh, we will," Denise said, and took the new blood bags with a glint in her eyes that I hadn't seen from her before. Sure, I'd seen that same look from many dangerous opponents in the past, and it had doubtlessly been in my own eyes several times, too. It was the look of anticipated violence.

"So, where do we crash this ritual?"

Ashael smiled. "Check your phone. I sent you a pin."

CHAPTER ELEVEN

"Watch where you're going!" Denise said for the third time.

If I didn't love her, I'd be annoyed. Had I flown us into the cliff face yet? No, so she should quit bitching. Sure, I'd come close to the rock walls to our left, but that was because we were being stealthy as we approached the rendezvous point.

Normally, you needed to hike almost seven miles to reach Alamere Falls. But I could fly, so we were arriving the easy way. Or, at least, it *would* be easy, if Denise didn't keep screeching in my ear and distracting me.

I had to give it to the witches; they'd picked a beautiful place for their ritual. The forty-foot falls landed on Wildcat Beach, where the surf was rapidly covering the sand as the tide started to come in. At this hour, no tourists were around since it was already a tough hike to Alamere Falls during the day.

It was only an hour before high tide on the full moon, when the second spell would kick in and the sea goddess would come for us. We were cutting it close, not that we'd had a choice. The witches hadn't been here earlier. I'd done multiple fly-bys and hadn't seen a hint of them. I'd started to worry that they'd concealed themselves with glamour—or that I was too drunk to spot them—when I finally saw a line of blue-robed figures hiking up the final stretch of trail leading to the falls. I tried to do a quick head count, and lost track after the mid-twenties. Whatever. I only needed to find and kill Morgana. She had to be here. This was the big shebang. Morgana wouldn't miss it.

I flew back to where I had left Denise, drank the last of Ashael's blood from the mostly empty second bag, and flew us back to the falls. Time to crash their party.

The witches were setting up a bonfire made of branches and the terrain's many loose rocks. No one had removed their hoods yet, so I couldn't spot Morgana's lustrous, dark umber hair.

Come on, Morgana. Where are you?

"Look!" one of them suddenly said while pointing up.

Dammit. We'd been spotted.

"Brace!" I told Denise as every hooded head looked up.

I dove us toward the tightest cluster of witches. We'd scatter them before landing near the bonfire—*Aw, shit!*

I crashed into the bonfire. Fire, wood, and stone burst out in every direction as we tumbled along the top of the cliff. Thankfully, a group of witches stopped our momentum, providing a much softer landing than the ground as we plowed into them.

I leapt up with as much bravado as I could muster after that epic fail of a landing.

"Give me Morgana, or I am going to fuck all of you!"

Denise shot an amazed look my way. That's when I realized I'd forgotten a very important word.

"*Up*," I stressed. "Give me Morgana, or I am going to fuck all of you *up*."

"Your first offer was better," an amused voice noted.

I knew that voice. Morgana.

I turned and flung several of my silver throwing knives toward the source of her voice. *Take that, witchzilla!*

The knives turned to liquid in midair before splashing to the ground near her feet. Worse, I suddenly felt a burning wetness, and looked down to see silver rivulets running from my now empty weapon sheaths on my arms, thighs, and ankles.

I stared at the shiny splotches in disbelief. *Please let me be hallucinating from Ashael's blood. Please don't let the bitch have just melted all my weapons!*

Morgana smiled. "How do you like my new spell?"

Oh, I'd be very impressed, if I wasn't the one covered in useless, melted silver. "Creative," I managed to say.

Morgana's smile turned smug. "I had a feeling you'd find a way out of the immobility spell, so I had that ready in case you showed up tonight."

"Cat..." Denise drew my name out in a concerned way.

I glanced over at her. Yep, Denise now had melted shiny streaks where all her silver weapons had been, too. Ashael had said his blood would shield us from any new spells they lobbed our way, but that protection obviously didn't extend to inanimate objects like our knives.

"It's fine," I said, cracking my knuckles. "Who doesn't love a good old-fashioned brawl?"

"Alas, I must decline," Morgana replied in a light tone. "We have our goddess' arrival to prepare for."

A high-pitched scream sounded behind me. I turned, seeing a brown-haired boy struggling between several witches. Freckles or pimples dotted his face, and his frame had that awkward, bones-too-big-for-his-skin look that some teens had. When his eyes met mine, horror, shock, and fear practically spilled from his gaze and his thoughts were a jumble of pleas and shrieks.

Firecrackers of rage went off inside me. "Another kid? What the fuck is wrong with you? If the goddess you worship *must* have a living sacrifice, chose a murderer or a pedophile like a normal person!"

"That's what I said," one of the nearby witches muttered, garnering her an instant censoring look from Morgana.

"We hold to the old ways of offering a pure sacrifice—"

My loud scoff cut her off. "First of all, you're evil. Second, purity is a spiritual state, not a sexual one, and third, wow are you dating yourself as an old, out-of-touch vampire if you think 'teenager' automatically means 'virgin.'"

"I'm done speaking with you," Morgana said, and picked up one of the sticks from the now-destroyed bonfire. Then, she poked it at a splotch of melted silver near her feet.

"I couldn't agree more," I spat and marched toward her, throwing aside the witches who tried to stand in my way.

Morgana didn't move. Instead, she threw the stick at me.

I didn't even duck. What was this, kindergarten?

The stick changed into a large snake that hit me right in the mouth. I flung it off, yelping in a very un-badass way, but I hated snakes, and now I'd just gotten to first base with one.

"Really?" I snapped when dozens of other branches suddenly morphed into serpentine life. Now, I had a field of snakes between me and Morgana. Gross, but did she actually think this would stop me from reaching her—

Ouch! One of the snakes bit me, and wow, it hurt. A lot.

I yanked the snake off, not caring that I ripped my flesh in the process. Its fangs were still oozing venom, only it wasn't normal-looking venom. It was shiny and metallic.

"Silver," I breathed out.

A single touch confirmed it. Only silver stung that much. All vampires were allergic to it, even freaky former half-breeds like me. Worse, liquid silver couldn't be removed with the same ease as yanking out a weapon, and until the silver was removed, I'd be weaker and I wouldn't heal as fast.

I hurled the snake aside. "Magic snakes? You need therapy!"

Morgana only tossed her hair. "And you need to sit quietly until our goddess comes to claim you, but I'm guessing neither of us is going to do what's in our best interest, are we?"

Denise grabbed my arm. "You okay?"

The bite in my calf burned like hell, but I'd be all right. I just needed to keep from getting bitten again.

"Fine," I said through gritted teeth. "Hold the other witches back while I kill her, will you?"

Denise dropped my arm and backed away a few feet.

"With pleasure."

I rose into the air, a little more wobbly than usual, but at least the snakes couldn't bite me up here.

"You're dead," I said to Morgana, and flew at her.

She shot upward right before I reached her, leaving me to plow into the spot where she'd stood. After I spat out a face full of dirt, I saw her flying in a graceful circle above me.

"I don't think so," she said in a pleasant tone.

Bitch could fly. She was also creative, powerful, and beautiful. If I weren't straight, married, and repulsed by child murderers, I might have developed a crush.

"Fellow coven sisters." Morgana raised her voice. "Teach this impudent vampire to show me the proper respect!"

The witches grabbed the magic snakes and hurled them at me. I flew up, avoiding most of them, but at least two sets of fangs sank home. That deadly silver venom scalded me from the inside out. I tumbled out of the sky, hitting the rapidly disappearing beach hard enough to scatter sand in every direction.

I staggered to my feet, cursing when I tried to fly and couldn't. Fucking liquid silver was weakening me by the moment, and only massive cutting could remove it. I'd do it, too, if I had any weapons, but thanks to Morgana, I didn't.

Screw it. I'd fight without flying *and* weapons, then.

"I warned you, motherfuckers!" I heard Denise yell.

Poor Denise, stuck up there with dozens of murderous

witches and God-knew-how-many magically venomous snakes. I had to get to her. Right now.

I started climbing up the cliff wall. Jagged rocks sliced up my hands, making my grip slippery from blood. I didn't care. All that mattered was killing Morgana.

The cliff suddenly shuddered while large rocks struck my head and bashed into my body. The heavy barrage made me lose my grip. I stopped my fall by shoving my hand into a crevice hard enough to shatter bones. Pain screamed through me, but now I was anchored to the cliff wall, and I ducked beneath the next onslaught of rocks.

What was this? An earthquake? We were in California; it was possible. Or was this more of the witch's tricks?

My bet was on the witch. "Is that all you've got, Morgana?" I shouted. "If so, I'm still coming for you!"

No answer except screaming. Hmm. That didn't sound like Denise. Instead, it sounded like several of the witches.

Another blast of rocks pelted me, and the cliff wall next to me crumpled before sliding off onto the beach. Shit, maybe this *was* an earthquake. I crab-crawled away from the growing hole, avoiding the worst of the landslide. Then, I raced toward the top as fast as I could. Two minutes later, I heaved myself over the still shuddering ledge...and stared.

I'm hallucinating. Wow. Ashael's blood is good shit.

A grayish-green dragon stomped after a group of witches. Every step from the massive beast made the ground tremble, and its thick, whiplike tail swept aside the snakes that tried to swarm it. When one of the witches got too close to its flank, a huge wing snapped out and flattened her.

Another witch grabbed a snake and hurled it at the dragon. The viper latched onto the dragon's neck while thin, shiny drops rolled down its thick scales as the snake tried to pump its magically derived venom into the beast.

The dragon's roar blasted the hair back from the nearby

witches. Then, its head snapped out with surprising speed. For a second, all I saw was the bottom halves of the witches' blue robes because the dragon's thick head blocked the rest of them. Then, the dragon reared back up, clenching several big, blue, bloody forms between its teeth.

That's when I realized I wasn't hallucinating.

Back away from her, or I swear I will turn into a dragon and eat every last fucking one of you! Denise had said two days ago. Morgana and the others had laughed, but no one was laughing now.

Except me.

"Ha ha ha ha! Oh, it's *on* now, bitches!"

CHAPTER TWELVE

Morgana tried to fly away. Denise swatted her back to the ground with one of those massive wings. Morgana rolled around, momentarily dazed, and I seized my chance.

I jumped on her. She tried to scramble away, but I climbed up her body with the same urgency I'd used to scale the cliff.

"I take it back," I said when I had crawled near her ear. "You don't need therapy. You need killing."

Morgana started screaming in that unfamiliar language. Instantly, it felt like dozens of invisible nails scratched me. Nothing else happened, though, and from Morgana's shocked expression, something more should have.

I laughed. "Nice try, but I've got friends in low, *low* places, so I'm temporarily immune to your spells."

She glared at me. "You will die screaming—"

My arm across her throat cut her off. I folded my other one over it, locking her neck in place between them. Then, I wrapped my legs around her torso and began pulling.

Her eyes widened, first in rage, and then in horrified understanding. She flung herself backward, knocking us against the ground hard enough to elicit an *oof!* from me, but I didn't let go. I kept tightening my grip and pulling harder.

"Morgana!" one of the witches screamed, seeing her leader's predicament. She ran toward her, only to be snatched up before she was halfway there. Several crunching sounds later, there was nothing left of the witch except the parts that Denise spat out.

Morgana's elbows slammed into my sides. Pain exploded as my ribs shattered. Every new movement caused ragged bits of bone to stab me, and I wasn't healing. I was too full of silver.

My arm slipped a bit from her neck. Morgana took advantage, rolling us across the ground while ramming her elbows into me again. Soon, I was vomiting blood between gasping screams, yet I didn't let go. I let her bash me while I readjusted my grip on her neck and kept my legs around her torso.

It's only pain. Keep pulling! Harder, harder, harder!

Morgana's head came off with a pop that sent me sprawling backward. Then I sat there, so dazed from agony that it took a few moments before I chucked her head aside. It rolled to a stop near her body, which was now shriveling into the state of true death for vampires. Soon, Morgana looked like a weird headless scarecrow that someone had dressed up in a bloody blue robe.

I lay back, relief briefly buffering my pain. It was over. Morgana was dead.

A roar made me sit up despite how much that hurt. Denise had chased a group of witches over to the cliff's edge. They had a steep drop behind them and a pissed-off dragon in front of them. They might have deserved either death, but I was eager to get the silver out of me so I could start healing, and I'd need Denise in her regular form for that.

"Enough," I called out. "Morgana's dead, so you can stop. Not you, witches," I added when they froze as if obeying a sternly worded command. "Denise, *you* can stop."

She did stop advancing on them, but the witches didn't move. Huh. Maybe they were literally scared stiff...or not.

I sat up more fully and looked around.

Now none of the witches were moving, even the ones that had been running down the path away from the edge of the cliff.

"The spell," I groaned.

As promised, it had infected everyone in our immediate vicinity. How ironic that the witches had gotten trapped in a hex of their own making. Still, that hex was supposed to end with Morgana's death, and the witches were freezing up *now*, after Morgana was dead.

Only one reason I could think of, and it was the worst possible scenario. Morgana's death hadn't ended the curse.

"She comes!" one of the witches suddenly screamed.

I thought she meant Denise, but she was still in her imposing stance in front of the cliff. The witches perched at the cliff's edge tried to turn around toward the sea and couldn't. They did manage to crane their necks a little though, so I stood up and followed the direction of their gaze.

The sea boiled. That's the only way I could describe the froth of white that poured from the tops of the waves. Then those white tips began to spin in a circle, forming a maelstrom that slowly approached the thin strip of remaining beach.

High tide was here. The sea goddess was coming, and Denise and I were still magically marked as her sacrifices. But we weren't the only ones. Not anymore.

"New plan!" I yelled, striding toward the witches even though every movement caused fresh spurts of agony. "Any witch that can still move better conjure something up to break Morgana's spell, or we're *all* about to be sea goddess chum."

"Blas...phemy," the witch nearest to me hissed.

Her broken speech concerned me more than her refusal. It meant the immobility spell had almost completed its work. The witches around her looked in equally bad shape. They must have been the closest to us since we'd arrived. They couldn't chant out a counterspell even if they wanted to.

I gave a frustrated look around. *Someone* had to be in better shape! We hadn't been up in every witch's face this entire time.

I heard a thump behind me and then gasps. I turned, shocked to see that the witch who'd said "blasphemy" would now never speak again, and it wasn't because of the spell. No, it was because her head was rolling near my feet while the rest of her body was still frozen upright.

"Who else wants to tell my wife that they won't help her?" a completely unexpected British voice said.

CHAPTER THIRTEEN

I swung around. Nope, I wasn't hallucinating this, either. Somehow, Bones was about fifty yards away from me and closing fast. Spade was behind him, moving slower because he had a canon-like object strapped to his back, multiple ammunition belts crisscrossed over his torso, and two mega-sized machine guns in his hands.

"Darling," Spade said as his spiky black hair blew around his pale, handsome features. "Love your new look."

Denise's expression was so openly shocked that I needed to get a picture. "Ooh, who's got a cell phone handy? A dragon making that face would be the *perfect* meme!"

Bones and Spade exchanged a look.

"She's even drunker than we are," Spade muttered.

Drunker than...huh?

Belatedly, it struck me that Spade's normally aristocratic tones were now distinctly slurred, and Bones swayed a touch as he strode toward me. I also hadn't felt them approach and they were Master vampires with auras that crackled the air around them with their power, so I *should've* felt them.

Unless they'd both dropped out of thin air.

"That devious demon!" I said, exasperated.

Ashael knew that Denise and I weren't involving our husbands while we were contagious, but had he respected our wishes? No, he'd teleported them here himself. At least it looked like he'd pumped them full of his blood first.

Bones flashed his fangs in something too feral to be a smile. "Exactly what I said when I learned he'd known of your predicament for days, but that's off-topic. What's on-topic"— he raised his voice—"is that if anyone wants to leave here alive, you *will* remove the hex from these women now."

"Or I will hunt down and slaughter everyone you love after I finish murdering you in the most painful way possible," Spade added in the coldest of tones.

"That's dark," I muttered while as a chorus of witches spoke. Unfortunately, most of what they said was barely intelligible from their broken speech. My teeth ground.

"They can't chant away a curse in their condition even if they wanted to, and since they're now marked as sacrifices, too, most probably *do* want to. But that immobility spell is hella effective. Did you-know-who leave you any extra blood?"

"No," Bones said before stopping mid-stride and turning to the nearest mostly frozen witch. He ripped his wrist open with a fang and held it to her lips.

"Drink," he said harshly.

Her eyes widened, but with Bones willing his blood into her mouth, she had no choice except to swallow.

Spade saw that and swung one of his guns over his shoulder. Then, he grabbed the witch nearest to him and fed her some of his demon-fortified blood, too.

"Now, start undoing this curse," Bones ordered.

Both witches started to chant in clear, unbroken voices. That's right, we could share our version of spell-buffering through our demon-altered blood. I immediately opened my wrist and held it over the mouth of the witch next to me.

She swallowed twice before her eyes widened and she fell over.

"Sil...ver," she gasped out before her eyes rolled back in her head and she spasmed as if I'd stabbed her.

Aw, shit! My blood was now vampire poison thanks to those damned silver-venom snakes. I'd probably be on the ground next to this witch, if not for all the demon blood I'd consumed. Guess I was too high to feel all the damage done to me, even though what I did feel was brutal enough.

A sharp whistling sound went off behind me, like a train barreling down the tracks. When I turned, sea spray was swirling so high in the air that it had reached the top of the cliff. It looked like a water spout, if one of those could trail a waterfall behind it like a cape. But this was no natural phenomenon. The sea goddess had reached the top of the cliff.

Suddenly, my silver poisoning was the least of my problems.

"You need to leave," I told Bones, swinging back around. "You and Spade have already been exposed to us for too long. If you don't go now, you'll end up marked as sacrifices, too."

"Not a bloody chance," Bones snarled. "And if any of these bitches want to survive the next five minutes, they'll undo your hex *right now* or they'll get this."

Another witch suddenly lost her head. I might not have mastered my telekinesis yet, but Bones was surgical with his abilities, if that surgeon was homicidally pissed.

"Wait, we can do it!" the witch Bones had given his blood to said. "Most of us never wanted to sacrifice kids anyway. We wanted to go after murderers or pedophiles like she said!"

"How...dare," another witch rasped. "We honor...old ways."

"Times change," said the witch Spade had given blood to. "I want to live long enough to change with them."

"Wise choice," Bones ground out. "Now, point to the most powerful among you, and be sure to pick those with good survival instincts because if they cross me, you'll eat your own heart."

The witch pointed, and Bones and Spade began giving more of their blood to the witches she'd indicated. At the same time, the dragon abruptly deflated like it was no more than a very elaborate balloon. Then, Denise rose up naked from the remnants of her leftover scales.

Spade yanked the robe off the witch he was giving his blood to, revealing that she was wearing jeans and a Miley Cyrus shirt under it. Then, he gave Denise her robe. She put it on, grabbed the next witch, and ripped her wrist across the witch's fangs.

"No!" Spade said as Denise's demon-branded blood spurted into the witch's mouth. Only Ashael's blood would have been more potent, and one taste gave away the source of Denise's powers. It also marked Denise as a vampire's version of a walking drug.

The witch's eyes widened as she swallowed. Then, she sucked at Denise's wrist as if she were starving. When Denise yanked her arm away, the witch howled, "Wait! I need more!"

"No more. Now, chant away that hex with the rest of them," Bones said in a steely tone.

The witch kept screeching for more...until her arm tore free and her own hand reared back and slapped her in the face.

"I said *chant!*" Bones roared.

Even high, being slapped with her own dismembered limb was enough to scare the witch into complying. She began to chant.

Denise shook her head. "Okay, I should give less of my blood to the next witch," she said under her breath.

That aquatic tornado came closer. I tried to back away and suddenly found that I couldn't. *What?* This wasn't the immobility spell acting up again. I could move closer to the writhing, spinning waterspout. I just couldn't move away from it.

Denise abruptly stopped giving blood to the other mostly

frozen witches, and from her expression, she hadn't wanted to. Then, the markings on Denise's forehead started to glow at the same time that my own forehead began to burn.

"Cat?" Denise said, her widened hazel eyes meeting mine.

I wanted to scream. I also wanted to hurl every weapon ever created at the towering funnel of water coming ever closer, and I couldn't. I could do nothing at all. Despite my best efforts, I'd lost and I wasn't the only one about to pay the price.

Tears made everything blurry. "I'm so sorry, Denise."

Why couldn't it just be me? Why did it have to be her, too? *I'd* gone after the witches! She'd done nothing to deserve this!

Bones was suddenly in front of me, blocking my view of the approaching sea goddess. He picked me up, but when he tried to carry me away, he couldn't budge me despite his feet digging furrows into the ground from his efforts. Then, his power flared until my skin burned from the residual energy and still, I didn't move a fraction. Whatever magic that marked me as her sacrifice now anchored me to her path despite Bones pitting all his physical and telekinetic strength against it.

I might not have been able to leave, but he could.

"Bones, you have to go *now*."

I couldn't let him die, too. I'd rather be fed to that watery monstrosity a thousand times than be the cause of that.

"Please go. Please," I said, and shoved at him with all my strength. "You can't let her take you, too."

"She's not getting either of us," he snarled.

I wished that were true, but I could only save one of us.

"It's okay." I forced back every screaming emotion enough to crease my face into a smile. "A little thing like death can't separate us. Not in any way that truly matters, so be the father that Katie needs and *leave*."

My voice rose on that last word, riding on the tears that I refused to shed. I wouldn't let his last memory be of me crying. In so many ways, I had nothing to cry about. I'd been so, so, so lucky. I'd had more love than I had ever dared to wish for, and I'd take the memory of that with me wherever I went.

His arms only tightened around me while he kept me locked out of his emotions.

"I *am* being the father Katie needs. That's why I'm not letting this waterlogged bitch take her mother." Then, he raised his voice. "If either one of them dies, every last one of you will beg for a merciful end, so bloody well chant!"

The witches' voices rose until their desperation was clear even if I couldn't understand what they were saying. Then, all I heard was a barrage of gunfire followed by a series of booms that shook the ground hard enough to make cracks appear.

Spade was unleashing his arsenal.

"No one stops chanting!" Bones shouted above the din.

Over his shoulder, I saw the waterspout part and then fall away like a discarded cape. In its place was a seven-foot-tall mostly humanoid woman. Frothy seafoam trailed from her head, reminding me of the Bible verse "it leaves a glistening wake behind, as if the deep had white hair." Her skin was the color of moonlight on water; not blue, not silvery white, but changing between each color with every glance. And her face...I shuddered even as I fought the urge to kneel.

Her face was the very essence of the sea; in one moment stunningly beautiful, and the next pitilessly violent.

The witches' chants grew until they were louder than the gunfire that had no effect on the sea goddess. Spade may as well have been firing his rounds into the deepest part of the ocean. When the gunfire stopped and all I heard was several futile clicking sounds, I knew Spade had run out of bullets.

He let out an anguished roar. Then, an assault rifle hurtled toward the sea goddess. It passed through her and disappeared over the cliff. Somehow, that got her attention better than all the bullets had because the swirling twin maelstroms in her face that marked her eyes now settled on Spade.

"No!" Denise shouted. "Leave, Spade. Hurry!"

"Like hell," he snarled, his voice sounding closer. "Wherever you go, I go." Then, "Crispin, you know what to do."

The sea goddess came closer, flowing over the ground like a river rushing over stones. The markings on my forehead that denoted me as her sacrifice kept burning as if they'd been set on fire. I knew it was useless, but I tried to back away again and didn't gain so much as an inch.

"Last chance!" Bones shouted, his power flashing out in rolling waves that made screams briefly interrupt the witches' chants. Then, the witches began shouting a single word so loudly that my whole head rang from the sound.

"Ustap."

The goddess looked away from Spade to focus her strange, swirling eyes on me. I shoved at Bones, begging him to leave. He only flared his power out again. The witches' shouts grew louder, until the ground trembled from them. Still, the goddess didn't look away from me. Then her arm rose, water falling from her fingers, as she reached for me—

"Ustap, ustap, ustap!"

The pain in my forehead stopped with the same abruptness that her arm dropped. Then, she recoiled from me as if I were foul. All of a sudden, I was moving, too, my surroundings blurring from speed as Bones flew us away.

CHAPTER FOURTEEN

"They did it!" I heard Spade shout, followed by Denise's glad cry. Then, I heard nothing except the wind whistling by as I saw the ground fall away and grow smaller.

Bones must have decided that flying us in the opposite direction wasn't enough. Now, he was flying us up and away, too.

For a few blissful seconds, I didn't care. All I focused on was the feel of his arms around me, the sweet sting of his hair whipping against my cheek, and his scent, like crème brûlée combined with the finest whiskeys. I didn't even feel pain from the silver or my many unhealed injuries. I was too happy.

At last, we were free. All of us.

Well...not all of us. Ashael had said if we broke the curse, the sea goddess would require a substitutional sacrifice for me and Denise. Morgana had mentioned the same. *We had to sacrifice the sister who survived your butchery because our goddess had already been summoned, and lifeblood is required after a summoning.*

The freckled boy's face flashed in my mind. He was still there, and the sea goddess still needed at least two sacrifices to make up for the ones she'd lost, assuming that Spade had rushed Denise away as soon as she could move, too—and he would have. That meant we'd left a helpless kid alone with a bunch of witches who'd shown no hesitation when it came to murdering innocents to appease their goddess.

"Bones, we have to go back," I said.

Either he couldn't hear me, or he was ignoring me because he didn't slow a bit.

"We have to go back," I repeated louder, punching his arm for emphasis. "There's a kid back there they're going to kill!"

That earned me a truly impressive curse, but he did do an aerial version of a U-turn. Soon, I saw the battered, half-collapsed side of Alamere Falls again.

The witches were still there, blue robes fluttering as they scurried about to rebuild the bonfire. That's all I saw before Bones headed toward the lower part of the trail further down from the bluffs. Once there, he landed, let me go, and then zoomed back up while I yelled at him not to leave me there.

He ignored me. Soon, I couldn't see him at all, and now I was a few miles away from the cliff.

"No, you don't," I growled as I ran up the trail.

Each movement felt like evil pixies were stabbing me inside, but I didn't slow down. Injured or no, I wasn't staying behind. The curse was off me now, so I was in no more danger from the sea goddess than Bones. He'd refused to let me face her alone earlier. I'd be damned if I let him do that now.

Still, it took several aching minutes to climb to the top of the trail, and I passed more than a few robed, headless bodies along the way. From how they were still in the process of shriveling, these looked like very recent deaths. Apparently, Bones had decided to make an entrance.

I was about to skirt by them when I heard frantic thoughts about staying hidden combined with a rapid heartbeat in the bushes to my right. Most of the witches had been vampires, but there had been a few humans among them. I yanked the thickest part of the bushes aside, and found myself staring into wide, panicked brown eyes.

"Don't hurt me!" the freckled boy wailed.

Thank God that he was still alive, and he'd had the presence of mind to hide, too.

"Good job," I told him.

His eyes darted in every direction, reminding me of a panicked horse. "Stay back. You stay away from me!"

I was anxious to get to Bones, but I couldn't leave the kid like this. He had every reason to be freaked out. He'd seen things tonight *I* hadn't seen before, and I'd seen a lot. That's why I didn't bother telling him to trust me (he wouldn't) or to calm down (in his state, he couldn't.) Instead, I fired up the glow in my gaze and put all the power I had left into my voice.

"You're okay now," I said in the resonating tone all vampires had. "You partied with the wrong girls tonight, and they slipped you drugs that made you hallucinate some wild stuff, but you'll be fine."

"Wrong girls...wild stuff," he repeated in the dazed way of a human under vampiric control.

"Yes, but none of it was real," I said, still holding his gaze. "It was just the drugs. Now, you're safe, and you'll be going home soon, so you're not afraid anymore. But for a little while, you're going to close your eyes and stay right here."

"Stay right here," he repeated, shutting his eyes.

Good. Now, he'd be calm and stay put until I could come back to get him. I put the thickest part of the bush back in place, concealing him again, and resumed my trek.

By the time I reached the top of the bluff, the bonfire was lit, the sea goddess was swaying in front of it, and Bones was emitting so much supernatural energy that approaching him felt like walking into an electrical storm.

"I don't care which ones you sacrifice, so hurry it up," he

snapped to a black-haired witch with high cheekbones and tawny skin.

I recognized her as the first witch who'd agreed to undo the hex, and I was struck with an idea.

"Don't pick just any witches," I said. "Point out all of Morgana's cronies that supported her child sacrifices. If the rest of you really want to change your coven's ways, now's your chance."

"No!" screamed a forty-something year old witch with parchment-pale skin and iron-colored hair.

I grunted. "Guess we know which side you were on."

Several witches tried to run. Bones's power flashed out, stopping them faster than the immobility spell. Then, his power reeled them back toward the sea goddess, who let out a noise that must've been the watery underworld's version of "nummy, nummy."

"That one, too," the pretty black-haired witch said, pointing at a witch that was trying to nonchalantly back away toward the trail. "And that one. Her, too."

When she was done, Bones held eight witches in front of the sea goddess, far more than the "substitutional" requirement to replace me, Denise, and the kid. Wow, she'd feast tonight.

A hard thump suddenly sounded to my left. I jumped until I saw that it was only Spade, Denise in his arms, landing near the edge of the bluff.

"Not finished yet, Crispin?" he asked, calling Bones by his human name as he always did.

"Almost, Charles," Bones replied, doing the same. Bones might have chosen his vampire name after rising in a shallow graveyard full of exposed bones, but Spade had chosen his as a reminder that he'd once been referred to only by the tool his prison overseer had assigned him: a spade.

"Quiet," said the dark-haired witch. "We're about to begin."

I didn't want to watch this, but I didn't trust them enough *not* to watch, so I stayed where I was and shut my mouth.

The eight sacrificial witches didn't. They screamed out threats that abruptly ended when Bones froze their lips as well as their bodies. That made it easy for the dark-haired witch to trace those burning patterns onto their foreheads, marking them as sacrifices. When she was done, she stepped back and the sea goddess surged forward. Then the goddess passed her hand over them, giving each a single touch, before backing away.

That was it? It hardly looked lethal—

The witches suddenly collapsed. In the split second it took them to fall to the ground, they had all turned into water, leaving only multiple splashes to hit the rocks instead of their bodies. The splashes were quickly absorbed into the sea goddess, until the former eight witches were nothing more than another sheen of liquid on her glistening form. Then she, too, turned into water that splashed back down the cliff and into the waiting sea.

I would've been less disturbed if she'd opened her mouth and eaten them whole. That, at least, would have left the witches *who they were*. But she'd reduced them to nothing at all, in less time than it took to blink, and the reality of that hit me like a brick to the head.

That could have been me and Denise. It was *supposed* to be us, and the sea goddess had been reaching for me right before the spell broke. She'd come so close to touching me...

Rage exploded through my subconscious, almost knocking me flat as Bones's shields cracked and his emotions burst through. Clearly, I wasn't the only one thinking about how close I'd come to being a splash on the ground that the goddess absorbed.

Then, that door slammed shut, and I only heard his fury as he said, "You were going to do this to my wife."

Death dripped from every word. The black-haired witch trembled as she backed away.

"We had no choice," she said in a hoarse tone. "You saw how powerful Morgana was. She ruled us for over four hundred years! Anyone who challenged her was fed to the goddess—"

"Oh, you'll wish for such a quick death," Bones said as his power cracked, whiplike, through the air.

Her eyes bulged and her neck stretched to an impossible length. So did all the other witches' necks, until they all resembled taffy being pulled by a machine.

"Stop!" I cried out.

Bones swung an amazed look my way. "Why? They meant this for you and Denise. They *did* this to who knows how many young lads, so they all deserve to die."

"They do, but then none of them will be left to tell other covens like theirs that the sacrifice of innocents stops now," I said in as strong a tone as I could manage. I wasn't sure how much longer I could speak, let alone stand, so I had to make this count. "We found this group through their magic. In the same way, we can find the others, too, so they all need to know that we'll be checking up on them to make sure that covens only sacrifice the worst of the worst of humanity from now on."

Bones's face was set in hard, unreadable planes, but for an instant, his shields cracked again, and I felt admiration threading through his vengeance-fueled rage. He recognized the logic of letting them live to warn the others about changing their ways even though he really, really wanted to kill them.

"Very well." If death had dripped from his other words, now reluctance coated his tone. "With these terms, you may live."

The witches' necks stopped stretching. The ones that were vampires recovered in a few seconds, but the few humans among them dropped to the ground, dead. Then, the black-haired witch gave a solemn nod first at me, and then at Bones.

"We'll do things differently from now on, and we'll make

sure that we're not the only coven, or you won't have to find the others through magic because I'll tell you where they are."

With that, a cloud of smoke poofed out. In the moments it took to clear, all of the witches had disappeared. Even their dead were now gone, and I blinked in disbelief.

"If they had the ability to teleport themselves out of here, why didn't they leave before now?"

"Because that's not teleportation," drawled a familiar voice.

No one had been sitting on the edge of the makeshift stone bonfire seconds ago. Now, Ashael perched there as comfortably as if he were getting ready to toast some marshmallows.

"That's a parlor trick," he went on. "It stuns the senses for a few seconds so it *looks* as if they've teleported away when in reality, they scurried out of here as fast as they could run. Still, it takes a bit of doing to momentarily daze vampire senses. Before they absorbed residual power from their goddess' feeding, they couldn't have pulled off such a trick."

That explained why they hadn't done it before, but I got why they did it now. "Fake" teleportation or no, it had still worked in getting them out of here before Bones changed his mind about letting them live.

"Ashael." Bones said his name as if it tasted sour. "Been loitering about, watching this whole time, have you?"

"Of course not," Ashael said with mock indignation. "My presence would have violated my race's treaty with the other gods. I would never do that, just as I would never add a dollop of magic to the witches' hex-dissolving-spell because the silly birds couldn't conjure up enough power to do it on their own."

My jaw dropped. *Ashael* had topped off the witches' undoing spell in time to save us?

Denise ran across the bluffs and threw her arms around him. "You beautiful, beautiful demon!" she choked out.

Ashael laughed as he patted her back. "I am, but as I said, I would never do such a thing. That's against the rules, and an obedient fellow like me *always* follows the rules."

"Of course you do," Denise said, laughing as she pulled away. "My mistake."

Ashael winked at her, and then held out a tiny glass bottle to me. "Drink this before they cut the silver out of you. It'll help."

I grimaced. "Thanks, but if that's more of your blood—"

Ashael was gone before I finished the sentence. Bones and Spade exchanged a look, and then Bones flew over to the stone bonfire and plucked the bottle off its ledge.

"Not blood," he said after pulling out the stopper and sniffing the bottle's contents. "Smells like flowers."

It could smell like fresh manure, and I'd still drink it if it wasn't more demon blood. Nothing against their kind, but I'd had enough of being high. Still, maybe I'd be lucky and Ashael had brought me the vampire version of Novocaine. If so, I'd never forget his birthday, assuming demons celebrated birthdays.

"If this stuff makes me pass out, or if the silver extraction does, the kid that the witches brought here is down the path in the bushes," I said. "He's bruised, but otherwise fine, and I gave him a new memory of what happened tonight."

"We'll see him home safely," Spade said. "Now, let Crispin tend to you. You look ghastly, Cat."

I let out a pained huff. "Thanks."

"Cat."

Denise came over and knelt in front of me. She didn't speak, and neither did I. We just stared at each other, and then we started to laugh because otherwise, we might have cried. We'd both been through so much these past few days that it would take time to fully process everything. All I knew right now was that I had the best friend in the world. Oh, and that I'd never forget *this* girls' getaway.

"Same time next year?" I quipped.

"Over my dead body," Spade muttered, but Denise laughed again.

"Sure, only next time, *I* pick the location and venue."

"Deal," I said and hugged her, ignoring her protest that she didn't want to hurt me.

"Everything's at maximum pain anyway, so don't worry."

"Speaking of that." Bones knelt next to me. "We need to get that silver out of you, luv. Want to try Ashael's potion first?"

I took the bottle and downed it. It tasted like rosewater and I didn't feel high, so Bones was right: it wasn't more demon blood. Hmm. Wonder what it was and how it was supposed to help. So far, I didn't feel anything...

Hey, I didn't feel *anything*. I poked myself in the ribs, which should have doubled me over since most of them still hadn't healed, but all I felt was the give where my finger pressed in.

"It's the magical version of anesthesia," I said with relief. "I can't feel anything, so go ahead and cut away."

Bones's cell phone started vibrating. So did Spade's. Bones ignored his, but Spade pulled his cell out and glanced at it. Then, he let out a sardonic grunt.

"It's Ian, texting over and over to say something's wrong with Cat and Denise, and to call him at once."

"It took him *three days* to listen to our messages?" Denise shook her head. "Remind me not to call him in an emergency again."

I only laughed. Sure, I'd almost died, plus I had a gruesome supernatural surgery in front of me, but now that I was free of pain, free of a deadly spell, free of the fear that I'd doomed my best friend, and free to go home with the man I loved, I was in the best mood ever.

"Yeah, well, better late than never, right?"

Three days later, I walked through the woods bordering our house in the southwestern-most part of Canada. Pine needles crunched beneath my feet, announcing my presence well before Katie could see me through the thick trees, but this time, I wanted her to hear me approach. I was done spying on her.

"Hey," I said when I reached the clearing where she was.

Katie's shoulders hunched ever so slightly as she glanced at the felled trees around her before meeting my eyes. They hadn't fallen from natural means, which would be obvious even if I hadn't known what she had been doing out here.

"Hi."

She sounded unsure, which wasn't like her. Katie normally had the poise of someone three times her age, which was another reminder of how her childhood had been robbed from her.

I nudged one of the fallen saplings with my foot. "Clean break all the way through. One kick did it, huh?"

"You know?" Katie whispered, turning a shade paler.

"Yeah, honey," I said softly. "I know. I'm not mad at you, either. I just want to know why you were hiding it from me."

She didn't say anything for several moments. I waited, schooling my features not to show anything except love and acceptance. I needed her to know that she could tell me anything, no matter what it was because nothing would ever, ever make me stop loving her.

"I didn't want you to see me this way," she finally mumbled while looking at her feet instead of me.

"What way?" I asked as gently as I could.

"The way I looked when I killed people."

Now she looked up at me, and her dark gray eyes contained more pain than any child's gaze should have.

"I never used to think about them, but now, I see them in my dreams, and it isn't like before because now I *care*."

Her voice rose at that last word, and if her speech had been carefully measured before, now she rushed through what she said as if she couldn't get it out fast enough.

"I only saw them as targets before. Messy ones because of all the blood, but just targets. So, when they begged, it was only noise, and when they died, I was glad because that meant I'd passed the test, and they were only *targets and tests* to me back then. But now, I know they were people who wanted to live, and I remember what they said when they begged me, and I know what I took from them when they died because now, I love people, too, and I want to take back what I did but I *can't*."

My eyes burned and my throat felt like a hot coal was stuck in it, but I refused to cry. This wasn't about me. It was about Katie, and I needed to let her get all of this out because there was so much more here than I'd realized.

"You're not to blame for their deaths," I said, my voice a little hoarse from the emotions I was holding back. "The people who turned you into a weapon are. You didn't know any better because you were only a child. They *did* know better and they used you anyway, so they're the real murderers. Not you."

Katie swiped a hand across her eyes, catching the single tear that had fallen. Then, she nodded sharply.

"Most days, I understand this. But then I see them in my dreams, and it brings it all back. Training is the only thing that makes them go away, so I keep coming out here to train."

My poor little girl! How she'd suffered, and worse, she'd suffered alone even though I'd been right there the whole time.

"How does training make them go away?" I asked, squelching my need to hug her and tell her I'd make it all better. I had to let her talk. She'd carried this inside her long enough.

"Because they know I'm doing this for them," she said, gesturing at the pile of felled trees. "I can't take back what I've done, but I'm going to make sure I'm strong enough and fast enough to stop other people from hurting those like them in the future. So, instead of being the weapon that kills people who need help, I'll be the person who saves them. Like you."

Like...me?

That was it; I was going to ugly cry. There would be rivers of snot. I might never recover from it. But first...

"Just be who you are." My voice was husky because that lump in my throat felt like it had detonated. "Not who you think you should be. Who you are is enough, Katie. It will *always* be enough. And you don't have to hide your training from me anymore. You don't have to hide any part of yourself, ever. I love all of you, and I always will. In fact, if you want to" —I shifted positions until I was in a classic fighting stance— "I'll even train with you. If you're going to do this, let's make it a little fun."

Katie's eyes had shone, hearing the first part of what I'd said, but at my training offer, her gaze clouded with skepticism.

"Thank you," she said, now sounding almost comically

polite. "But I don't know if that would be a good idea. I'm a very skilled fighter. I don't want to hurt you."

I almost burst out laughing in addition to still wanting to cry myself into a state of snotasia. Oh, she had a *lot* to learn. First was that I'd always love her and be there for her, no matter what. Second was that her mama might not be able to cook, sew, or hold a conversation without dropping at least one f-bomb, but she could fight until the cows came home.

Or, at least tonight, I could fight until Bones finished with dinner in about an hour.

"Come on, sweetie," I said, circling her while I cracked my knuckles and rolled my head around my shoulders to loosen up. "*This* is what your mama does best."

The End

EXCERPT OF CURSED LUCK

by
Kelley Armstrong

AVAILABLE now!

Aiden Connolly is making me an offer I can't refuse, even when I know I should.

For the past two years, I've run a small antiques showroom in Boston. Business isn't exactly booming. I recently downgraded to a micro-apartment tiny enough that my cat is ready to serve me an eviction notice. So when this guy walks in and offers me a "unique opportunity," it's hard to say no, though if my gut warns me his job is a million miles out of my league.

Also, in the last five minutes, I've formed a very definite opinion of Mr. Connolly. He's kind of an asshole. He strode past my By Appointment Only signs as if they didn't apply to him, marched up and said, "I'm Aiden Connolly," as if I should recognize the name. I do not.

He stands there, looking down at me. Way down. He's not overly tall—maybe five eight or nine—but Connolly is one of those guys who could manage to look down their nose at someone standing at eye level. The smell of old Boston money wafts from him like fine cologne, and from his expression, my perfume is clearly eau de working class.

It doesn't help that Connolly is a ginger. I know that's usually an insult, but I have a thing for redheads, especially ones like this with red-gold hair and eyes the color of new grass and just the barest suggestion of freckles across the nose.

Combine "rich asshole" plus "hot young guy" plus "job that's beyond my skill set," and I should send him packing. I really should. And yet, well, I'm reaching the point where I drool every time I pass the fresh fruit stand but have to count my pennies to see whether I can buy my apple a day.

"My office needs redecorating," he announces.

I look around my dimly lit showroom, crammed with antiques. "That . . . isn't really—"

"You are not an interior designer," he says. "But I believe you could be, of a sort. I'm envisioning a different process, one that begins with set pieces and builds around them."

It takes a moment to understand his meaning. "Start with antiques and design an office to suit?"

"Yes. Someone else would do that design, of course. What I want is an expert to select the base pieces. Roger Thornton tells me you have a unique collection and an eye for quality."

I brighten at that as Connolly's odd offer begins to make sense. Roger Thornton is one of my best customers.

"My collection is indeed unique," I say. "Every piece is one of a kind. Not a single factory-produced item."

"I will take your word for that. I've collected a few antiques over the years, but I wouldn't even know their period of origin."

This admission could come with chagrin or self-deprecation. It could also come with pride, someone wanting to be clear their brain has no space for such mundanities. From

Connolly, it's a simple statement of fact, and I grant him a point for that.

"Now what I'd like—" he begins.

My front door opens, bell tinkling. I wait for the intruder to notice the By Appointment Only signs. Instead, a man strides in clutching a box. He looks like a professor. Maybe forty, tall and slender with wire-rimmed glasses and silver-streaked hair. He even wears a tweed jacket with leather patches on the elbows.

"I'm sorry," I call. "We're open by appointment only."

He keeps heading straight for me.

"I'm sorry," I say again, a little firmer now. "If you have a piece to sell, you'll need to make an appointment. I'm busy with—"

The man thrusts the wooden box at me. "Fix this."

I glance down at a hanging hinge. "I'm afraid I don't offer repair . . ."

I trail off. The box is a tea caddy. Regency period. Rosewood. Perched on four cat paws, with a mother-of-pearl inlaid top showing a kitten playing with yarn. That yarn seems to slide off the box and snake toward me, whispering a soft siren's call of devilry. Joker's jinx.

I clear my throat. "I do purchase damaged items, but if you want me to take a look at this, you'll need an appointment—"

He thrusts the box into my stomach. "I mean the curse. Fix *that*. Take it off."

I force a light laugh and try not to cast a nervous look at Connolly. "I'm afraid that's a whole other level of repair. I'm not sure why you think this is 'cursed'"—I air-quote the word with my tone—"but that is definitely not my department. Maybe you have the wrong address? There's a psychic two doors down, upper apartment."

"Are you Kennedy Bennett?"

"Er, yes, but—"

"From the Bennett family of Unstable, Massachusetts?"

"It's pronounced Unst-a-bull," I murmur reflexively.

"Owners of 'Unhex Me Here,' also in Unstable?"

"Er, yes." I tug at my button-down shirtfront, straightening it. "But I . . . I'm not part of the family business."

"Your sisters sent me. They say this curse is a joker's jinx, and that's your area of expertise. Now unhex my damn box, or I'll leave a one-star review."

"Go," Connolly says.

The man turns and blinks as if Connolly teleported in from an alternate dimension.

"I said, go," Connolly says. "Ms. Bennett clearly has no idea what you are talking about. Just as clearly, she has another client. Now take *that*"—his lip curls—"piece of kitschy trash and leave."

The man's face flushes in outrage. "Who the hell are you?"

"The person Ms. Bennett is currently dealing with. The client with an appointment."

"Y-yes," I say. "Mr. Connolly absolutely had an appointment, and I must insist that you make one yourself if you're interested in selling that box. As for anything else you think I can do with it, my sisters have a very weird sense of humor. I'll totally understand if you one-star *their* business."

The man's jaw works. Then he plunks the box on a sideboard. "Fine. You know what? You just bought yourself a curse, young lady. *That's* my one-star review."

He stalks out, leaving the box behind. As the door bells jangle, Connolly murmurs, "That was interesting."

I force a laugh. "Right?" I ease the cursed tea caddy off the sideboard and tuck it safely out of reach. "So tell me more about this job, Mr. Connolly."

———

I AGREE to stop by Connolly's office after lunch so I can see the space. Once he's gone, I exhale and slump over the sideboard. Then I lock the door, place the tea caddy on my desk and peer at it.

While Connolly called it kitsch, it's actually a valuable antique like everything in here. As I told him, all my goods are one of a kind. That's because they're cursed. Formerly cursed, I should say. The *former* part is very important.

I come from a family of curse weavers—a gift said to stretch back to the Greek *arae*. While we can weave curses, we can also unweave them, and that's our true calling. Most times we're asked to uncurse an item, though, we fake it. Not that we leave the curse on. That would be wrong. The problem is that those who show up on our doorstep rarely suffer from an actual cursed object. Instead, they suffer from an anxious mind that needs settling, and for generations, the Bennett women have provided that service, pretending to uncurse some heirloom or other.

People who have a real cursed object usually don't realize it. They may only know Great Aunt Edna's jewelry box gives them the creeps. Worse, no one wants to buy it because it gives *them* the creeps, too. That's where I come in. I will take that box off your hands. I'll even pay you for it. Then I'll uncurse it and resell it.

One might think that the ethical thing to do would be to offer to uncurse the object. I tried that a few times. The owner stared at me as if I'd sprouted a turban and hoop earrings. Lift a *curse*? What kind of wacko was I? They just wanted to sell their dead aunt's weird jewelry box.

A couple of times, when I felt really bad about buying an heirloom, I tried quietly uncursing the object and giving it back. Didn't help. They wanted it gone. That explains the tea caddy suddenly in my possession. While the owner obviously believed in the curse, he decided dumping it on me was safer than keeping it. Or he just got pissy and wanted to storm off with a grand gesture . . . which ultimately benefited one of us more than the other.

I'll uncurse the caddy tonight, and if the former owner returns, I'll buy it from him. Fair and square. Right now, though, I have a far more important task: texting my sisters to tell them I'm going to kill them in some fresh new way that is totally different from the other two times this week I threatened to do it.

Kennedy: Suffocation. Inside an antique tea caddy.

It only takes a moment for my younger sister to reply.

Hope: I don't think we'd fit.

Kennedy: Oh, you will when I get through with you.

Our older sister, Turani, joins in.

Ani: Pfft. I'm not worried. To kill us, you'd need to come to Unstable. Which apparently has fallen off your GPS.

Kennedy: I missed one weekend. ONE. Also, the highway runs both ways. You could come here.

Ani: To that den of iniquity?

Kennedy: We call it 'Boston.'

Hope: Can we go pub-hopping?

Ani: Yes. When you're twenty-one. Now what's this about a tea caddy?

Kennedy: Joker's jinx Regency tea caddy. Guy barged in during a client showing.

Ani: I didn't send him. Hope?

Hope: Hell, no. I learned my lesson. I hate you, by the way, K. I had a date last week. Made the mistake of offering to drive, forgetting that every time I sit in the driver's seat, it makes a fart noise. 🐺

Kennedy: Unhex it. Oh, wait, you can't. Jinx.

Hope: Hate. You.

Kennedy: Well, whoever sent the guy, please just don't do it again.

Ani: We didn't, K.

Kennedy: Confer. Get your story straight. Gotta run.

They don't text back to protest. They know better. One of them sent that guy, and I don't care which—I just want it to stop.

My sisters aren't trying to ruin my business. They just don't understand why I need to run it in Boston rather than Unstable where I'd pay a fraction of the rent and have a steady stream of tourist clients. Except I don't want bargain-hunting tourists. I also don't want to live at home. Not right now.

Mom died of cancer a month before I fled to Boston. Three years earlier, a car accident claimed our father. That time I fled in the opposite direction—quitting college to come home and be with my family. After Mom died, I needed out. I needed to breathe, to be somewhere that didn't have my parents—our family, our memories—imprinted on every damn blade of grass.

Besides, I'm twenty-five, and if there is an age when I should be living wild, this is it. Yes, there are times when I miss Unstable and my sisters so badly I could cry. Times when I must admit that "living wild" means "going to a bar, telling myself I'm going to hook up with a hot guy, and then spending all night chatting with the bartender instead." But I just . . . I want to give this a shot. I want to prove that I can make it on my own, even if I don't need to prove it to anyone but myself.

EXCERPT OF THE WICKED & THE DEAD

By
Melissa Marr

AVAILABLE now!

Chapter One

Autumn in the South was still both humid and hot. New Orleans was always a wet city. Wet air. Wet drizzle. Beer soaked streets. *Other* things spilling out from behind trash bins. Sometimes, the heavy air and frequent rain was just this side of too much.

Most nights, there was nowhere else I'd rather be. We were a city risen from the ashes, over and over. Plagues, floods, monsters. New Orleans didn't stop, didn't give up, and I was proud of that. Tonight, though, I watched the fog roll out like a cheap film effect, and a good book in front of a warm fire sounded far better than work. The nonstop rain this month would wash away evidence of the things that happened in New Orleans' darkened corners, but I could prevent bloodshed. It was more or less what I did. Sometimes, I spilled a bit of blood, but if we weighed it all out, I was fairly sure I was one of the good guys.

More curves and sass than actual *guys*, but the point held. White hat. Dingy around the edges. I blame my persistent nagging guilt.

A *thump* on the other side of the wall made me pause.

Could I hurl myself over the wall into Cypress Grove Cemetery? It wasn't the *worst* idea ever—or even this month—which said more about my life than I'd like to admit.

I listened for more sounds. *Nothing.* No scrabbling. No growling.

I needed to be on the other side of the wall where tombs were lined up like miniature houses. The tree branches I'd used last time were gone, probably trimmed by someone who saw their potential. Now, there was no graceful way to hurl myself over the ten-foot wall.

Every cemetery in the nation now had taller walls and plenty of newly-opened space for the dead. Cemeteries had become "stage one" of the verification of death process. Honestly, I guess graves were better than cold storage at the morgue. The lack of heartbeat made it impossible to know if the corpses would walk-again, and those of us who advocated for beheading all corpses were deemed callous.

I wasn't sure I was callous for wanting the dead to stay dead. I knew what they were capable of before the world at large did.

At least I was prepared. A moment or so later, I shoved a metal spike into the wall, cutting my palm in the process.

"Shit. Damn. Monkey balls."

A ripple of light flashed around me the moment my blood dripped to the soil. At least the light was magic, not the police or a tourist with a camera. While the laws were ever-changing, B&E was still illegal. And I was breaking into a cemetery where

I might need to carry out a contracted beheading. *That* was illegal, too.

It simply wasn't a photo-ready moment—although with my long dyed-blue hair and nearly translucent skin, I was far too photogenic. I won't say I look like I've been drained of both blood and color, but I will admit that next to a lot of the folks in my city, I look like I've been bleached.

I fumbled with my gloves, trapping my blood inside the thick leather before I resumed shoving climbing cams into gaps in the wall. Normally, cams held the ropes that climbers use. Tonight, they'd be like tiny foot supports. If I were human, this wouldn't work out well.

I'm not.

Mostly, I'd say I am a witch, but that is the polite truth. I am more like witch-with-hard-to-explain-extras. That smidge of blood I'd spilled was enough to send out "wakey, wakey" messages to whatever corpses were listening, but the last time I'd had to bleed for them to rest again, I'd needed to shed more than a cup of blood.

I concentrated on not sending out a second magic flare and continued to insert the cams.

Rest. Stay. I felt silly thinking messages to the dead, but better silly than planning for excess bleeding.

At least this job *should* be an easy one. My task was to find out if Alice Navarro was again-walking or if she was securely in her vault. I hoped for the latter. Most people hired me to ease their dearly departed back in the "departed" category, but the Navarro family was the other sort. They missed her, and sometimes grief makes people do things that are on the wrong side of rational.

My pistol had tranquilizer rounds tonight. If Navarro was awake, I'd need to tranq her. If she wasn't, I could call it a night —unless there were other again-walkers. That's where the beheading came in. Straight-forward. Despite the cold and wet,

I still hoped for the best. All things considered, I really was an optimist at heart.

At the top of the wall, I swung my leg over the stylish spikes cemented there and dropped into the wet grass. I was braced for it, but when I landed, it wasn't dew or rain that made me land on my ass.

An older man, judging by the tufts of grey hair on the bloodied body, in a security guard uniform had bled out on the ground. Something—most likely an again-walker—had gnawed on the security guard's face. Who had made the decision to have a living man with no special skills stand inside the walls of a cemetery? Now, he was dead.

I whispered a quick prayer before surveying my surroundings. Once I located the *draugr*, I could call in the location of the dead man. First, though, I had to find the face-gnawer who killed him. Since my magic was erratic, I didn't want to send a voluntary pulse out to find my prey. That would wake the truly dead, and there were plenty of them here to wake.

Several rows into the cemetery, I found Alice Navarro's undisturbed grave. No upheaval. No turned soil. Mrs. Navarro was well and truly dead. My clients had their answer—but now, I had a mystery. Which cemetery resident had killed the security guard?

A sound drew my attention. A thin hooded figure, masked like they were off to an early carnival party, stared back at me. They didn't move like they were dead. Too slow. Too human. And *draugar* weren't big on masks.

"Hey!" My voice seemed too loud. "You. What are you . . ."

The figure ran, and several other voices suddenly rang out. Young voices. Teens inside the cemetery.

"Shit cookies!" I ran after the masked person. Who in the name of all reason would be in among the graves at night? I ran through the rows of graves, looking for evidence of waking as I went.

"Bitch!"

The masked figure was climbing over the wall with a ladder, the chain sort you use in home fire-emergencies. Two teens tried to grab the person. One kid was kneeling, hand gripping his shoulder in obvious pain.

And there, several feet away, was Marie and Edward Chevalier's grave. The soil was disturbed, as if a pack of excited dogs had been digging. The person in the mask was not the dead one in the nearby grave. There *was* a recently dead *draugr*.

And kids.

I glanced back at the teens.

A masked stranger, a dead security guard, a *draugr,* and kids. This was a terrible combination.

The masked person dropped something and pulled a gun. The kids backed away quickly, and the masked person glanced at me before scrambling the rest of the way over the wall—all while awkwardly holding a gun.

"Are you okay?" I asked the kids, even as my gaze was scanning for the *draugr*.

"She stabbed Gerry," the girl said, pointing at the kid on the ground.

The tallest of the teens grabbed the thing the intruder dropped and held it up. A syringe.

"She?" I asked.

"Lady chest," the tall one explained. "When I ran into her, I felt her—"

"Got it." I nodded, glad the intruder with the needle was gone, but a quick glance at the stone by the disturbed grave told me that a fresh body had been planted there two days ago. That was the likely cause of the security guard's missing face. I read the dates on the stone: Edward was not yet dead. Marie was.

I was seeking Marie Chevalier.

"Marie?" I whispered loudly as the kids talked among themselves. The last thing I needed right now was a *draugr* arriving to gnaw on the three dumb kids. "Oh, Miss Marie? Where are you?"

Marie wouldn't answer, even if she had been a polite Southern lady. *Draugr* were like big infants for the first decade and change: they ate, yelled, and stumbled around.

"There's a real one?" the girl asked.

I glanced at the kids. I was calling out a thing that would *eat* them if they had been alone with it, and they seemed excited. Best case was a drooling open-mouthed lurch in my direction. Worst case was they all died.

"Go home," I said.

Instead they trailed behind me as I walked around, looking for Marie. I passed by the front gate—which was now standing wide open.

"Did you do that?" The lock had been removed. The pieces were on the ground. Cut through. Marie was not in the cemetery.

Shaking heads. "No, man. The ladder the bitch used was ours."

Intruder. With a needle. Possibly also the person who left the gate open? Had someone wanted Marie Chevalier released? Or was that a coincidence? Either way, a face-gnawer was loose somewhere in the city, one of the who-knows-how-many *draugar* that hid here or in the nearby suburbs or small towns.

I pushed the gates closed and called it in to the police. "Broken gate at Cypress Grove. Cut in pieces."

"Miss Crowe," the woman on dispatch replied. "Are you injured?"

"No. The *lock* was cut. Bunch of kids here." I shot them a look. "Said it wasn't them."

"I will send a car," she said. A longer than normal pause. "Why are *you* there, Miss Crowe?"

I smothered a sigh. It complicated my life that so many of

the cops recognized me, that dispatch did, that the ER folks at the hospital did. It wasn't like New Orleans was *that* small.

"Do you log my number?" I asked. "Or is it my voice?"

Another sigh. Another pause. She ignored my questions. "Details?"

"I was checking on a grave here. It's intact, but the cemetery gate's busted," I explained.

"I noted that," she said mildly. "Are the kids alive?"

"Yeah. A person in a mask tried to inject one of them, and a guard inside is missing a lot of his face. No *draugr* here now, but the grave of Marie and Edward Chevalier is broken out. I'm guessing it was her that killed the guard."

The calm tone was gone. "There's a car about two blocks away. You and the children—"

"I'm good." I interrupted. "Marie's long gone, I guess. I'll be sure the kids are secure, but—"

"Miss Crowe! You don't know if she's still there or nearby. You need to be relocated to safety, too."

"Honest to Pete, you all need to worry a lot less about me," I said.

She made a noise that reminded me of my mother. Mama Lauren could fit a whole lecture in one of those "uh-huh" noises of hers. The woman on dispatch tonight came near to matching my mother.

"Someone *cut* the lock," I told dispatch. "What we need to know is why. And who. And if there are other opened cemeteries." I paused. "And who tried to inject the kid."

I looked at them. They were in a small huddle. One of them dropped and stomped the needle. I winced. That was going to make investigating a lot harder.

Not my problem, I reminded myself. I was a hired killer, not a cop, not a detective, not a nanny.

"Kid probably ought to get a tox screen and tetanus shot," I muttered.

Dispatch made an agreeing noise, and said, "Please try not to 'find' more trouble tonight, Miss Crowe."

I made no promises.

When I disconnected, I looked at the kids. "Gerry, right?"

The kid in the middle nodded. White boy. Looking almost as pale as me currently. I was guessing he was terrified.

"Let me see your arm."

He pulled his shirt off. It looked like the skin was torn.

"Do not scream," I said. My eyes shifted into larger versions of a snake's eyes. I knew what it looked like, and maybe a part of me was okay with letting them see because nobody would believe them if they did tell. They were kids, and while a lot had changed in the world, people still doubted kids when they talked.

More practically, though, as my eyes changed I could see in a way humans couldn't.

Green. Glowing like a cheap neon light. The syringe had venom. *Draugr* venom. It wasn't inside the skin. The syringe was either jammed or the kid jerked away.

"Water?"

One of the kids pulled a bottle from his bag, and I washed the wound. "Don't touch the fucking syringe." I pointed at it. "Who stomped on it? Hold your boot up."

I rinsed that, too. Venom wasn't the sort of thing anyone wanted on their skin unless they wanted acid-burn.

"Venom," I said. "That was venom in the needle. You could've died. And"—I pointed behind me—"there was a *draugr* here. Guy got his face chewed off."

They were listening, seeming to at least. I wasn't their family, though. I was a blue-haired woman with some weapons and weird eyes. The best I could do was hand them over to the police and hope they weren't stupid enough to end up in danger again tomorrow.

New Orleans had more than Marie hiding in the shadows.

Draugr were fast, strong, and difficult to kill. If not for their need to feed on the living like mindless beasts the first few decades after resurrection, I might accept them as the next evolutionary step. But I wasn't a fan of anything—mindless or sentient—that stole blood and life.

Marie might have been an angel in life, but right now she was a killer.

In my city.

If I found the person or people who decided to release Marie—or the woman with the syringe—I'd call the police. I tried to avoid killing the living. But if I found Marie, or others like her, I wasn't calling dispatch. When it came to venomous killers, I tended to be more of a behead first, ask later kind of woman.

———

EXCERPT OF SHADES OF WICKED

By
Jeaniene Frost

AVAILABLE now!

Chapter One

This had better be the right whorehouse.

It didn't look like the seedier brothels I'd recently been to. This three-story structure could pass as the meeting place for an elite social club. Despite its unexpected prettiness, if I had to wade through another flesh-fest only to turn up empty-handed again, I wouldn't be responsible for what I did to my quarry when I finally found him.

To vent my aggravation over weeks of fruitless searching, I kicked the door open. Politeness had been wasted at the last several establishments anyway. No smart proprietor willingly gave up a well-paying client, and I'll say one thing for the bordello-loving vampire I was after: He obviously paid well.

To my surprise, I didn't see anyone in the elegant foyer. Brothels usually had several prostitutes lingering around the entryway to welcome new customers. I was further surprised when I didn't hear sounds of carnal activity coming from the upper floors of the house. I pulled out my mobile and checked the GPS pin. Yes, this was the right place. What's more, it certainly smelled like sex, once you got past the choking scents of various perfumes and colognes.

But where was everyone?

Faint vibrations in the floor made me stride toward the hallway. Ah, so the party must be downstairs. I followed the strongest scents of perfume until I found a staircase that descended two floors. It ended at a locked door that I also kicked in. No point in being dainty now.

Noise blasted out. The basement must have been soundproofed for me to miss it before. Now, I wished I couldn't hear what was going on. A boisterous chorus assaulted my ears, repeating over and over. Thunder and Blazes, the favorite opening song of the former Barnum and Bailey circus.

And I *had* walked into a circus, I saw now, although one without any real animals. About a dozen naked women and men frolicked on the ground, doing woefully inadequate impressions of the creatures their full body paint represented. No work ethic, I thought when three faux lions appeared more interested in petting each other than in more realistic fights for dominance, and don't get me started on how they ignored the two faux gazelles that walked by them.

The dozen or so prostitutes dressed in clown suits showed more dedication for their roles. They emerged from a fake car in the far corner of the room, some falling forward in rolling somersaults once they exited, some tripping each other with comedic exaggeration, and some blowing up balloons into explicit body parts that they then graphically connected.

An eruption of fireworks yanked my attention to the other side of the room. They were going off around what looked like a throne, haloing its occupant in a blaze of sparks, fire and smoke. The mini pyrotechnic display was so bright, I couldn't make out the enthroned person's face, but when he called out, "Act Eight will now begin!" I heard a distinct English accent.

Then the smoke cleared enough to show a tall man wearing a blue circus-ringleader jacket. The smoke still concealed him from the waist down, but I didn't need to see more to know I'd finally found my target. The vampire who'd blazed a trail through a dozen whorehouses in only two weeks had a face as beautiful as an angel's, not to mention that his fire-and-umber hair was as distinctive as his looks. When he got off the throne, revealing he wore nothing beneath the ringleader jacket, I realized those weren't Ian's only notable attributes.

For a moment, I stared. What vampire in his right mind would pierce himself with silver there?

I was the only one shocked by the silver piercing through the tip of Ian's cock. Everyone else stopped what they were doing and rushed toward him. Even the glitter-covered acrobats leapt from their swinging perches near the ceiling, gracefully landing near the pile of limbs that now formed around the red-headed vampire.

It wasn't enough that I had to be burdened with a vampire so mentally deficient that he'd willingly given himself a case of perpetual cock burn. He also had to be depraved enough to indulge in carnival-themed orgies. I wasn't about to find out what the rest of Act Eight entailed. I made my way to the growing flesh pile and began flinging people aside, taking care not to throw them too hard. Their heartbeats meant they were human, so they couldn't heal the way my kind could.

"What's this?" Ian asked in an annoyed manner when I

reached the bottom of the bodies. Then he let out an appreciative noise when I yanked him up with none of the care I'd
shown the other people.

"Why, hallo, my strong blonde sweeting." Now he didn't
sound annoyed at all. "Are you the surprise I was promised?"

Why not let him believe that? "Sure," I said. "Surprise." And
I grabbed him by the cock. I had one more thing to verify
before I went any further.

Ian chuckled. "That's the spirit, poppet."

I dropped to my knees. I wasn't about to do what he
thought. Still, this act allowed me to zero in on my goal with
the least amount of resistance from him. Once I got a good
look at the smoke-colored brands near the base of Ian's groin, I
released him. Only one demon branded people with these
particular markings, and it was the same demon I'd been after
for thousands of years.

"Ian," I said as I straightened. "Say good-bye. We're
leaving."

He laughed outright. "I don't think so. You might be lovely,
but two's lonely, while a dozen is a party."

I gave a disparaging look around. "No great loss. The clowns
were fine, but none of your faux animals fought each other or
even attempted to jump through the fire rings."

At that, he gave the animal-painted prostitutes an accusing
look. "You didn't, did you?" Then, his eyes suddenly narrowed
as he looked back at me. "Wait a moment. I know you."

We'd only officially met once before, so I hadn't thought
he'd remember me. Someone with his tendencies had to have
crossed paths with vast numbers of blonde women.

"Veritas, Law Guardian for the vampire council," I
confirmed. Then my hands landed on his shoulders. "And as I
said, you are coming with me."

His eyes changed from their natural vivid turquoise into
glowing, vampiric emerald. "Leave it to a Law Guardian to try

and ruin a perfectly good orgy. Sorry, luv, I'm not going anywhere. Now, take your hands from me before I remove them."

He couldn't mean that. Merely striking a Law Guardian was enough to garner a death sentence, if the council was in a testy mood. Only the vampire council itself was above us in undead society. That's why I ignored his threat and tightened my grip.

"There's no need for empty threats—"

The next thing I knew, I was thrown several meters away. I blinked, more startled by his quickness than by his reckless disregard for the punishment his actions merited.

"No need?" he repeated, contempt edging his tone now. "I remember the last time I saw you. I'd say your complicity in the murder of my friend's daughter more than qualifies as a need."

She isn't dead.

The words rang in my mind, a comfort I drew on whenever I thought back on that awful day. But if Ian didn't know that the child's supposed execution had been nothing more than a clever ruse . . .

"That was the council's decision, not mine," I said, my voice roughening from the memory. I'd nearly lost my position as Law Guardian arguing against the girl's execution, but fear and bigotry had made the council unmovable. At least they hadn't succeeded in taking her life as they'd intended to.

Ian snorted. "Sleep better telling yourself that, do you? You make my sins look forgivable, and that takes some doing."

"Enough." How dare he judge me? "Now, come."

His brows rose, as if he couldn't believe I'd spoken to him the same way some people called their dogs. Well, if he insisted on acting like a beast, I'd treat him like one.

"All of you, leave," Ian said to the prostitutes, who'd been watching us with more boredom than interest. They'd probably thought our exchange was more role-playing. "My compliments for the day's entertainment, but now it's over. Go," he stressed when some of them hung back instead of joining the ones that began to file out the door.

I bit back a disbelieving laugh. "Are you getting them out of the way because you're intending to fight me?"

Ian flashed a smile that increased the intensity of his unusual beauty. "You must not have done your research if you thought I'd come willingly."

The silver from his piercing must have gotten into his bloodstream and damaged his brain. That was the only explanation. "I'm more than four thousand years older than you."

"Really?" he said with mock surprise. "Here I was thinking you didn't look a day over twenty, little Guardian."

I'd been older than that when I was changed into a vampire, but his guess was a common mistake. People put far too much emphasis on appearances. "Is 'little guardian' supposed to be insulting? If so, do better."

"Not being insulting," he replied in an easygoing tone. "But if you're half my weight, I'd be surprised."

Yes, I currently looked more delicate than formidable. Even if that were true, it wouldn't help him. With age came strength, and I had thousands of years on him. "Stand down, Ian, and I won't punish you for attacking me."

"Why don't you try begging me to stand down?" he suggested. "Make your plea interesting enough, and I might consider it."

I was done negotiating. I plowed into Ian hard enough to shatter the bones in his upper body. To my surprise, he did nothing to block the blow. Instead, he flung me upward with a strength he should never have had. I hit the ceiling with such force, I went all the way through. For a stunned moment, I stared at him through the hole my body made in the floor.

"Stop now and perhaps you're the one who won't get punished," he said in a pleasant tone.

I suppressed the urge to immediately charge him

again. Never underestimate an opponent twice, if you're lucky enough to survive the first time. My vampire sire, Tenoch, had taught me that. Following Tenoch's advice had saved my life many times, so I pushed back my urge to retaliate.

Ian was wrong—I had done my research on him. It hadn't revealed anything unusual except for a voracious sexual appetite, an open disdain for rules, and a penchant for collecting the rare and expensive. My previous assault should have left him on the ground, not whistling along to that awful circus tune while looking more bored than concerned.

Maybe his unusual strength came from the demon brands? They did more than act as a leash between Ian and the demon who'd seared them onto him. Over time, those brands would also endow Ian with some of that demon's strength and power. Ian had only been branded for a few weeks. Not nearly long enough for him to manifest parts of the demon's strength or abilities.

I'd find out his secret later. Right now, I needed to take him down, and thankfully, I had some surprises for him, too.

I gave Ian a level look. "My turn."

His smile grew into a grin. "Come and get me, little Guardian."

ABOUT THE AUTHORS

Kelley Armstrong believes experience is the best teacher, though she's been told this shouldn't apply to writing her murder scenes. To craft her books, she has studied aikido, archery and fencing. She sucks at all of them. She has also crawled through very shallow cave systems and climbed half a mountain before chickening out. She is however an expert coffee drinker and a true connoisseur of chocolate-chip cookies.

Visit her online:
www.KelleyArmstrong.com
mail@kelleyarmstrong.com

Jeaniene Frost is a New York Times and USA Today bestselling author of paranormal romance and urban fantasy. Her works include the Night Huntress series, the Night Prince series, the Broken Destiny series, and the new Night Rebel series. Jeaniene's novels have also appeared on the Publishers Weekly, Wall Street Journal, ABA Indiebound, and international bestseller lists. Foreign rights for Jeaniene's novels have sold to twenty different countries. Jeaniene lives in Florida with her husband Matthew, who long ago accepted that she rarely cooks and always sleeps in on the weekends. In addition to being a writer, Jeaniene also enjoys reading, writing, poetry, watching movies, exploring old cemeteries, spelunking, and traveling – by car. Airplanes, children, and cook books frighten her.

Visit her online:
https://www.jeanienefrost.com

Melissa Marr is a former university literature instructor who writes fiction for adults, teens, and children. Her books have been translated into twenty-eight languages and have been bestsellers internationally (Germany, France, Sweden, Australia, et. al.) as well as domestically. She is best known for the Wicked Lovely series for teens, *Graveminder* for adults, and *Bunny Roo, I Love You*. In her free time, she practices medieval swordfighting, kayaks, hikes, and raises kids and chickens in the Arizona desert.

Visit her online:

http://www.melissamarrbooks.com

ALSO BY KELLEY ARMSTRONG

Rockton thriller series

City of the Lost

A Darkness Absolute

This Fallen Prey

Watcher in the Woods

Alone in the Wild

A Stranger in Town

A Stitch in Time time-travel gothic

A Stitch in Time

A Twist of Fate

Cursed Luck contemporary fantasy

Cursed Luck

Standalone Thrillers

Wherever She Goes

Every Step She Takes

Past Series

Cainsville paranormal mystery series

Otherworld urban fantasy series

Nadia Stafford mystery trilogy

Young Adult

Missing

The Masked Truth

Darkest Powers paranormal trilogy

Darkness Rising paranormal trilogy

Age of Legends fantasy trilogy

Middle-Grade

A Royal Guide to Monster Slaying fantasy series

The Blackwell Pages trilogy (with Melissa Marr)

ALSO BY MELISSA MARR

Signed Copies:

To order signed copies of my books (with free ebook included in some cases), go to MelissaMarrBooks.com

Adult Thriller

Pretty Broken Things (2020; psychological thriller)

Adult Fantasy

Graveminder (HarperCollins, 2011)

The Arrivals (HarperCollins, 2012)

Cold Iron Heart (2020; *Wicked Lovely* adult)

The Wicked & The Dead (2020; Urban Fantasy)

The Kiss & The Killer (2021; Urban Fantasy)

Young Adult

Wicked Lovely series (HarperCollins, 2007-2012)

Made For You (HarperCollins,, 2013)

Seven Black Diamonds (HarperCollins, 2015)

One Blood Ruby (HarperCollins, 2016)

Middle Grade

The Hidden Knife (Penguin, 2021)

Loki's Wolves (with Kelley Armstrong, 2012)

Odin's Ravens (with Kelley Armstrong 2013)

Thor's Serpents (with Kelley Armstrong, 2014)

Collections:

Tales of Folk & Fey (2019)

Dark Court Faery Tales (2019)

This Fond Madness (2017)

Co-Edited with Kelley Armstrong (with HarperTeen)

Enthralled

Shards & Ashes

Co-Edited with Tim Pratt (with Little, Brown)

Rags & Bones

ALSO BY JEANIENE FROST

Author's Note: The Night Rebel, Night Huntress, Night Prince and Night Huntress World series all contain stories set in the same paranormal universe. The Broken Destiny series is set in a different paranormal universe that's unrelated to those series. Thanks and happy reading!

– Jeaniene Frost

Night Huntress series (Cat and Bones)

Halfway to The Grave

One Foot in The Grave

At Grave's End

Destined for An Early Grave

One for The Money (ebook novelette)

This Side of The Grave

One Grave at A Time

Home for The Holidays (Ebook Novella)

Up from The Grave

Outtakes from The Grave (Deleted Scenes and Alternate Versions Anthology)

A Grave Girls' Getaway (Novella in The Hex on The Beach anthology

Night Huntress World novels:

First Drop of Crimson (Spade and Denise)

Eternal Kiss of Darkness (Mencheres and Kira)

Night Prince series (Vlad and Leila):

Once Burned

Twice Tempted

Bound by Flames

Into the Fire

Night Rebel series (Ian and Veritas)

Shades of Wicked

Wicked Bite

Wicked All Night

Broken Destiny series (Ivy and Adrian)

The Beautiful Ashes

The Sweetest Burn

The Brightest Embers

Other Works:

Pack (A Werewolf Novelette)

Night's Darkest Embrace (Paranormal Romance Novella)

CPSIA information can be obtained
at www.ICGtesting.com
Printed in the USA
LVHW030858110721
692392LV00003B/289